KNOCK AT
A STAR

Pamela Hill

Chivers Press   •   G.K. Hall & Co.
Bath, England   Thorndike, Maine USA

This Large Print edition is published by Chivers Press, England, and by G.K. Hall & Co., USA.

Published in 1998 in the U.K. by arrangement with Robert Hale, Ltd.

Published in 1998 in the U.S. by arrangement with Robert Hale, Ltd.

U.K. Softcover   ISBN 0–7540–3393–7 (Camden Large Print)
U.K. Hardcover   ISBN 0–7540–3137–3 (Chivers Large Print)
U.S. Softcover   ISBN 0–7838–8319–6 (Nightingale Collection Edition).

Copyright © Pamela Hill 1981

The text of this Large Print edition is unabridged.
Other aspects of the book may vary from the original edition.

Set in 16 pt. New Times Roman.

Printed in Great Britain on acid-free paper.

British Library Cataloguing in Publication Data available

Library of Congress Cataloging-in-Publication Data

Hill, Pamela.
    Knock at a star / Pamela Hill.
        p.   cm.
    ISBN 0–7838–8319–6 (large print : sc : alk. paper)
    1. Large type books.   I. Title.
PR6058.I446K56   1998
823'.914—dc21   97–36724

And once more yet, ere I am laid out dead,
Knock at a star with my exalted head.

Robert Herrick

AUTHOR'S NOTE

I should like to thank the following; the Duke of Buccleuch and Queensberry, KT; Colonel John Scott, DSO, Major E.M.W. Cliff McCulloch; J. Ridley Brown, Esquire, OBE; as always, the Dumfries and Galloway Library Service and the National Library of Scotland.

P.H.

CHAPTER ONE

'I'll have my rights. I'm married to the King of England, and there'll be trouble for any scum who lays a finger on me or my child.'

The crowd milled about the brown-complexioned young woman in worn finery, mocking and laughing while they still had some sympathy even if she owed them money; it was hard for a lone woman to be dragged off to prison for debt, and one or two whispered that the King had indeed married her at Liège, they'd heard; oh, a while back now. The Princess of Orange, that was the King's sister, had taken to do with her, and the old widowed Queen too; it had all happened a while back. She'd been prettier then, this Mrs Barlow, before the hard times; they admitted she still had rich chestnut hair and magnificent eyes, and these flashed fire at the Flemings with their well-fed faces and coats of new-woven drab and fine linen, or sometimes lace if it were a gentleman. But the crowd were mostly shopkeepers. Lucy Barlow's eyes turned frantically to a man in a fair peruke who was trying to take away her little boy; and she spat. 'Scum,' she said again. She swooped down and clutched the child fiercely to her; he might have been six or seven years old, and a small girl, even younger, clung to her skirts. But it was the

1

boy who drew the eye; he was princely, with a sturdy graceful body, long dark curling hair and great shining eyes of a hazel colour.

He had been standing quietly enough when his mother seized him, for he was neither afraid nor surprised. There were always scenes where Maman was. 'Who's going to pay us our guilders? Not King Charles, he's a beggar like all his kin since they chopped his father's head off. They batten on honest folk this side the Channel. Get out of here to your King, if he'll take you; we want none of you.' Such things hurt Maman more than they hurt him. He was sorry for her and if he had been a man, would have taken his sword from its scabbard and dispelled the crowd with ease; but he did not yet wear a sword. For his own part, he ought to be used to men who came and tried to prise him away from her. Why did his father the King not come for himself instead of sending the men? He could not ask Maman at present, for he was clutched against her satin bodice which was thin in places, so that he felt the threads rough against his cheek. The warmth of Maman's body was beneath; he could feel it, and smell the scent she used which had gone stale. She held him so tightly that the fingers of the fair-wigged man, whose name was Edward Progers and who was an Englishman, could get no hold. Lucy was in tears by now and telling the crowd, some of whom hooted, that her people were descended from the Plantagenets, in fact

2

from Cadwallader, and had owned a castle in Wales that Cromwell's men burnt to ruins. That stirred the crowd; they knew of Cromwell.

James wriggled a little against the frantic hold. They had taken him away from her before; once when he was a baby at nurse at Schiedam, when he had slept in an ebony cradle carved with mermen and mermaids and strange beasts, that would rock by the hand. He knew what he had looked like then, for there was a portrait of him, helplessly bundled in linen and narrow lace; but he could remember nothing. Later they had seized him again and had held him for two weeks at a place called Loosdymen, but Maman had come and taken him away to a rich house she had rented. Sometimes they were rich and sometimes poor, as now; it depended when the pension arrived. James knew all about the pension and how it was sometimes not paid, because the King, his father, was poor; a beggar, like these people said. A king should not have to beg. He himself was a prince, for his mother told him so; the King of England's eldest son. It made him different. He had always been certain of it, as they traipsed from town to town; Antwerp, Rotterdam, The Hague, Paris, Brussels. This was Brussels, where the houses had curly gables and most folk were rich.

'James.' His mother's voice sounded, and

suddenly they were almost alone in the street, for the crowd had gone at somebody's approach. Even Progers had vanished. He heard someone murmur, 'The Governor hath heard of it; now there will be debts to pay.' But at least they were no longer going to prison, for the creditors had gone. A grand personage in livery was before them; but Maman did not curtsy to him, which meant he was a servant. Presently a plain coach was brought and they were ushered into it and made off, not too far, to a side door in the Governor's dwelling. James glanced up at the sugar-icing curls upon the brick, and the many windows whose shutters were drawn against the sun. Then it was cool darkness, and a clashing of salutes from the guards who stood in the corridors; they wore great helmets and carried swords; he envied them.

A personage then received them whose clothes were all of silk, with much lacing; he kissed Maman's hand and spoke to her, while his shrewd eyes ranged over the children. Mary was holding James's hand by then; she was only five, and very quiet. The Governor stroked her hair.

* * *

Don Alonso de Cardeñas, His Spanish Majesty's Governor in the Netherlands, had met Lucy Barlow before. The situation was

4

somewhat delicate; friendly as Spain was towards the dispossessed Charles II, there were as yet few prospects of his being restored to his throne; one must not offend the powerful Protector of England, Oliver Cromwell; and the rumoured marriage between Mrs Barlow and the King was being tacitly denied nowadays by the very actions of Charles, who desired to take his boy away from the mother as soon as possible. But it had been unnecessarily cruel to try to have poor Lucy conveyed to prison for debt while they took possession of her son. Swift action from Don Alonso had dispersed the crowd, and as for Progers, he could be dealt with later, and so could his colleague Colonel Slingsby. There were always hangers-on intent to oblige the King, who might one day come into his own; when that happened, he had a fine heir in this handsome boy.

'You are welcome here till other provision may be made,' the Spaniard heard himself saying. 'None will touch you here.'

*   *   *

James was remembering the Tower.

They had crossed to England at a time he could just recall, and Maman wore a dark hooded cloak and carried packages; he and Mary had been told to make no noise, for it would be better if no one noticed them. They had crossed from Flushing on a smooth sea and had come at last to a great grey river, about which buildings lay; this was London, and Maman knew where there was a house that would shelter them; Maman had been strangely calm. Afterwards when they were alone in a room of the house she had spoken to James and had told him that he must guard Mary, who was too small to understand; but James had understood, and had realised that they were here on some business of the King. It involved money, though he did not know more, and he heard and saw strange men slipping into the house and out again, and the chink of silver. This had not happened for very long when a guard came, in plain helmets and carrying pikes; he had known they were pikes for someone must have told him. They had been taken before a man with warts on his face, who questioned Maman; his eyes were beautiful, like clear water, but in all other ways he was ugly, so much so that one would always remember him; he wore soiled linen and his clothes were stained with mud and sweat. It did not seem to matter, though, when the eyes looked at one, and they had roved over him, Maman, and settled briefly on Mary, then returned to James again.

'This is Charles Stuart's son?'

And Maman's fingers had tightened on his shoulder as she replied that Charles Stuart's son was dead, and this was her child by a Dutch

6

husband. James had known that he must be quiet even though Maman was telling lies; oddly enough the man, whose name was Oliver Cromwell, knew also, he was certain. But he said nothing more then, only Maman and James and Mary had been taken by water to a grim high place, and lodged there. He had felt cold and had shivered, which was not like him; but he was afraid of the Tower. Perhaps it was because Maman had said there, standing calm and set-faced by a window, 'Your grandfather, King Charles I, did not demean himself on the scaffold; he died bravely. Those were the men that murdered him.'

But they had let them out of the Tower after a few days, and had even set them on shore in Flanders again, which was an honour not given to everybody. But Maman was sobbing by then, because a man named Bradshaw had taken away a paper from her that said she was married to the King.

*   *   *

Other things had happened. They reflected the turmoil in his mind in that he could never afterwards remember the order in which they occurred; they shifted always. Some scenes stayed sharp and clear in his memory, such as the day when they had received a visitor in the house they were in in Antwerp. Antwerp was like all the other towns in Flanders, with its rich

7

booths, high houses and sour well-dressed burghers in the street; but the visitor was different. He was very tall and everything about him seemed dark; dark clothes, dark hair and dark swarthy skin and yet, surprisingly, grey-green eyes beneath his black brows. 'It is the King,' they had whispered, and from the first he knew that he and the King belonged to one another. The strong arms had tossed James up and had held him—at what a height!—and a deep voice had said, 'This one is all mine, Lucy. The other—well, so be it.' That was Mary, then a small yelling scrap of humanity; a girl did not matter. Later the King sent money for Mary too. But Maman had complained then and Jemmy's father had set him down and had said patiently, 'My poor Lucy, I would not have you harried.'

'Yet you believe anything they may say about me.'

'Where there is smoke there is always fire.' The light eyes dwelt on Jemmy, and there was laughter at the back of them. Always after that, when Jemmy saw his father, he had looked for the presence of that laughter. But now Maman was angry. 'You can say that to me, after all we have known together!' There were red patches on her cheeks that had not come there with rouge, and her eyes were bright with tears. As though he were sorry, the King bent and kissed her; then began to talk again, gravely as though he were much older than his years.

'This is my son and I would have him reared in a manner befitting his station. You tell me he can neither read nor write; that will not do.' James had looked up then and had seen two long lines deepen between the King's nose and mouth; next time they met they were deeper still, because the King had been to England and had fought a battle which he lost. But still the voice from that earlier time persisted and teased, as though it described events which later came to pass. 'Come to me, Jemmy, and you will meet your grandam the Queen, who is French and hardly taller than you are; and your uncles York and Gloucester, and your aunt Minette. I swear I cannot think of Minette as an aunt; she is young enough to play with you.'

James was pleased, and would have said he would like to come; but Lucy surged forward and clutched him to her, exactly in the way she had done lately with Progers in the street. He writhed, but she would not let him go.

'I swear I will do Your Majesty's will in all things, even though you come to me no more. But let me at least be in the house where he is; if we were parted it would break my heart and I would die.'

'Lucy, Lucy, who said I never came to you? I am here now, the same man who left you. Come, send the boy away and cheer me as you can do; you have done naught but weep since you set eyes on me again.'

So James was taken away, and presently there was the sound of a lute and of laughter. There were three things he would always find when he thought of his father; great love, the laughter, and a kindly evasion.

*   *   *

On the following morning his mother had sent for him before he was dressed. Still in his flapping shirt, he climbed on to her bed. The maid, Anne Hill, had left chocolate in a pewter jug. Lucy ran her finger round the rim; other folk had silver.

'Hath my father gone?' asked James.

'Why, yes, alas, and God knows when they will let me see him again; they tell him all manner of things about your poor mother to suit their book. Come here to me, my Jocky, my treasure, and give me a kiss. You are all they have left me, and Mary; and if they had their way they'd take you too, for they know you are the King's true son.'

He stared at her; her eyes were wide-set and she seemed to be looking at something, or someone, not in the room at all. She hugged him to her suddenly and he was aware of the scent of stale perfume, lace and night-sweat; he wriggled free of it, for he was fastidious. 'What may a true son be?' he asked her. It was the best thing to do with Maman, for it took her mind off present troubles. One could never be

10

certain of her; look at the way she called him Jocky, Jemmy, James.

Lucy lay back and let her rich hair settle over her brown shoulders. Her eyes regarded him with an expression he knew well; childlike, and yet wise.

'A child conceived between two married folk is a true son, and I had the lines, but Bradshaw took 'em from me in the Tower. Was it not a merciful day when they set us free of that place? Other folk have rotted there, or else come out that they may have their heads taken from them.' The long lashes blinked away tears. 'I have other papers, say what they may. You ain't a bastard, like he got on a woman in Jersey before we were together. I know naught of that. But he and I were wed, and he got you before ever he was King; ten weeks after his father's beheading you were born, and it comforted him.'

She shifted position and the coverlets rustled softly. 'Never forget you're the King's heir, for he knoweth it himself; he's fond of you, and maybe still he's fond of me, but men change in such ways. The King hath had his fill of adventuring, and of danger, with his enemies looking for him in folk's houses all over England, and beneath an oak tree where he hid. A young woman named Jane Lane helped him to escape disguised as a servant, and I chaffed him, but he says he didn't lie with her. So he won safe again to Holland, but God

11

knoweth when he will ever see his crown.'

'When will he come to us again?'

'I know not.' She turned her head away and the full lips were petulant. They were against her now, all his kin, his sister the Princess of Orange and his mother the Queen. Once she'd served them well enough, when he was mad for love of her, and nothing would do but a marriage. Now they'd disown it if they could; oh, she knew them well enough.

James shut his eyes and pictured his grandam, tiny and French like his father had said. Here he never met anybody, unless Maman owed them money; and even then they would sometimes slip him a coin and ruffle his hair. He was aware of a growing curiosity about the unseen relatives his father loved and his mother hated; surely he would meet them some day? He asked Maman, who hitched her lace wrap higher about her brown bosom.

'The old Queen? Why, no one in England could get their tongue round her name; they used to call her Queen Mary. Mary's the Princess of Orange too, her daughter; you won't catch her coming here, or sending for me, now. The Queen's name? Henrietta, after her father Henri Quatre, who was a great soldier. Will you be a soldier, my Jocky? You must be very brave, for I'm proud of you; and so is he.'

It was always back to that, to his name, to the King, her lover and her husband, even

12

though he'd been only a boy. Now they weren't so young, and maybe wiser; but Jemmy should have his rights. She'd see he did; even though Bradshaw had availed himself of that bit of paper.

*   *   *

... 'and granted His Majesty made you a yearly allowance of five thousand livres while he was at Cologne, his finances are much straitened. It would be wise to have some proof of the obligation His Majesty is under to provide so large a sum, otherwise his advisers may...'

'Advisers? Scum, the lot of 'em, and you no better than they. The boy's flesh and blood, and cannot you see how like he is? There have been folk who never set eyes on Charles Stuart who know this is his son.'

The plausible gentleman seated on her right, who was no other than Progers, hid a smile at this lack of logic; it was like a woman. The boy, Jemmy, sat staring at him solemnly; it was true he looked like the King, but handsomer; there was something else, which in a woman could be called beauty, but it sat on Jemmy in manly fashion. He was a son of whom anyone would be proud, if only the mother would go away.

But Lucy was all of a bustle and determined to prove her rights, for how could they live without the money? Progers told her if she had a bit of paper to let him see it; she hurried out of

13

the room, saying her things were all in disorder since coming to Don Alonso's house, but she would look; it might take a little time. The small girl Mary, brown curls bobbing, trotted after her; James, as behoved a man, remained in male company. As soon as the two had gone out Progers leaned towards him and winked, saying that he had a very fine pair of carriage-horses to show, if they might step outside.

James went eagerly, as he had been disappointed already about a coach Lucy said the King had promised her, lined with red velvet and gold fringe. He walked past the Governor's guards, who presented arms; if he had thought, he should have known the matter was arranged. But he did not know till he had climbed into the coach and the horses started, and there on the opposite seat was Colonel Slingsby, the man who had already tried to take him from his mother. He tried to jump out, but Progers and Slingsby prevented him, and the horses were making some speed by now in the street. He began to be frightened, and Progers, who had a kind heart, said, 'No need to fear, sir. Know you where we are bound? Why, to your gracious father, and to meet the Queen's Majesty, and the young Princess and the Dukes.'

'May not my mother come?' He was excited and trembling; it was good if it was true; but Maman would weep when she found he had gone. Why must they be cruel to her?

'Later, maybe.' The coach got up more speed; presently they left the curly-gabled town behind and were fairly flying over the flat roads. He began to be excited by the journey and the good speed of the horses; certainly they were a fine pair.

If he had known, a further coach was following already with Lucy in it, her tears having prevailed on Don Alonso. But she never caught up.

*   *   *

Day had turned to night, and still they travelled. James had fallen asleep, with his head nodding against the cushions. Day came again, and they stopped at an inn to have some food; then on and on, until it seemed the longest journey in all his life of journeying. The countryside changed and steepened, there began to be avenues of trees and great châteaux; then at last the outskirts of a city, where chickens and pigs foraged in the dirty streets, and coaches grander than their own lurched and passed them. Once there was a great grey building whose attics jutted in a row, and to Jemmy it was faintly familiar; in fact had he not once lived here? He asked Progers. 'Ay, sir, you and your mother lived at the Louvre for a while, and the King was there, and the Queen and Bishop and all.' It sounded, he thought, like a game of chess: but the

15

players had been cold and hungry.

'And Maman. I can remember her, in a green gown. There was no fire and we were frozen.'

'There was no fire for anyone then, sir. Things are somewhat better now.' He went on to speak of the boy King of France who lived nowadays at the Louvre, and of how apt he was at games and wrestling, and forward with his languages, as befitted a King. 'I can remember some French,' said James. His mind was a jumble of that and Flemish, which was a strange language unlike any other; and English, which he had spoken with Maman. His eyes filled with tears as he thought of her. Would she come again and take him back to a rich house? Would the King come to them both?

Progers answered. 'The Queen's Majesty will have a tutor ready, to teach you French and all manner of things a young man ought to know, and the ways of Courts.'

James was uncertain about the tutor, but the rest sounded well enough. And soon the coach stopped at last and he was ushered into the presence of a little old lady who wore a black head-veil and whose teeth stuck out, and her eyes were red-rimmed as though she wept a great deal. He was made to bow to her, which he did finely; and she held out her hand for him to kiss. It was a thin hand, freckled with age but still delicate.

'He hath grown *à merveille*,' said Henrietta

Maria, the widowed Queen of England.

*   *   *

There was other company; the maids in waiting, for although she was poor and exiled the Queen kept a certain state about her; and a pretty young girl, her youngest daughter Henriette, whom King Charles called Minette because she was like a kitten. There was a tall fair young man, the King's next brother James, Duke of York; he looked down his nose sourly at times. He did not believe, or chose not to believe, in the King's marriage; this was Charles' little bastard, and a spoilt one at that; he should not have been admitted to the company. York was sorry his younger brother Gloucester, with whom he generally saw eye to eye, was not present, but Gloucester had quarrelled with the Queen, who had tried to make him a Papist. Mam was interfering; she would not so change *him*.

He raised his eyes and saw the child Jemmy measuring him; he did not smile. Jemmy knew he was not liked; this was the first time it had happened to him, and he would remember.

CHAPTER TWO

But everyone else at the exiled Court petted and made much of him, so he was never solitary. Once there was a special day; he was taken to visit a plump opulent lady in black who he was told was the Queen's sister-in-law, Anne of Austria, Queen Dowager of France. James saw her two sons, the elder Louis XIV of France and too grand to play with small boys; even the younger, Philippe, was no longer good company and seemed concerned not to spoil his clothes. James thought Philippe girlish with his mop of dark frizzed curls like a poodle; but one was not permitted to say so. Later someone—it might have been Progers— whispered to him that Philippe was thought to be the son of Cardinal Mazarin and not of Louis XIII, the latter having been a poor sort of husband for many years.

But his own King did not come.

Progers excused him, and so did Minette, who adored her brother. 'Charles has to travel all over Europe, even to Spain, to try and find aid to regain his kingdom, for Cromwell hath made everyone afraid,' she said. Minette played with James a great deal, as his father had foreseen; and told him what she knew, which was a lot, for there were not servants enough to ensure that the young people did not overhear what went on audibly. But Minette would soon be grown up. 'Then you will be married,' said Jemmy disconsolately, for he enjoyed her company. Minette laughed, showing her pretty teeth.

'We are too poor and not important enough

18

for anyone to want to marry me,' she said. 'When Charles is on his throne again it will be a different matter.' That was the theme which lay beneath all their talk and doings here at Court; when the King shall enjoy his own again, seated in Whitehall.

Jemmy mentioned Whitehall one day to his grandmother and she turned her head aside. He was anxious at once. 'What is wrong, madame? What have I said?' For this imperious little lady could not be called grandam to her face, though her children called her Mam and good-naturedly resisted her constant efforts to rule their lives. But Jemmy watched his grandmother now and saw that she was in deep grief.

'Whitehall,' she said. 'Do not name that name to me. It is not a lucky place. They led my husband out to die there on a day of snow. He was so brave that even his enemies paid tribute to his bravery. Now he is dead my life hath ended. I live only for my children, in particular the King and Henriette. I would see her make a good marriage and then I can die.'

Minette had already been received into the Catholic Church; she did not remember her father, who had died, they said, for the rights of the Church of England; Jemmy had heard them whispering about it. Minette had been in her mother's care almost since her birth; she had been brought out of England in disguise. Another of the children, Princess Elizabeth, had died there, it was said of grief. How did grief kill? To think of it was strange.

Shortly news came of Maman; who had, perhaps, died so. Jemmy was sent for by the Queen Mother and found her at her prie-dieu; when she heard him come in she crossed herself and rose, worn black robes crackling. She came to him and took him in her arms.

'You must be very brave, my child. It is bad news for you.'

'The King?' he faltered, and drew a breath of relief when she said, 'No.' There could not be worse news than that; an accident or a knife-thrust, and his father dead.

Henrietta Maria stroked the rich curls. 'Not he, thank God. But your mother is dead. We must pray for her soul.'

And she led him by the hand into her chapel, while he tried to disentangle his relief about the King from sorrow over Maman. He felt sad, he decided, but it was a long time now since they had met and she had written few letters. He could not picture her dead face; where she was, there had always been tears, scenes, laughter, a lute playing; never stillness, as now. Why had she died?

Queen Henrietta pursed her lips. It would not be fitting to tell the child of York's coarse boast when he heard of the death Lucy, he said, had brought on herself. That might not be true; York was harsh in his judgments. She herself remembered poor Lucy at the Louvre when

20

they were all together with Jemmy, then a baby just learning to crawl. A fine fellow now! She looked down and smiled tenderly. 'You have all your life before you, *chéri*,' she said.

Jemmy heard her out with downcast lids. He felt tears pricking his eyes and it was not manly to shed them. Poor Maman was dead, and could never come now to take him away. But did he want to go? In truth he admitted that he was happy with the company here, despite his uncle York's dislike; and despite Father Gough.

*　　*　　*

Father Gough was the tutor, and there was something in his face, a thing grim and withdrawn, that had not come there because he was a priest and fasted often. How he discovered it James could never remember, but discover he did that Gough's brother had been one of those who, in England, had signed the death-warrant of King Charles I. Whatever had led this man to abandon his country and his faith, and after rigorous training be sent here to serve the widowed Queen, no one ever knew, and Father Gough did not speak of it. He was open, however, about the fact that he had once been a Protestant, but had come to see the error of his ways. What errors? thought the boy. Why should it be an error to be a Protestant? I am one, and so is York, and

21

though I do not like him or he me it is a bond between us. 'I will not change,' he said one day to the tutor.

Father Gough smiled gently. It was his hope, and he knew it was the Queen's also, that Jemmy would indeed change. He did not force the pace; a year or so, the company of other lads at Port-Royal, and accustoming; then the boy himself might request instruction, and he prayed that it might be so. Meantime, young Master Jemmy's education was sadly lacking; he must work hard in order to face the world that one day, please God, might be waiting for him.

And so they worked at mathematics and grammar and Latin and the globes, and increased the smattering of languages Jemmy already had: and all the time with a word here, a word there, Father Gough tried to accustom Jemmy to the notion of Catholic truth, Catholic faith, the old proscribed Faith of England. If sad, estranged England might one day return to the fold of Rome, it would not matter how many names were forgotten. God had already played a part of His hand. A priest named Father Huddleston had aided the King after his flight from Worcester field. He would not be overlooked when the King enjoyed his own again.

But James wrote slowly, stubbornly, in a gradually forming hand, his tongue slightly protruding from his mouth with the effort of

22

concentration. It would be a long time before higher truths need concern him. But after a space he did not see even Father Gough any longer, and instead there came a pawky Scotsman, the first he had met, named Thomas Ross. Jemmy missed the black flapping robes of the Oratorian for a time, and Father Gough's wit; but Ross was apt at beguiling hours away, and lessons grew less tedious than before. The Queen Mother went about with tightened lips; it was against her wishes that the King had changed his son's tutor.

There was also Lord Crofts. It seemed as if he had been there in the background ever since James had come to Court, yet that could not be; only the man had a way of insinuating himself. It was not clear what post he held; Queen Henrietta was as cool with him as she was with Ross; neither of them would aid her cherished hope that Jemmy should turn to Rome. Also it was certain Crofts was in touch with the King wherever the latter might be, whereas she herself was not always informed on this head. Crofts would bring Jemmy little messages of affection, small gifts, letters, salty sayings; and it was to Crofts that Jemmy one day said the forbidden thing. He knew by now that it was forbidden, though nobody had told him this; deep in his mind he kept the knowledge of it, and guarded it carefully. Then something made him blurt it out the day they were laughing, Crofts and he, about the King's reluctant suit of La Grande Mademoiselle, the richest spinster in Europe; very tall and angular and pleased with herself, for she was the King of France's cousin. 'She is a Papist too,' said James; Crofts was his ally against all this Papistry. James and he strolled and talked together, the boy having grown almost as tall as the man; his graceful curls stirred in the wind, while Crofts put a hand to his own stiff periwig. 'The King must marry a Protestant princess if he will please the English people, and get an heir,' he said.

James drew his dark brows together. '*I* am his eldest son.' His bearing had become consciously princely. Crofts frowned quickly, then tacked about. 'You know that meantime the King will have you take my name,' he said. For some time the boy had been written about in despatches as James Crofts. 'It is not yet time for him to acknowledge you openly.'

'For the time only I am called Crofts. My father calls himself Mr Jackson in letters. Soon he will acknowledge me.' The assurance was too swift for the mind of a child; who had been influencing his thoughts? Crofts made a mental note to speak to the tutor. Meantime he changed the subject, smiled, and made the talk gay. It was the swiftest way to win the heart of this boy who would never be serious for long; he seemed as bright and errant as a butterfly. God grant that he fall into no danger, Crofts prayed. He was fond of Jemmy.

24

That night he wrote to the King. A very short while after, Ross the tutor was dismissed. In one way this suited Jemmy very well; there were no more lessons, only shooting across rough country with Lord Crofts, or travelling by my lord's side into Paris. He was growing up unlettered, therefore; but nobody remarked it after the news came from England.

For Oliver Cromwell was dead. Instantly—so it seemed to any observer of affairs in Europe—the different countries breathed again, looked about them, plotted, smiled. Who would rule England? For a while it was Richard Cromwell, the dead man's son. But Queen Dick was known to be too effete to hold the reins of government without letting them drop. After so long a time as eleven years, would matters fall out so that the King could enjoy his own again? Everyone prayed for it; and the education of a half-lettered boy did not seem of prime importance. Quite suddenly a cautious joy seemed to make itself felt at the intrigue-ridden little Court; even the Queen sensed it. James asked Lord Crofts, and that nobleman put a finger to his nose and said, 'Wait and see, my boy, wait and see!' This was not enough, and James escaped upstairs to his aunt Minette, coaxing her to come down to play battledore and shuttlecock with him. Lately she had seemed to grow up and wore her hair in a combed-out frizzed style he thought ugly. She turned the coxcombed head and laughed at him, and came.

Afterwards she said, 'There is a secret, but I should not tell you for you never keep them. No matter, it will be all over Court soon.'

'Tell me.'

'Shall I? Well,' and she edged nearer to him and talked very low, 'they speak of a General Monck, who was one of Cromwell's, but now wants to call my brother home as there is none other to rule England. Think of it! The King will reign at last, and we ... we will all be made different.' She sounded forlorn at the last and James bent and kissed her. He watched her pale long fingers smooth the feathers of the shuttlecock she held. Under her excitement she did not look happy. 'Will you come to live in England?' he asked her, hesitating for fear of what her reply might be. Yet surely the King would send for both of them?

But it was not to be. The King sailed from Breda in May, to be welcomed on his thirtieth birthday by all the citizens of London crowding on balconies and in the street, and Tom Wentworth's old father—Tom was much with the King—had a body of a thousand men all dressed in buff and silver, following on, and the crowds threw flowers and cheered the King's homecoming. Oliver had ruled well, but made England sad; now there would be dancing again, and necklines would be low, and hair curled and cheeks painted. Now this Merry Monarch—they called him so already as his glance raked the women in the streets and along Cheapside as he rode by—would make a different England, one of his own. All of it came back to the Queen's Court in letters, but there was as yet no word of their setting sail.

Meantime there were things to be seen in Paris. They had all sat on tiered seats to watch the King of France go by with his bride, an Infanta of Spain. Louis had been handsome on his horse beneath the gilded canopy, with a great white plume in his hat; but the new Queen was homely. James thought Minette would have made a better Queen of France, and said so. 'Hush,' she answered. Her long lashes closed for an instant over her eyes, then she was gay again.

'There is always Philippe for me. I would not want to live anywhere except in France, although they say our cousin Rupert spoke about me to the Emperor. But that would mean going away.'

Philippe! That little monster to marry with Minette! 'But you will have to bed with him,' blurted out James, on whom the facts of life had never been lost. To think of Philippe's frizzed head on a pillow beside Minette's was unpleasant. She had blushed a little.

'Whoever one marries, that is so,' she replied gently. 'And there are other things. I shall be at the Court of France, and Charles will write to me as he always does, and that will be delightful.'

'But will you not see him again? You love him as I do.'

'It depends on what is arranged for all of us, James. You are always impatient. Wait and see.'

*　　　*　　　*

He waited; and in the end it was Minette who sailed for England, not himself. The Queen and her daughter would spend Christmas at the new Court, and then would return for Minette's wedding to Philippe d'Orléans. James was sick with disappointment; he was to stay with his tutors. They must have forgotten that he had none. It would be dull enough.

Word came soon. There had been great joy at their meeting, all the members of that family parted through the years of war; even Mary, Princess of Orange, the eldest daughter, came, leaving her little son William at The Hague; and thereby was sadness. For Mary died of smallpox in England, murmuring on her deathbed her regrets at having slandered Anne Hyde, her brother York's new wife. York had secretly married Anne, who was a maid-in-waiting to the Princess; she was plain and plump, but clever, for she was the daughter of Clarendon. The Queen was furious; everything was in turmoil until the death steadied all. Queen Henrietta was induced to receive her new daughter-in-law, and forgive her; not before time, for Anne was with child. Of other slanders, made long ago about Lucy Barlow, the dead woman had said nothing.

CHAPTER THREE

Wait and see, they had all of them said; and he had waited almost two years, which was not in his nature. Now, very quickly, a great many things had happened, and at last the ship heaved towards Greenwich in a storm that sent everyone but himself below. He stood on deck riding it out, recalling that earlier time he had crossed the Channel and how it had been still as a pond. Staring at the high waves washing on deck, he reflected on the talk of marriages. Minette was married, and already wretched with her nasty little Philippe; and his own father the King had married again, these two months past, a Portuguese princess who was supposed to bring a rich dowry and then had not brought it after all. 'And she is a Papist, and that will not please the people,' thought James, looking round for Lord Crofts who was below. It was true that it might cause trouble; when all was said, the Civil War had partly been begun because grandam had befriended priests as far as she could, and had refused to be crowned by a Church of England ceremony.

So in the end she had not been crowned at all, and Cromwell had made use of the fact to stop her allowance. But in any event this Portuguese Queen and her offspring should not affect him. 'You are the King's true son,' he heard his mother's voice saying. He often heard that voice, with the Welsh lilt, and pictured her face clearly while the salt winds tore at him.

But there was a plan further to advance him; he remembered that he himself was to be married when they reached England. His bride was a Countess in her own right, a little girl of eleven named Anna Scott of Buccleuch. 'It was that villain Lauderdale put it into His Majesty's head,' Lord Crofts had told him. 'Trust a Scot to see which way the wind blows.' And he was marrying another Scot, or Scott: the pun was poor. It would not affect him greatly for the present, except that he was to change his name again and take his wife's, by some law of the inheritance.

So they would all of them be married, himself and the King and York. His uncle Gloucester, whom he had never met, was dead long ago of the smallpox; the circle was lessening. York's wife had given birth to a boy baby who had died almost at once.

The spray blew high on deck and Crofts came for him, battling against the wind. 'Best come below, sir,' he said, 'a nasty gale's blowing up. At this rate we'll not make Greenwich before morning.'

But to Greenwich they came at last; up the sludgy mouth of Thames, past green flats where sky almost met water, past scattered cottages and farms. A few folk stood on shore to watch the ship pass, wondering who might be aboard her; then more houses, thickening into streets, higher land, trees; the trees of England, some of which had been part of the ancient forest the Romans saw. They were already green, the trees of England; to look upon them made him glad.

Then came London; spires, bridges, crowds crossing on foot and horse. There was the smell of London, which he remembered now the more strongly when it was with him again; a smell of soot, leather, dung, horseflesh, rain, humanity. And last of all Whitehall itself, and a tall swarthy figure waiting; older than James remembered, for the King's travels had scarred him and the lines on his face had grown deep and cynical. Out of the press of courtiers he came, and caught James to him in a mighty hug. 'I cannot lift you now, my son,' the deep voice told him. 'You are much grown. You are a courtier now, Jemmy; come and make your bow to the Queen.'

He went, glad in his heart because the King had called him his son in front of them all. What had he been so afraid of? There was nothing to fear. He was indeed the King's acknowledged son.

The new Queen Catherine received them with grave, formal courtesy; she was very young. At first sight she was plain, with her hair frizzled out after the ugly Portuguese fashion till it resembled a wig. But one noticed then the shy almond-shaped hazel eyes, which were beautiful, and her skin was clear. She was much in love with the King; her eyes followed him wherever he went, a little sadly. James pleased her; he had bowed and kissed her hand as he had been taught, and she smiled at him and stroked his sleeve.

'You are a handsome boy. You are like your father.' The English came with difficulty for she had not yet fully mastered it; she and the King spoke Spanish together. Why was she sad? James found out later, for it was common knowledge at Court. In fact it was Lord Ashley, a little man with a small hunched body and the head of a god, who sidled up to him and told him.

'It is the old story. The King's Castlemaine bore him a son during the honeymoon, and His Majesty could do naught but leave his bride and go to see the brat. Then the fair Barbara cozened him into putting her at the head of the list of ladies of the bedchamber. The Queen refused it, and fainted when they met, bleeding greatly from the nose. That did not please the King, and was the cause of coolness. Now, to

32

atone, the Queen is over familiar with Barbara; she had better have kept her distance.'

Jemmy was diverted; this little man spoke to him as if he were grown. 'Who is Barbara?' he enquired. The other laughed, his curved narrow mouth widening while the long eyes stayed almost shut. 'Well seen you have been long abroad who do not know of great Barbara! A fine wench, but a virago; her husband, Roger Palmer, was in so high a dudgeon at the birth that he had the child christened a Papist, and spoke of leaving the country. I do not know whether or not he is yet gone, but it signifies nothing one way or t'other.'

James saw Lord Crofts seeking him among the crowd, and excused himself. When he found him he asked instantly, 'What of Lord Ashley? He diverts me greatly.'

Crofts looked at the ground. 'Beware of him; he hath a certain power.'

'Is he a Papist?'

Crofts laughed. 'Of all men, never! He hates any such, and will be your friend because you are Protestant.'

'Then I need not fear him.'

Crofts looked at the young unsullied face. 'Fear all men, sir, till they are proved. There will be many out to entrap you, for you are high in favour. Listen to all, ay, and weigh it in your mind; then form your own judgment.'

But Jemmy thought that sounded dull and

weighty; he delighted in knowing everyone, in being sought out by everyone; after Paris, where nothing ever happened, this was paradise. He loved the sight of the richly-dressed women, with their rustling skirts and white forearms showing, and bosoms half so; they excited him. And the men were as often as not dressed as coxcombs, with ribbons tied at the knee, much lace, and the great heavy periwigs that had come into fashion here lest a man should have had his locks cut short in Cromwell's day, and now would sooner not have it known.

'You do not yet know the ways of Courts,' murmured Crofts, his thick brows drawn together. He looked at the boy again; innocent, guileless, beautiful as a young god; both women and men would seek him out, and neither for his good. 'Have a care to whom you speak, sir!' he said again, and again 'Have a care!'

But Jemmy was looking at a handsome sword-hilt on a satin coat, and did not heed him.

*   *   *

He had been found lodgings in the Privy Gallery for the time, but soon would have a house of his own at Whitehall; in the Cockpit, above the old tennis court, still to be rebuilt. Meantime he saw the King every day, and the

Queen most days. And he saw the King's Castlemaine. He would never forget her.

*   *   *

He had held his breath; he had never seen such beauty. Evil she might be, greedy and false and promiscuous; it did not matter. He had seen fair women before; there had been the elfin prettiness of Minette, his own mother's brown beauty and fine eyes and hair; Cardinal Mazarin's lovely nieces; some others, about Court here, whom the King would ogle; but never the like of Barbara. She had red-gold hair which shone with health, and her breasts were a marvel of symmetry; beauty itself, pagan and indestructible, was here. Not even childbirth had destroyed the opulent figure, fair skin and throat, the delicate caressing hands; these roved over the boy, and it would seem she was as pleased with this son as with her own. 'We are rogues both, are we not?' she murmured, and petted and caressed him before them all. They began to whisper that had he been a year or two older, his father had been made jealous; but the King only laughed. It pleased him that both Catherine and Barbara loved his son.

*   *   *

He had his portrait painted; once scantily

attired as John the Baptist, clasping a banner and a lamb; once again for a portrait in an oval, with Lucy painted holding it. The artists had not, he thought, portrayed her truly, but how well could one paint the dead? He dimly remembered in her time when they were in England having a miniature of himself taken by Samuel Cooper, who had painted Cromwell; his own child's head confronted him accordingly in the King's rooms. He was embarrassed at being made childish; he no longer thought of himself as anything but a man. He was to be married soon; was that not almost proof of it?

*   *   *

He was married in April, when the newly planted lilacs in the King's garden at St James's had burst into tender leaf. The little bride Anna Scott had come to Court with her mother Lady Wemyss, who was stout, twice married, jolly and friendly and made much of James. Anna herself was shy and unsure; she had been Countess of Buccleuch for only two years, since the death of her elder sister Mary, whom they had not even saved by having her touched for the King's Evil. Anna had long fair hair of which she was vain; otherwise she would sooner have read a book than spoken with anyone, though later her tongue would spill much wit. She was a good dancer, and loved it;

36

she and her young husband would tread the boards gracefully together. The marriage took place in the King's great chamber; afterwards the bride was kissed by the King and Queen, by her mother and, somewhat unwillingly, by her husband. James had decided that she was too clever for him, and her nostrils had a haughty set. He was glad he need not see her often; despite his manhood, the marriage was not yet to be consummated. He gave Anna his hand in the bridal dance; everyone said they made a pretty pair; the King danced also, and the Queen; afterwards there was great feasting, and later still they were put to bed, but James was permitted only to lay his leg over the bride and was then taken away. He was vexed at the company's laughter; he could have done much more.

At any rate, he was no longer James Crofts; he was James Scott, Duke of Monmouth and Buccleuch, Earl of Doncaster, Earl of Dalkeith, Baron Tynedale, Lord Scott of Whitchester and Eskdaill. They would have made him Baron Fotheringay, but the King had stopped it; the Queen of Scots had lost her head at Fotheringay, and there was no need to pair such luckless fate with Jemmy.

*   *   *

A week later the Court was at Windsor. The evening had drawn in and, again, there was music for dancing. Monmouth had the Queen as his partner; her small body moved formally and correctly, and she had had herself dressed in the English style, with her hair combed smooth and curled over one shoulder, and threaded with pearls. Monmouth was taller than she by many inches, and all eyes were upon them; in his mind he knew what they were saying. She bears no heir; he is a Protestant, the King they say married his mother. How handsome he is! What a King he would make, our Jemmy!

The rebecks and fiddles sounded high and clear. Among the dancers were those he knew, Castlemaine with her red-gold curls dressed elegantly, Lord William Russell with his wife, who ruled him always. They moved in a glitter of gold and soft bloom of velvet, sheen of silk, hush of lace. Monmouth's own costume was superb, stiff with gold. The plumes of his hat, held in his hand, whirled as he went through the complicated motions of the dance; he danced well that night. The King watched idly. Queen Catherine smiled bravely, her slightly prominent teeth making her look like a little good-natured animal, her flat feet padding the measure beneath her gathered gown. The music increased in pace; Monmouth handed the Queen lightly, her skirts whirling. They wheeled and circled as His Majesty stalked to the floor, but not to dance. He kissed Monmouth and, taking his plumed hat, clapped it on the boy's head. A murmur arose from the watchers; this was the royal accolade, permitted to none except princes of the blood. Some kept their eyelids lowered; it had been foolish of the King.

CHAPTER FOUR

The Court was gay three seasons of the year, but in summer the London streets stank and there was danger of the plague and of sweating sickness. All who could do so went into the country. Monmouth accompanied his father to Windsor, where King Charles loved to go out fishing, rain or shine; to Newmarket for the horse-meetings, where a strange thing happened as events were to fall out. A soothsayer sat in cap and gown, nearby the straining beautiful horses; Monmouth at once went to him. He had always had faith in luck and fortunes, though some said they were folly. Ashley the amusing dwarf was one of those who agreed with him; he would do nothing without consulting his horoscope, and now odds were shortening on the horses, one of which belonged to the King.

The soothsayer looked up, saw a tall young gallant, and began to speak rapidly, for time was money and they had not yet gone off to the pistol. 'Which will win, say you?' asked the boy eagerly. The soothsayer predicted such a one, and such another, and another; in the end not one he had named came through. He told Monmouth also to beware of the river Rhine and that fifteen was his unlucky number. Monmouth hurried off to put his money on the winners, and lost all he had. 'You will never be near the Rhine, and you have poured good money after bad,' said the King, and would write of it to Minette. But all his life Monmouth was to believe in soothsayers.

They made progresses about the country; everywhere the King's son was to be seen at the King's side, and could almost by now rival Charles' long striding walk, for he had grown as tall as his father. His energy was boundless; he was foremost in the hunt, highest at the vault, first to climb, run, shoot at pigeon, take joy in his own youth and in his splendid body. Everything whereby it was put to use was a pleasure; 'the most leaping gallant ever I saw,' wrote Pepys somewhat sourly in his diary. Like others, Pepys had noted Monmouth's coat of arms wherein, borne on his coach, there showed no sign of bastardy, no bar sinister. Among its arms of England, Scotland and France the stag passant and star of Buccleuch showed proudly. And Monmouth had been seen to admiration in the gorgeous robes and white-plumed hat of the Knights of the Garter, and the King had given him one of diamonds and another of pearls to show off his shapely calf. Fortune favoured him, and most of fortune's children; everyone who was anyone sought him out, with the possible exception, as a rule, of his uncle York. Generally in any case their ways fell separately, for York was by now a heavily married man; his Duchess was pregnant again, watching from her windows in the Mall as the crowds loitered, uncertain which way to follow; they loved it best when the King was at home and would go down to the water to feed his coloured fowl. But the King had other prowess; Barbara Castelmaine was pregnant also. 'You only have to look at her and she bellies out like a ship in full sail,' quipped Charles. But his Queen still bore him no children.

CHAPTER FIVE

Monmouth was back in town for the spring gaieties; by now he was accustomed to doffed hats, and felt himself to be of great importance; yet he was uncivil to no man. They had solemnly conferred Master of Arts degrees on him at both Oxford and Cambridge, but he still found it laborious to write a letter. His house at the Cockpit was building; soon it would be ready, but meantime there was yet another, at Chiswick, very pretty and neat; at the time of their entry into it King Charles gave the little

Duchess of Monmouth a pair of diamond earrings. Her spouse was pleased enough that she made friends—one of them was York—with her learning and wit as long as she did not trouble him; and she did not.

Barbara Castlemaine's child was born and proved another boy. The Duchess of York went into labour and gave birth to a girl, which pleased nobody; but it was a pretty little thing with dark eyes and hair, and would live, and be christened Mary. Monmouth, bored with talk of births, saw a good deal of Ashley, a good deal also of Lord William Russell, a solid friendly good fellow, son to the Duke of Bedford. Prince Rupert had taken a house in Spring Gardens and they all three went there to see his combustible furnace used for making chemicals. They saw and marvelled, but were not treated to Rupert's common remedy for fools, which was to throw sulphur on the fire and make so nauseous a smell that visitors left. Instead, they talked of the great battles of the Civil War, when Rupert had formed the body of horse which became famous as his Cavaliers, so much so that Cromwell had copied them in making his New Model Army. Monmouth's blood warmed at the tale of the mounted charges; he would like to be a soldier. He watched his host's saturnine face beneath the great periwig: they said Rupert's skull was open to the size of a shilling beneath it, and he suffered much pain also from a leg wound got in France. But he was as full of fire as ever. 'There will be trouble with the Dutch soon,' he barked out, 'you may yet see war.' This was odd talk for a man whose family had sheltered in Holland all his youth; but in war the enemy was no friend, even were he Jan de Witt, the Grand Pensionary.

*   *   *

Rupert was right; the trouble with the Dutch came to a head that summer. The day came when the King laid his arm on his son's sleeve and said, 'Now, Jemmy, you shall taste war.'

He assigned him to York, who was not pleased to be at such a charge; as Lord High Admiral of the Fleet he had other matters on his mind, and Lucy Barlow's brat would make a holiday of it. He stood stiffly, Monmouth eagerly, when matters turned out as they did; Monmouth was to serve in the Red squadron under York. They sailed from Lowestoft on the third of June.

*   *   *

He watched the flat Suffolk coast melt away in the sun's heat and let the summer wind blow through his dark hair. It was a sou' wester and good fortune, the sailors said. He looked about him with the shy curiosity of a novice at the rigging, the tarred ropes, the three-deck rows

43

of cannon that would fire in line ahead, so that the fire could rake the enemy. The *Royal Charles*, the Admiral's ship on which he stood, had seventy-eight guns shining in the day. And the enemy was not far off; soon, a shout came.

'They are eastward of us!' A cheer rose; the wind was with England and they were ready for a fight. Monmouth stayed in his place and watched the White squadron, with Prince Rupert in command, sail ahead, rigging spread proudly. Rupert had harried Commonwealth England at sea long enough to know the men under him. He held his fire till the Dutch discharged, then waited his moment for a full broadside; it came, and time after time shook the sea like thunder for an hour, smoke and flame searing the calm of the day.

The Dutch squadron tacked about when it could, sails furled; majestically, the White followed suit, placing Sandwich, who commanded the Blue at the rear, now in van. The guns roared on and the enemy could not pass to gain advantage of the wind. There was exhilaration on the English decks; to get at them now, hand to hand! Now there would be revenge for the Dutch plague in the seas about Africa; now there would be old wrongs righted, and the smell of blood! Monmouth glanced at the upright figure of the Admiral on his quarter-deck; this copybook battle would no doubt please his uncle, who liked things to happen predictably.

But York gave orders to ram the enemy fleet, and the Red squadron burst through the line. Now no one could see the next man's face for smoke, and again the cannon thundered. Monmouth felt the heedlessness of battle come on him; he did not care that he was in danger, but gloried in it. This was to be a man. The Dutch line was presently cut in two; he heard the sailors shout the news to one another cheerfully, as though they feasted, and he was one of them.

The *Royal Charles* opened fire full blast at Opdam's *Eendracht* with her seventy-eight, and the conflict raged in sound and flame, each ship engaging her own. Once there was a grating collision, and men prepared to rush across decks to where the grim-faced Dutchmen stood, swords ready. But the *Charles* made away; a shot was fired then which killed three men standing next to the Admiral, and his armour was smeared with their blood. 'He might have been among them,' Monmouth thought. His uncle was cool in danger; despite everything, he admired him this day. He had drawn his own sword and the blade was red; he stared at it unbelievingly.

A sudden growing roar, and the *Tendracht* blew up. Afterwards he learnt that their shot had fired the powder-magazine, spewing bodies and tackle to the waves. Some of the crew still lived, struggling in the churning water. Only five were to be saved of all the ship's company; these are men, he thought, and we can watch them die. He felt pity for them.

The Dutch fleet limped off at last. He was surprised that it was already near evening. The day had seemed short, yet the Admiral had been on duty eighteen hours. No one had eaten anything since breakfast. After the roads were clear York came down to get some sleep. He and Monmouth surveyed one another, faces black with powder, showing white runnels where the sweat had run down. The older man's stiff lips moved, the eyes surveyed him.

'You did well,' said York, then with difficulty, 'I will see that the King hears of it.'

*   *   *

Bad luck dogged York even after victory. They stayed in pursuit; at dawn next day a man named Brouncker went up on deck and said the Admiral's orders were to furl sail. In this way they lost the escaping enemy fleet; the chance of annihilating it was gone, perhaps for ever. When York came on deck and found what had been done he was angry; nevertheless, his enemies would use the story later to accuse him of cowardice.

*   *   *

They went home, to cheers and a heroes' welcome; Monmouth grew used to the sound every time he rode abroad. Monmouth Jemmy, folk called him now; he heard the name shouted in friendly fashion in the streets. Monmouth Jemmy, sixteen years old, having acquitted himself as well as any, appraised himself; but results were not always fair. When the King, delighted with his prowess, sent him to report on the defences of east-coast towns, he did his duty as well as he might. But Pepys, again feeling sour, wrote only that the Duke of Monmouth had ridden down to debauch the women.

*   *   *

Christmas of 1665 they spent, King and Court, with Lord Crofts at his Suffolk home of Saxham. There was skating on the ponds, the men would shoot by day, etiquette was lax and everyone spoke to anyone. Of an evening, they danced; Monmouth chose partners for their pretty faces, but he did as much in Whitehall. Among the company was a little child with silver-fair hair and a missing milk tooth; they called her Lady Harry. It was not until near the end of the visit that he learned who she was; Tom Wentworth's daughter, handsome Tom who used to be much about the King in his travels, and who was lately dead. This child had inherited his title and his half-ruined estate of Toddington in Bedfordshire. She was some kin to Crofts. Monmouth heard no more and he soon forgot her. But that was their first meeting.

*　　　*　　　*

There was ill fortune also in London, though it would eventually turn to good. A baker's shop in the City took fire, and the wind spread the flames to all adjoining houses. Shortly the streets themselves, with their overhanging timber buildings, were ablaze with rats running screaming from underfoot. The King rode in, and ordered the blowing-up of certain houses to stop the spread. He and Monmouth and the Duke of York stood among the rest passing buckets of water to throw on the flames, while shocked women with bundles crowded into the clear places and fields beyond town: but the fire smouldered on for days and would burst out afresh when it was thought to have subsided. In all, by the end thirteen thousand houses were said to have been destroyed, and many landmarks such as St. Paul's.

Good came, but not what it might have been. The Mayor and aldermen rejected the new plans the architect Wren made for a city with wide streets. When houses were put up again it was as the common folk wanted them, leaning close and narrow so that a woman might stand at an upstairs window and talk to her neighbour. So the plague would rise anew, at least in the crowded alleys; later it was realised that the fire had almost done away with it, for the time.

*   *   *

Other matters moved apace. The relations between York and his nephew were less strained since the battle at sea. They attended the Charlton Hunt near Chichester together, and York was pleased enough with his nephew's poise in the saddle, plumes streaming, thighs gripping, hair flying; Monmouth never failed to be in at the kill. That the boy was no coward York now knew, and grudgingly acknowledged; but then the same boy incautiously said a thing which put him out of favour again. He was in love with the beautiful Charlton country; once at the end of a long day's hunt he stretched himself in the saddle, looked over at the green woods, and said, 'When I am King this is where I shall hold my Court.'

York said nothing, but noted it.

CHAPTER SIX

'I believe that you may readily guess that I am something concerned for this bearer, James, and therefore I put him in your hands to be directed to you in all things, and pray use that authority over him as you ought to do in kindness to me.'

He watched the bent, curled head of Henriette Anne, Madame of France, and her pearl ear-drops swinging as she read. Outside in the cold, there were the formal gardens of St-Cloud. Where he stood were riches and warmth, painted ceilings and tapestries, lacquered chinoiserie, gilt chairs. But Minette was not a happy woman; her face was peaked and pale below her rouge. Not long ago her only son had died; and her marriage was known to be obscene. Monmouth had been glad Philippe Monsieur had not been there to greet him on arrival; he might have kicked the little fuzz-headed pervert who paraded his male favourite in front of his wife.

Minette raised her head, smiling at her tall nephew. It was a fair prospect; Monmouth had grown till he was fully the height of the King, and his well-marked brows showed the planes of a face which would have delighted a sculptor; a pale oval, with a full mouth and cleft chin, and framing it the magnificent hair, combed long and full in the latest fashion. His attire was fashionable too; a young blood! She felt tenderness rise for this son of Charles, who was so far away. 'Do you remember,' she said softly, 'when we played battledore and shuttlecock at Chaillot? And now I am to have authority over you.'

'I will obey you in all things.'

'How young we were then! And you are still young. We must show you to the King at Versailles at Christmas, or maybe Twelfth Night, for that is merrier.'

'I have a gift of horses for him from His Majesty.' He spared a thought for the horses, who had made the crossing well. He was about to describe them—they were superbly bred and matched—but he saw his aunt's long eyes slide warily towards the door; she was spied on. He dropped his eyes quickly. What could one do to aid her, alone as she was here in a foreign land? Yet he remembered her saying that she would not live anywhere but in France. They still whispered that Louis XIV had been in love with her. Now, many others were so. He wondered if she took lovers to console herself for the distasteful Philippe. In England it would have caused no comment; here it would be fatal. They said Madame was gay, and he could sense the gaiety, a quality like froth and flower-essence; underneath was great unhappiness.

He said, 'I was sorry for the death of grandam. I should have liked to kiss her hand again.'

'Poor Mam. She died in her sleep, which was merciful. Her life was not a happy one, except for her marriage. Whatever else may be said of them, she and my father loved one another. Come; I will show you St-Cloud, and this

51

afternoon we will go for a drive, and in the evening there will be a play, and tomorrow night Lulli can be heard at Versailles, but perhaps it is not yet time to take you there till you are recovered from your journey.'

But he was fully recovered. The days passed in a round of feverish enjoyment in which he took full part; Minette was glad of his escort, for at least there could be no scandalous gossip concerning aunt and nephew; or so one would have thought, but the Court smeared everything. Monmouth met the Roi Soleil, splendid and coruscating, still recognisable as the formal young man of the days at Chaillot. Louis had two mistresses, one the shy, unworldly La Vallière, who loved him, and the other the flamboyant Montespan, another man's wife. In the way that he had once admired Barbara Castlemaine Monmouth admired La Montespan; her opulent white flesh, her golden hair—everyone knew she dyed it, but it became her—and the flaunting insolence she brought to the position of King's favourite, although as yet unrecognised, for poor La Vallière was the *maîtresse en titre* and the King and Montespan even used her house for their assignations. 'The Church frowns on the adultery and each Lent, they separate for a time,' said Minette, and Monmouth remembered the suspicion he had once had that she was herself in love with Louis; but all that was long ago.

He found Paris amusing, and would have stayed a long time; but word came from England that his wife Anna had injured herself while dancing, and he must return at once. He did so with regret, keeping the memory of Minette's little peaked rouged face long in his mind as his carriage rattled towards the sea. He knew well enough that the Chevalier de Lorraine, Philippe d'Orléans' odious *mignon*, had started gossip about her and himself. For everyone's sake, it was time, no doubt, that he took his leave. His thoughts were of Minette on the journey, never of Anna. When would she come to England? He had asked her on parting. The dark eyes had filled with tears.

'If I could but do so, it would be worth everything else in the world to me.' Then she had recollected herself and had sent her dear love to His Majesty. 'And have a heed to yourself also, Jemmy; you are heedless, as I was once. It does not do in the end; one must be prudent in this world. Farewell, and treat your wife kindly; she is young.'

Anna was at Bath, hoping for recovery with the waters. He went straight to her room, where she lay in bed. Her fair locks were loose about the pillow; she grimaced when she moved, for she had sprained a thigh. The blue, long-lidded gaze turned on him; it contained no warmth.

'How do you fare?' he asked her. He was sorry she was in pain. She shrugged her shoulders a little.

'It will take time, they say. The doctors set it badly at first and it had all to be done again. I cannot walk yet. I am sorry to have drawn you away from your pleasures in Paris.'

Her tone was languid, to hide the pleasure she felt at seeing him; she was aware he cared nothing for her, but she found in course of her recovery that he could be kind; any hurt thing had his sympathy. But for her own part she was bitter: she might be his superior with her shafts of wit for which she was becoming celebrated, but no longer would the perfection of her dancing match his own. She knew before the physicians told her; for the rest of her life she would be lame, and walk with a limp. Monmouth broke the news to her, however, and she wept.

'It is the only thing we could do together, and now I shall dance no more.' Her voice rose on the last syllable to a wail, like that of a child. She was hardly more, and he seized her hand and kissed it.

'Sweetheart, there is one other thing we may do, that we have not done yet: but that must wait on your recovery.'

She blushed; the marriage had yet to be consummated. They were almost twenty, and it was time.

The thing was done, as soon as she grew better; Monmouth found enjoyment in becoming a husband in deed as well as in name.

For a time he was constantly in Anna's company, though her sharp tongue chilled him.

*　　　*　　　*

There was a greater joy; the King promoted him captain of the Life Guards, to the thunder of ordnance and glitter of ceremony. The polish Monmouth had acquired in Paris enabled him to go through it perfectly, mounted in his new saddle, a gift from the King. It was made of scarlet velvet, embroidered with gold powdering and arabesques in gold and silver, and a plumed helmet which showed behind his thigh.

CHAPTER SEVEN

Moll Kirke hitched her bedgown round her naked shoulders, and turned from where she sat on the bed's edge to survey her lover. Monmouth Jemmy was delicious, fresh, and eager; a change from Mulgrave, who was good-natured enough, and York, who was pedestrian; but it added some little savour to the task of waiting upon the Duchess to know that one also served the Duke. But this ... this was youth, godlike, abandoned; if only he could come to her openly! She watched him as he lay asleep, his full lips parted a trifle, as if after kisses; his fine hand, which had caressed her so knowledgeably, flung out of the sheets, so that its texture and symmetry showed to admiration. Beautiful hands; the King's hands. It was almost better than having Charles himself here, a favour she had not yet sought to attain.

He turned his head into the pillow, and Moll put out a warning arm to shake him. 'Best go, sir,' she whispered against his hair. 'There will be others in here, and you must not be taken or we'll both fare ill.'

'Taken?' He blinked awake, cherry-lipped, dark-eyed, flush-faced. He reached out to her. 'I'll take you again, sweetheart, for certain: who is to say nay? It's not morning yet.' He brushed a hand across his eyes and was suddenly full awake. 'Come here, jade; what a jade you are, eh, Moll, Moll...'

'And you are wickedly demanding, sir ... Ah, have a care, they'll come soon, but now...'

'They? The devil take 'em, whoever they are.' But being broad awake he knew very well who they were; Mulgrave would come to her tonight, and his uncle at any time. He laughed within himself at the thought of York, staid, straightforward, stupid, a lover of such flesh. Yet there were many beautiful women at Court; he'd only taken Moll for the jest of it. He had a plan that would ensnare Mulgrave and infuriate York; it should happen tonight, before the taste grew sour. He sat up in bed and began pulling on his breeches. He, the captain of the guard ... York made a fool of ... they said York had become a Papist in Ghent last year. In a way it suited him, he wouldn't have to think for himself, but he hadn't mended his ways with such as Moll ... ah, Moll. His head ached. He passed a hand through his hair, smoothing its ruffled strands. He'd never wear a wig; they were hot, and inconvenienced a man needlessly. In bed, for example ... but it was time to be gone. He dressed himself, yawning, and went; leaving her with the memory of a kiss at the end, uncertain whether he would or would not be back again. So many wenches, so little time ... Monmouth Jemmy.

*   *   *

He knew York had been displeased over the Life Guards appointment. That was not all; his uncle had opposed the notion of his being on the Privy Council, still more his promotion to the Lord Lieutenancy of Ireland. They might keep their rain-swept bogs, however; he'd stay in London, among good company; Ormonde, York's man, could go to Ireland. He himself had his own friends; Ashley loathed York, and had made Monmouth known to others who did also. The King? He kept his own counsel, and treated both brother and son with affection. The Duchess? She bore children

57

yearly who died; only the little Mary, who would be a beauty, and Anne, a plump stolid infant, lived. York they said was fond of his children, nearly as fond as he was of plain ugly women; but Moll Kirke was not ugly, otherwise he himself would never have bedded with her. Mulgrave...

That night he played the jest on Mulgrave, as the latter emerged from Moll's chamber fastening his small-clothes; the guard were told to arrest him and detain him till morning. York would be furious; perhaps he would debar Mulgrave from the promotion he wanted in the Foot Guards.

It happened as planned; and Mulgrave retorted by telling the Duke of York that his nephew had been in Moll's bed as often as himself. The cold eyes of York grew colder as they surveyed the distant, gorgeous and nonchalant figure of the people's Monmouth Jemmy. One day retribution would fall on that handsome, careless and elegantly dressed dark head. Perhaps it had been a mistake not to let Monmouth go to Ireland; but Ormonde was already appointed there at the Duke's urging.

So, through Moll, any goodwill lingering from sea-fights and hunting days withered. Monmouth continued to behave himself as the King's heir, flouting his uncle. Put to the test, the King swore, in presence of witnesses,

'I would sooner see him hanged at Tyburn than make him my heir.'

But the sun shone and wenches were kind, and Monmouth had eight thousand pounds a year which were always spent by midsummer. Soon there came agreeable news; Madame was to visit England, not having seen her brother the King for almost eleven years, in her girlhood.

*   *   *

She sailed into Dover with an escort of the King's ships, for Charles had sent the French escort home in mid-Channel. White sails unfurled to a cloudless sky; the King strode on deck, and they embraced, the brother and sister, after so long; held back and looked at one another, and laughed and sighed. Tall Prince Rupert, who had once vowed to betroth her to the Emperor, bent low and kissed her hand. The Duke of York stood silent, never able to speak easily to those he loved; and Madame turned and smiled at the tall splendidly attired young man who had come on board with the rest. 'We are old friends,' she murmured. Monmouth was handsomer than ever, she decided; marriage had matured him. She forgot him for moments, as the next pressing visitant came forward; everyone waited to see her, meet her, have speech with her. Monmouth had withdrawn, and went and stared at the blue-green water; behind him the sounds of pleasure and welcome ran on.

Madame was happy now, in a moment of happiness snatched from time; was happiness so fragile a thing, to fade, leaving nothing? Was he himself happy? Until today he had not thought about it; even now, he could think of nothing he wanted that he did not possess.

He did not dwell on it again in the round of dancing and gaiety which marked Madame's three-week visit. Nor did he know of the real reason for the latter; that in Madame's possession were certain secret documents, which in due course King Charles would sign. It made him a pensioner of France, bound to help that country against the Dutch; bound also to embrace the Catholic Faith as soon as might be. That was already the King's private desire; but, as he said, he had no wish to be sent on his travels again.

*   *   *

Often there was laughter. An actor named Nokes was among those hired to entertain the company during Madame's visit; they had dressed him in a ridiculously short coat in mockery of those now fashionable at Versailles. Monmouth took him behind the scenes and buckled his sword on, and the dragging weight made the abject garment odder than ever. Nokes made his entry to howls of laughter from the audience, and 'the French were shagrinned.'

Minette had received the King for the last time and had opened her jewel-case; it was a matter of hours before she must sail back to France. The jewels lay there, sparkling and gleaming; a young Breton maid-in-waiting held them in her white hands. One of her blue eyes had a delicate cast.

'Take what you like best, as a gift from me,' Minette said. She could not take her eyes from the tall swarthy figure; so greatly beloved, and to part again so soon! Yet she herself could not be happy forever in England now; too much had come between.

Charles raised his eyes; he had hardly looked at the jewels. His gaze was set on the little maid, who blushed; the colour came up evenly in round cheeks devoid of paint; her hair was dark and fell in curls. 'Give me this jewel,' the King said, but Madame demurred; the child was young, and must return to France.

Her name was Louise de Kéroualle.

CHAPTER EIGHT

Monmouth sat with Ashley over a bottle of wine. The light from the candles flared on the two handsome faces, fair and dark; disguising Ashley's stunted body in their shadows. Was it because Crofts had told him long ago that Ashley was dangerous that he, Monmouth, so relished his company? The little fellow was amusing, always ready with the latest gossip; what harm could that do?

'You are not the King's eldest son, sir.'

The long fair-lashed eyelids raised themselves a trifle, the clumsily fashioned hands curled beneath the table's edge out of sight. Ashley waited for the expected anger and astonishment; it came. 'You are feeble in your wit today,' Monmouth finished cheerfully. He could never hold a grudge against a friend.

'I have said it and it is so. There is an elder than you by three years.'

'What, did my father get a son when he was sixteen? Yet he was not married to the mother.' He always, knowingly, defended his own mother's honour; there was no one else to do so.

Ashley sipped his wine. 'I know no more of it than the next man. But this other hath become a Papist, and is in fair way to becoming a priest. He is to travel here in due time, as His Majesty's confessor when he, like your uncle, turneth Papist so that all the world may know it.'

Monmouth swore an oath. His father was neither Catholic nor Protestant, but open-minded, like himself; for the argument of the thing he would place himself against York. The flattery of such as Ashley pleased him. He poured more wine.

'What is this man's name and where is he now?' As well to know of it; but the whole thing was a chimera.

'James de la Cloche,' said Ashley slowly. 'He is with the Jesuits in Rome. France hath other ties with the Court of England. Saw you Madame's little maid of honour the King ogled?'

'There are many women, I know not if they be maids, and the King ogles every one.'

'Well, we shall see. Her name was Louise de Kéroualle; mark it.'

'Why should I do so? What the devil ails you?' He was angry; both at the news of James de la Cloche and of Louise. It was as though some worm gnawed away the foundations on which he stood. Ashley had not done talking, fixing him always with those long eyes that missed nothing. He spoke softly, leaning across the table to the other, fingering his glass.

'That the devil may be in't is true. Think you Madame came to England only to visit her brother, when her odious husband was so greatly set against it that he slept with her each night in order to get her pregnant, so that she would not be permitted to leave France?'

'I do not like your talk,' said Monmouth. 'How do you know all of this? You are like a carrion crow, tearing at vitals before a man is dead.'

'Dead men tell no tales. And I have my ways

of knowing. You and I may yet be the richer for this eagerness of France to be served with what's afoot here.'

'You go too deep for me.'

Ashley smiled. 'Think you Louis would welcome a strong England united within herself? I say to you that he wishes us divided. In such a way we can be no menace to him in his ambitions to own all Europe. The little Dutchman is tough, but without allies his strength will fail. King Louis would pay men here to divide the counsels of the nation, Protestant against Catholic. Our soldiers may fight for him, ay, and be slaughtered cheaply for his cause. But there is another army among us here; and we want you, sir, to lead us.'

'I am loyal to my father,' said Monmouth hotly. The other smiled.

'That goes without saying; all of us are loyal to the King. Nothing will be asked of you save that you put your name at our head; then the forces will have a rallying-point against ... foreigners.'

'Who else have you?' Monmouth recognised the sidling avoidance of the name of York; he would be happy enough to oppose his uncle.

'Russell is one.'

'He is a good fellow.' Monmouth liked Lord William Russell and his loving termagant of a half-French wife, and his wistful beautiful mother who had been the only child of the scandalous Somersets. 'Who else?'

'There is Pembroke, and Danby, and Essex, and Holles, and more.'

Monmouth was nodding over his wine. The resentment he had felt at mention of James de la Cloche receded. If the young man in truth existed and came, he had best tread warily; none should usurp his, the heir's, place. But perhaps de la Cloche would not come.

'More wine,' said Ashley gently, and brought his ugly hand again up out of the shadows to refill the glasses. The light shone on his Grecian profile and fair wig. If he had had a body to match his face, he might not have been so readily consumed with envy at the sight of Monmouth, tall, graceful, and half drunk, lolling back from the table. But as a figurehead he would be superb; with Ashley's brains behind the enterprise. 'Pay no more heed now,' the latter said, 'but remember.'

'Remember what?' His wits were indeed fuddled with wine; what had Ashley been saying?

'That we are all together in this.' The small man raised his glass, and drank deep.

*　　　*　　　*

Ashley had a weakness, odd in one so self-sufficient; he doted on astrologers. He had been told, he said, that he would have much power and three wives, and would die of the gout. As yet he had none, but it would come.

'And my good wife Margaret is my third, as he said.'

'I went to a soothsayer also,' yawned Monmouth. 'He bade me beware the Rhine and the number fifteen; I have put myself to some trouble concerning the latter, but the former eludes me. And there was another in France that cast my horoscope, which I carry.'

'It cannot avail you here. This I speak of is no charlatan, but a man grown rich with prophecy. He was a poor farmer's son who could not abide the plough, and so he came to London as the servant of a man of wealth. When the man died he married his old widow, who had had two husbands before. So now he may do as he pleases. He hath spend her money on astrological books, a great library he hath, and much custom.'

'What is his name? I should like to meet with so enterprising a fellow.'

'Lilley. He boasts of telling each man the truth about himself.'

'No man doth that.'

'Come and see.'

So they entered a coach together, making their way through empty spaces where streets had been burned down in the fire and were not yet rebuilt. Presently they came to a pleasant house, set back in its own garden. Ashley smiled as Monmouth ascended the steps; he had said nothing of it, but Dr Lilley had several lawsuits presently on hand, some from

66

Members of Parliament, for telling the truth to them.

Above on the stairs an old woman peered down; no doubt this was the wife whose money had been spent on books. Monmouth jangled the gold coins in his purse, and looked about him as he was shown into a room, larger than the hall and shadowed by a leaping fire. The furnishings were fantastic, and included an astrolabe and also a device, which Monmouth had not before seen, for registering the turning of each planet about the sun. It stood in a square frame, and contained globes and squares, each diminishing inside one another till they came to the centre.

'I bid you good-evening.' Dr Lilley did not stir from his place before a great cabinet of books; it was for the customer to come to him. He wore a velvet coat and a skull-cap such as philosophers had worn a generation since. He knew Monmouth well enough, but said nothing of it.

'I would know the future.' He heard his own voice echo in the room, catching strange responses from the metal machinery and books. A sense of excitement rose in him; he was grateful to Ashley. He sat on one of the chairs, crossing one silk-clad beribboned leg over the other.

'I do not speak to flatter,' said Dr Lilley. 'I predicted, as long ago as Cromwell's time in 'fifty-one, that London would burn beneath the sign of Gemini; and many other sayings of mine have come true for certain folk, who do not always like it.' He smiled; he had an uncommon charm, a narrow face and short beard.

'Let me have a particle of your truth, then, and I'll pay you well for't.'

Lilley rose presently, set a hand on the great machine, and spun the planets in their squares; a humming noise came from the metal, and Monmouth shivered. He had always been superstitious, a legacy from his Welsh mother. Some said it was folly, but he carried charms and amulets, and consulted them.

There was silence in the room; the machine had stopped spinning. Dr Lilley stood staring down, his lids concealing his eyes.

'Well?' said Monmouth. 'Out with it, man; have I good fortune or ill?'

The man's voice was hoarse. 'You say your birth date is the ninth of April; that is in Aries, and you are affected by the head, which ... is impulsive. You must guard against impulses. I will say no more.'

'No more? But you have not told me the half of what you have there; what do the stars say?'

Dr Lilley closed his eyes in pity. 'They are silent,' he lied. 'The stars are silent. I will take no money.'

*   *   *

There was a rumour flying about Court;

68

Monmouth heard it when he returned and met Bab May walking in the grassy space where there had once been a tennis court. Behind, the façade of his own new house reared brash and unweathered. He looked at the other's shocked face. 'What ails you?' he asked, for Bab was a cheerful fellow. They had met often in taverns and at Ashley's house, and trusted one another.

'Have you not heard? They say Madame is dead.' Bab's grimed hand flew before his eyes to hide their feeling; men called him the King's creature, but he loved the King.

Monmouth was still. He was thinking of Minette, graceful and laughing in the garden at Dover Castle only seven weeks since. 'But she is young,' he heard himself blurt out. The words fell heedlessly on the summer air.

'Ay, and for that reason they are saying—'

'What are they saying?'

'I should not be telling you; you will hear more of it than I, and from closer at hand.'

'Tell me now. Perhaps it is not true.' How could she be dead, while the old lived on? Twenty-six was young to die: even he, who was not yet near that age, saw the truth of it. 'They are saying,' said Bab, 'that it was poison.'

'They say that whenever anyone dies. Pray God it be not true.'

'Here is a messenger for you,' Bab said.

A servant in the Queen's livery came hurrying across the grass. Monmouth waited, his mind shut off and blank, forgetting the soothsayer. He took the note the man held out, scanning the few words quickly.

'The Queen would see me without delay,' he said. 'What of the King?'

'They say he will see no one.'

Monmouth hurried to Catherine's apartments. She was usually at Somerset House these days, but had come to Whitehall on hearing the news. She held out her hand absently for his kiss, and as soon as they were alone fell into rapid talk, gesticulating as she sought for words. 'He will not let me comfort him,' she said sadly. 'Only you can do that, Monmouth. That is why I wished to see you; they will try to prevent you, but go to him. He loves you more than anyone who is left, more than his play-actresses.' She spoke without bitterness; that had been laid aside since the days of Barbara. Jolly Nell, pretty Moll, all the rest, drew only shrugged shoulders. Acquiescence came strangely from Catherine's lips; eyes bright with tears, she looked up at him.

'How did it happen?' he asked curtly. They have forgotten, he was thinking, that I knew her as a child; that I was with her not so many years ago, in Paris. A hundred memories of Minette rushed back; he was certain now that the news was true.

'They say she had been bathing in the river at St-Cloud, and later asked for iced chicory water, and when she drank it she cried out with pain. She took to her bed, and was many hours dying. I have had a mass said for her.' The tears had spilled over on the Queen's sallow cheeks; she too remembered the charming woman at Dover, and before that, long ago, the young girl who had come to Hampton Court in the days of her own happiness.

'Was she poisoned, think you?' He was vehement. Catherine crossed herself.

'How can one think it? It is too terrible a thing—' She came to him suddenly and gave him a little thrust, with both her hands laid flat against his chest. 'Go to the King,' she said again. 'Show him your love and comfort. He needs love now.'

Monmouth went to his father's apartments, and at first was refused entry, as orders had been given that no one was to be admitted. But he found a way. He came upon Charles seated staring at nothing, his hands stroking his little dog who sat in his lap. On the table lay a paper. Monmouth took it up and then put it back in its place.

'Father.'

There was no reply; the long fingers continued stroking, stroking. Monmouth went and laid his hand on his father's sleeve.

'I came at once,' he said awkwardly; he was not adept at finding the right word. 'You and she ... loved one another, and I also ...'

His voice dropped hoarsely into silence. The

71

grey-green eyes looked at him sideways, their lids red. Then Charles stretched out a hand, and touched his son.

'That little French rat,' he said. 'He had the doing of this, if it was done. She spoke to me, when she was here, of leaving him. I should not have let her go back.'

'How could you know it? And she was happy to be with you, even for so short a time.'

'I shall miss her letters ... Jemmy.'

Monmouth knelt by him and pressed his lips to the long fine hand. 'Many mourn with you,' he said. 'She was well loved.'

The little dog jumped down. The King laid his free hand on his son's head, caressing the dark hair. He must have something to stroke and caress, Monmouth thought; a dog, a child, a mistress. But he stayed by the King.

* * *

Charles wrote to King Louis to demand an autopsy, and this was done; no trace was found of poison, after half a dozen doctors had argued and prodded and failed. In time, the sadness eased; the Court could again be gay. For to England, sent by Louis himself, there came the young Breton beauty, Louise de Kéroualle, whom Charles had admired on Minette's visit and had demanded for himself. The new mistress diverted the King, almost, it was said, consoling him for his sister's loss. But the common people hated the baby-faced Louise, who was a Papist; they loved best witty Nell.

*   *   *

Monmouth himself had found a mistress by then; it happened almost by accident. Her name was Eleanor Needham, and she was a shy uncertain dark girl, as unlike Anna as could be found. He took her maidenhead in the garden, and some from Court came upon them and made a scandal, which angered Eleanor's father, a knight of Lambeth. But he could say little, for Eleanor's sister, Jane Middleton, was already set on a life of affairs. Eleanor had not her sister's beauty or her bold ways; it was like caressing a little soft animal, a shrew or harvest-mouse. Monmouth placated Sir Robert, who ended dazzled by his daughter's protector; promised to set her up in a house, and found one in Bloomsbury. Soon Eleanor was expecting a child; and so was Anna.

CHAPTER NINE

Christmas was merry enough that year, with the advent of a stranger; young William of Orange, the son of the dead Princess Mary. The King had last seen William as a swaddled baby in the uncertain days of his own exile; he found the Dutchman a shy lad, with good manners that were a trifle stiff, but William had matured early in the bitter war after the French had invaded Holland, which he himself had defended bravely. Monmouth and the young man took a liking to one another. They went together to admire the Christmas gift of twenty horses the King and York had made William. William had also been made Master of Arts and Knight of the Garter, like Monmouth before him; they emerged into the cold wind with the great cloak and plumes blowing about the Dutchman's slight form.

There should have been another arrival in January. Anne, Duchess of York, with her many dead children to remember, went into her last labour; and all the princes of the blood must stand in her chamber for the duration of it. The smell of sweat and the heavy air were almost too much for William, who suffered from asthma. Monmouth saw his discomfort and edged him near the door. The woman on the bed was enormously fat; Anne consoled her other miseries with food, and ate incessantly. York stood nearby the bed, his fair wig's curls falling about his face; he was in as much discomfort as any husband under such circumstances. Monmouth stared at him between half-closed lashes; they did not often meet face to face, but he knew York to be much about the King. They were, after all, the last surviving members of their generation; Minette's death had drawn them close.

York's lips were moving; perhaps he was saying Popish prayers for his wife, whom once, they said, he had loved. He had been constant in his religion to his own undoing; the people resented it, and it was becoming difficult for the King to keep his brother in his post as Lord High Admiral of the Fleet. James filled the post with devotion and courage, but these went for nothing. What was this faith that caused its faithful to cut their own throats rather than deny it? Monmouth let the question drift through his mind to divert it from the waiting crowd, the labouring woman's half-stifled groans. He glanced at William of Orange and surprised a glint of compassion in the dark eyes. He has never witnessed such a thing before, Monmouth thought; in Holland they brought him up strictly, and both his father and his mother are dead. He felt much sympathy with the young man, though he had laughed with the rest when they had lately made William drunk at a supper of Buckingham's, so much so that the Prince of Orange had tried to fight his way to the maids of honour in their rooms, and had had to be held back. The following morning so vile a head had he that King Charles himself came in with beaten eggs in milk, flavoured with chocolate, which he said was a sovereign cure.

The Duchess gave her final groan and the

75

child was delivered. It was a girl, to be named after the Queen, and would not live long. The York nursery still held only Mary and Anne, and neither were considered old enough to make the acquaintance of the Prince of Orange. Meantime, the sharp bright eyes of the young Dutchman were occupied with much coming and going of French ambassadors to Whitehall.

*   *   *

The trees in the Mall were bursting into bud when Anne, Duchess of York, at last lay dying. The air was stuffy and close in the curtained room. She had cancer, was pregnant again, and her husband had given her syphilis. She saw the swollen mound of her body beneath the covers as if it belonged to someone else; by now, pain had dulled in her. Soon, they would come, the black-robed priests her husband favoured, and would give her the last rites for the dying. It had been to please York that she had lately become a Catholic; everything she had ever done was to please him. He had long since ceased to care for her body, but he was concerned over her immortal soul. She had never been a deeply religious woman and now went through the prescribed observances as with any other form of etiquette; it meant as little. Soon she would be dead, whether in purgatory or in the clean-washed heaven of her father's faith she did not know. She thought of her father, Clarendon, now, recalling his broad face and good mind and how he had been angry at her marriage. So many had been angry with her; James himself, the old Queen, the rest. It did not matter now except that she did not feel that she had sinned greatly and it would be difficult to make a last confession. All of her thoughts were on the things of this world still; was that a sin? Her children; she could not stop thinking of her children; what would become of them? They had been brought in wide-eyed lately, in some awe at the news that she was dying. It was their first experience of death, except for the little wasted babies; she herself, constantly and uselessly pregnant, had been left much in their company. How beautiful Mary had grown, with her dark eyes and roseleaf skin! Yet she was a girl and all the boys had died. York needed a male heir; no doubt he would marry again. Anne considered the prospect impersonally as if it concerned someone she hardly knew. It seemed a lifetime ago that they had been in love with one another at Breda. Now he was tired of her. She was ugly, she knew, and made more so by childbearing; but his mistresses were as ugly as she. He needed wit, not beauty, to entertain him; Arabella Churchill, his most lasting paramour, was plain and clever. Anne's mind strayed and she remembered Arabella's handsome brother John, who was in a fair way to becoming a soldier. He was in Monmouth's regiment of foot, at present in France. He had curling hair, bright blue eyes and a face like a girl's; why should such beauty go to a man?

She stretched a white arm—her arms had been beautiful—towards where the children knelt, and whispered admonishment to them. They wept dutifully. Presently York came in; he leaned towards the pillow on which her head lay and told her that the priest had come. That was all; no word for herself. He cared only for his mistresses, his priests, and the navy. He was brave, dutiful and diligent, she knew. If only . . .

*   *   *

She died, and after she was coffined the bloated corpse burst the seams of the wood. Not even in death was Anne permitted dignity. She was buried, and they forgot her.

CHAPTER TEN

The death of Minette, his own lack of contentment in his marriage, the applause of the crowd, a kind of recklessness in himself—who was to say which, or all of them, caused Monmouth to do the things he did that winter and spring? Many were shocked, but not the young nor yet the mob; the young kept him company, the mob would always love him.

The first outrage concerned Sir John Coventry, who had insulted the King in Parliament. Afterwards he went to the Cock Tavern in Bow Street, drank deep, and made his way alone on foot to his house. He did not reach it; certain men, said to have been hired, set about him and slit the poor devil's nose. Sir John staggered on his way, maimed for life and with blood pouring down his face; the world blamed Monmouth, hot in defence of the King.

Next time it was a beadle. There was a wild party at a house near Lincoln's Inn Fields, and Monmouth was there; the beadle and watch came to secure the peace, and swords were drawn. 'We will drink as we will,' they shouted. 'Nay, sirs, nay, but to keep the peace.' Monmouth said no word, but drew his sword. The familiar hiss of metal against leather revived him and made him cool; a thrusting against bone and flesh, and the beadle somehow lay dead. They took the King's son before the King.

'It was for your sake, Sire.'

'The first offence, not the second.' Charles was grave. Had York been by him, he had been harder; but he still doted on his son. In the end he issued an edict pardoning 'all Murders, Homicides, and Felonies' committed alone or with others. At the same time he murmured a warning; lesser men than 'our deare sonne

James' would have been tried and strung up to a gallows. Perhaps the lad had not enough to do; there was no way at present of using his sword lawfully, and he wasted his time on brawls and women. The King invited him to come on a tour of the east coast, and they set out in the changing colours of autumn.

The invitation was not entirely disinterested. At Euston Hall, on the way to Yarmouth, the French Ambassador was a hidden guest; with him was baby-faced Louise de Kéroualle. Much was decided regarding the fate of nations in the languid autumn sunshine; but the King went through a mock marriage with Louise, and a stocking filled with salt was flung at them in bed. Witty Nell, who called the new mistress Squinterella, was forgotten for the time. Monmouth liked Louise, and practised his French. They parted, and went on to Blickling, where some said Anne Boleyn's body had been secretly buried; and to the house at Oxmead where the Paston letters had been penned; and to Raynham Hall, and Cambridge, and at last Newmarket again, with the beloved smell of horseflesh and the challenging racing bays. Monmouth betted heavily, to the disapproval of sober John Evelyn, who had been at Euston.

After it was all over Monmouth was again at a loss for occupation. 'Have no fear,' said the King; war, he knew, was imminent, and he would find good use for Jemmy's sword.

'Now you shall see war,' said Charles a little later.

This was the result of the Treaty of Madame, the Secret Treaty of Dover. It had been read and passed by Parliament in February, with certain clauses concealed. France was England's ally, in an unjust war to add to Louis' glory. The King of England did not conceal the truth from himself; but he needed his French pension. He had proved himself; there had already been a swift attempt against a Dutch merchantman off the Isle of Wight. That small brave nation had held out for long in this war, defeating Louis by flooded towns and fields and roads.

Charles brushed it all aside, and took comfort in looking at his beautiful insouciant son. Jemmy would make a handsome soldier and a fair fighter, despite the beadle. He would think nothing of the whys and wherefores; all he wanted to do was fight.

*   *   *

That was true enough; but for the moment he was a model husband. That summer he had stood by Anna's bedside and looked down on their new-born son. He kissed his wife warmly; he had never been nearer to loving her. 'We will call him for the King,' he said. The child was sallow, dark, a Stuart; that would put paid to the rumours which said that he himself was not the King's son.

The baby's delighted grandfather created the child Earl of Doncaster. For some time Monmouth took pleasure in watching the Earl at nurse, learning to crawl, learning to talk. As for Eleanor, she bore him a son too, a fine lusty fellow whom he would call James Crofts, after his own name in childhood. James Crofts thrived; but Anna's son died at a year old. Monmouth comforted her as best he might; many lost their children, but he missed the little fellow. 'There will be more such,' he said. He saw her regard him with the sardonic look in her eyes he had learned to dread; he could not answer her wit. 'Without a doubt, there will be more,' she said, and turned to some embroidery she was at. Well, he would father children on this stranger; had he and she ever known one another?

He was glad when the King found a task for him in the Netherlands. Six thousand men had been promised to Louis under the Treaty, and Monmouth was to take his regiment and go. He recalled that first campaign as in the nature of a dream; the flat land and flat water, desolate as far as the eye could see, for nothing had been left for the French. He took ghost towns that only needed a flag run up after they marched in; Orsoi, Rhineberg, Wesel, Emmerich, Doesburg, Zutphen. He saw the terrible Rhine run high, but paid no heed to early warnings, swept away by the excitement of war. He went home again and then returned, to further triumph, for what it was worth. Despite the glory he was sorry for the ravaged homes, the starved, raped peasantry. But one must say nothing; the French command did not, and they were the allies with whom he fought.

*   *   *

They were besieging Maestricht, in the strange narrow neck of land that ran down between Flemish Brabant and the German Rhineland. The city, which reared on a height, had held out all through the war. Below, the country itself was flooded like the rest, with William of Orange's ferry-craft plying; but they themselves could expect no aid there. The opening of the dykes last year had almost defeated Louis' flamboyant offensive; there was never an enemy to be got hold of, only the wretched peasants in their homesteads still drenched from the tide that drained downwards again with summer. The French had ravished and plundered accordingly; there was abiding hatred among the people for the invader who had come almost idly here to show how swiftly arms, and the Sun King, could conquer. But he had not conquered yet. The young Dutch Stadtholder whom Monmouth remembered at Whitehall being made drunk at a supper party had matured and hardened; small, delicate yet tough, watchful of every endeavour, determined with a sharp clear faith that his people and his country should not be overrun and chained in conquest, William was everywhere; but he would lose Maestricht. They fired at the town and brought up siege-cannon to replace those which the late commander, Luxembourg, had taken away; Monmouth directed them, and by his side was that handsome youth John Churchill, brother to Arabella, primed with the latest military expertise from the School of Marshals in Paris. His keen blue eyes surveyed the ditches surrounding the beleaguered town. 'A man might leap those were he long enough of leg,' he murmured, looking up and down at Monmouth and himself. Both men were tall by contrast to the little dapper Frenchmen who paraded about in coats almost as short as the one Monmouth had himself made mock of long ago, on the occasion of Minette's visit to England. Minette's little catamite of a husband was married again by now to the enormously fat and witty daughter of the Elector Palatine, Prince Rupert's brother. The royal Court, trailing behind the King with waggons and mistresses, was likewise in Flanders; but Louis had not yet come to the siege of Maestricht. There was little for him to do but wait for the water to go down, bringing fever and ague in its wake. There would be richer places for His

Most Christian Majesty's war machine to display itself. Later he would come to Maestricht, after it fell.

Later, it was also said that the Duke of Monmouth showed exemplary courage there. Within himself he still loathed this harrying of a wretched people; they were starving in the town while the French ate sweetmeats. He tried to jest with Churchill; but the other was still intent. 'Shall we take the ditch, Your Grace?' The hazel eyes looked into the blue.

'If it can be done.'

'Today, then.' He was right; best lose no time. The two men had spoken each into the other's ear, for the cannon were sounding. But soon a handful of Life Guards, with Monmouth, Churchill, Arlington, and a Scot named Armstrong who would follow the Duke all his life, leapt the ditch and captured the demilune. They battled on till the town fell.

*　　　*　　　*

Added to his previous victories this meant triumph for Monmouth. A year hence he would re-enact the scene of the breach with, amicably enough, his uncle York, and real cannon, before the King and Court at Windsor. Meantime, King Louis presented him with a diamond-studded sword worth thirty thousand livres; yet, he thought, looking deferentially at the Sun King, whose teeth had blackened despite his glory, it would not sell for as much. But Turenne, the great commander, complimented him; that was worth more.

The regiment was sent to Dunkirk after that, and he himself returned to London, somewhat unwillingly; nowadays he felt himself to be more successful in war than in peace.

CHAPTER ELEVEN

At a window of his apartments in Whitehall, a tall erect man in a fair periwig stood looking out, seeing nothing of the world outside and the day. The Duke of York was no longer Lord High Admiral of England. He had had to resign from the profession he loved and had followed since he was a boy in France, newly escaped there after his father's murder. He had fought often and well at sea, notably in this late war; understood the disposal of ships in battle, could direct them without fear of danger; was adequate, honest, and punctual in command. Yet he had had to resign; for that other cause which by now was dearer even than his ambition. Shaftesbury, Monmouth's friend, had caused to be passed the Test Act, whereby any public servant must be seen to take the sacrament of the Church of England: and York had refused.

He thought back over his life, for old hurts seemed less; remembering how, as a boy, he had followed his father in all things because they were so greatly alike in nature; rigid, humourless, and united in a common dislike of the Queen's faith. York remembered the last time he had seen Charles I, and how that beloved father had made him promise to remain a Protestant, like his brother Harry who had died. He had promised, and had kept his promise even to the extent of quarrelling with their mother; then, in the year of her death, he had found himself convinced of the very matters which earlier he had denied; and being an honest man would not hide it. He had been received into the Church because he had become gradually convinced that her teachings were right; and by that conviction he would abide for the rest of his days. There had been no other decision which was possible to him.

That it would not make matters easy for him he had known; had known also that his second marriage to an Italian princess would not please the people. He had prevaricated on that; had begged the King to let him marry his old friend, the widowed Lady Bellasis, for whom he had some feeling which might have been respect. Charles had said 'No man should be permitted to make a fool of himself twice,' and had arranged the Modena marriage. The bride was a beautiful child of fifteen, with jet-black hair and eyes, and so devout that she had begged instead to be allowed to enter a convent. After their wedding York had taken her by the hand and had brought her to his daughters, saying to Mary, the elder, 'Here is a playmate for you.' He still thought of his wife as a child, and continued in his own pleasures though by now, accepting their marriage, she herself had fallen in love with him. The thought made him sad; he had no feeling for her, and nothing could console him for his lost ships. He still remembered the brilliant fight at Solebay last year when he had defied adverse winds and a sluggish ally to bring home victory. The people of England might have taken more pride in their Admiral.

A sound behind him made him turn. It was his wife, dressed for riding which she loved despite his disapproval; it irritated him to see women in quasi-masculine dress. With her were his daughters Mary and Anne and the little Countess of Sussex, great Barbara's girl by the King. York tried not to frown at them; he had not wanted to be disturbed. Yet he felt guilt at the little heed he paid his wife; she was a fine rider and must take what pleasure she could. She held out a gloved hand now, deprecating, almost pleading.

'Your Royal Highness will come with us?' She spoke careful English. He smiled, and shook his head, drawing his finger along young Mary's smooth cheek; he loved her best of his children. 'No,' he said gently, 'I have some

88

business which detains me.' It was not true; he could easily have gone with them, for nowadays he had more than enough time to spare. But he disliked the thought of jeers in the Park at the Papist Duke who had fallen from his high place. He wanted to be alone, to learn to live with the sensation of outrage, to know himself justified. Presently he would seek his confessor for the sin of the lie he had just told, and also for comfort, which the Church never failed to give.

Mary Beatrice of Modena turned away, her dark eyes full of tears. She must master them before she rode out with the children and their attendants. It was not fashionable to love one's husband, but she and the Queen defied fashion. Men might scorn her for it, as they scorned the Queen, but she cared nothing.

*   *   *

There was to be a masque at Court. Preparations would take some weeks, and the scenery to be erected was as elaborate as anything in James I's day, the great age of masques; at that time costumes had cost many hundreds of pounds, but gods and goddesses nowadays wore scanty attire and no longer blacked their faces. Jupiter, who was enamoured of a nymph named Calisto, was to be played by Lady Harriet Wentworth, newly come to Court. She would be noticed by the

King, for she was the daughter of his old companion in arms Tom Wentworth, now long dead; the only daughter. Lady Harry had combed out her thick fair hair—it was guinea-gold now, no longer silvery fair as in her childhood—and Jupiter's crown had been set upon it by the mistress of ceremonies; otherwise, Harry's dress was draped knee-high to show Greek boots and her neat turn of ankle. It was said she would outshine Sarah Jennings, the Princess Anne's outspoken friend, who would take part, as would the Princess herself as the problematical nymph Nyophe. Harriet looked dreamily in the mirror, surprised at her own appearance; she seldom troubled with it, or had to. 'Don't dream; you will need to stay awake to remember your lines,' said Sarah crossly, tossing her red-gold head; as Mercury, she had less to say than other people, a state of affairs which was not usual. She cast a critical gaze towards the Princess Mary, who was darkly beautiful as Calisto herself; all the nymphs were young ladies, and the gentlemen, dressed as shepherds, would only dance. Harriet recalled that her cousin, John Lovelace, was taking part, and she felt glad to know one face among so many. 'Don't be shy; you will do well enough,' her mother assured her, but mother was always positive about everything. 'To be sure it is a way of letting everyone see you, for with no dowry you must needs show yourself to attract offers.'

'Mother, you think always of offers. There are other things.'

'Maybe, but the offer must be sought first,' replied Lady Philadelphia practically.

* * *

Monmouth was bored. He had been glad enough to return to England, for he disliked King Louis' war; even great names like Condé and Turenne palled in face of so much misery. Yet he missed the excitement, the very sound of firing, the knowledge that one might not lie down at night to rise at dawn. He had attempted to pass the time in different ways; he had had his portrait painted in the glorious robes of a Chancellor of Cambridge University, and had studied the head they gave him, its painted planes seeming broader, wiser than before. They had feasted him lavishly and had watched him depart by river, and there was an end to it; he did not take seriously the suggestion King Charles made that he might watch over the behaviour of Cambridge divines, though he had sent a letter protesting at their modish lawn sleeves and idle reading of sermons.

Now, he took his place among the shepherds almost reluctantly. He had not troubled to attend rehearsals with John Lovelace and the rest; he knew very well how to dance. He adjusted the sheepskin over his shoulder, swept back his hair—he had had it cut short in the army—and was ready. The others came dressed likewise, Lovelace, Dunblane, Daincourt, other young men who had been boys when he left for Flanders. He felt old and outmoded among their gilded youth.

He stifled a yawn as the music struck up; then stared, fascinated, at Jupiter.

*   *   *

It was John Lovelace, of course, who introduced them afterwards. That she should be Lovelace's cousin, and he had not known of it! Yet he had known her always. He said it, almost as he straightened from bowing over her hand. 'But we have met before.'

She smiled, unlike so many women not with the mouth only, but with her eyes; they were deep sapphire, and he could picture their compassion for suffering or unkindness. She had slender fingers on a broad hand, and he would have liked to hold them longer; but others watched. He was unfit even to speak with this pure creature, this grown child; she was no more.

'We met at Saxham, sir. It was many years ago. I was a child, and you took no heed of me.' The voice was deep for a woman's, amused, rueful. 'I remember you danced very well; everyone spoke of it.'

All those years ago; how old did he seem to her? Later he was to find that Lady Philadelphia's ambition could be satisfied; at least four noblemen had taken heed of Jupiter that night, and would make offers. He was powerless against that, shackled as he was to Anna.

He heard himself reply to her 'I must atone.' He must have put his meaning into his words, for he spoke from the heart; he saw a flush come up over her delicate skin, as though the saying disquieted her.

*   *   *

He could not put her out of his mind, and for the time could not bear to go home, where Anna, still querulous after the birth of a second son in May, was pregnant again. He ordered his carriage to go to Bloomsbury, to the house he had taken there for Eleanor Needham and their children. Eleanor would soothe him, would not ask questions or complain; and he could watch his son playing soldiers. Young James Crofts wanted to be a soldier and nothing else; his father was pleased enough. He ruffled the small boy's hair, kissed Henry, who knew nothing yet; and went with the mother to her room. Once there, he seized her compliant body in his arms and refreshed himself in her. Eleanor had no talents, no mind to speak of, only much loving; she would smooth his forehead if she knew things were amiss, and otherwise did not trouble him. Yet he was troubled now; he knew he could not win Harriet Wentworth for himself without scandal to her, and perhaps for the first time in his life he took thought to the effect of scandal on another than himself. It was strange; after half a lifetime of success with women who dropped before him like ripe fruit, he felt fearful, uncertain, tender. Yet how could he say that he could no longer live without a child he had seen twice in his life? But it was so; in Eleanor's very arms, he thought of that other.

Eleanor moved a little in order to watch his face. She loved her splendid lover unquestioningly; it had been worth braving her father's anger and her sister's scorn to come and be his mistress openly. The head that lay on her breast was the handsomest in England, the short hair essenced, the clearly-marked brows serene. She hoped she made him happy; she knew enough to know that his wife did not. She herself, if she had to, would perform any service, make any sacrifice, lay down her life for him. This hour, and others like it, should be hers, should mean all of joy; and yet somehow she knew him far away.

* * *

The masque had been successful and was repeated the following week. This time

Monmouth foresaw Jupiter, and trembled with expectation, at the same time amused with himself; he, a man of the world, and this child! Yet when Harriet came out on the stage she sought his eyes, and he knew that she had been thinking of him; the very joints of his body turned to water with the gladness it brought.

Afterwards they met as if by chance, and walked together out of the great hall, out to the open grass beneath the cold December stars. His hand was in hers, his absurd sheepskin about her shoulders to keep her warm in her thin god's clothing. Behind them the Palace loomed darkly, forgotten. They did not speak until she made him stop and look up at Orion, sparkling threefold in the frost.

'Do you watch the stars?' she said quietly. 'I sometimes think I hear the spheres singing. That is talking to God, I believe. Do you pray?'

'Not till now.' His voice was hoarse. He could not take his eyes from her face, raised in rapture beneath the night sky; her lips were parted, and her little pearly teeth gleamed in a half-smile. She grew grave and turned to him.

'I am often alone. I think that you, too, are lonely.' He did not smile; he, the favoured of fortune, had all his life been alone till this hour, and it was right that she knew it.

'What is your birth-sign?' he asked her, and the smile came again for him, and she drew close so that only her hair shone in the starlight, her face hidden. 'Leo,' she said, 'and yours is Aries. Maybe that is why they put you in a sheepskin.'

'You knew of mine?' He was pleased; he heard her laughter. 'I know many things about you,' she said. 'You must know that they talk of you a great deal at Court.'

'What do they say?' he asked lightly. He half expected a child's chatter, but she spoke with the quiet assurance of a much older woman.

'Why, that there is nothing you will not dare, and that you are too handsome ever to fail. All the ladies are in love with you except the Queen, who loves the King, and the Duchess of York, who loves the Duke.'

'And you?' he said. She slipped her hand back into his; they had drawn apart briefly.

'I am fourteen years old,' she said, 'and I have loved you all my life. When we left Saxham that time, I left my heart with you. Now I will take it back.'

'Take my heart,' he said, 'for it is yours. You are brought here that you may make a good marriage; do not. It would break my heart if any other called you wife.'

'My mother will be angry.'

'Do not heed your mother.'

He thought she trembled then with cold, and took her back into the warmth. The scent of guttered wax candles was strong in the hall and they were shifting the elaborate scenery; the company had mostly gone. We are like two travelling players who have met again, and are left to find our way together, he thought. He put aside his deep feelings lest they betray him, and said lightly, 'We had country dancing at other times in Saxham, but I never saw you again. Where did they hide you, Harry?'

'At school in France.'

'And now?'

'Now, when we are not at Court, I shall be at Toddington. I should like you to come there, although it is half ruined and no longer rich. We have a long gallery and towers, and the trees are beautiful, and there is a maze in which one may get lost.'

'We will not try the maze except together.' He could not help talking to her thus; even so early they belonged to one another. He knew he would not harm her without her wish. 'I will come,' he said.

'Sir William Smyth, my guardian, is very disagreeable. He and my mother talk of money always, and he grudges pence.'

'I will come,' he said again, and kissed her hand.

*　　　*　　　*

At Christmas they danced together, but the Court for once found no scandal; Harriet was young, a protégée of the Duchess of York and known to the York princesses. No doubt it was to please his uncle that Monmouth danced with the child. Also, another scandal promised abundantly; great Barbara had had John Churchill in her bed, the King had come in, and Churchill had escaped out of the window without his breeches. But Monmouth and Harriet already noticed nothing except one another; their horoscopes had been cast, they compared them, and found that the stars were conjunct.

*   *   *

At home, Anna was heavy with child; in February she gave birth to a daughter. He tried to treat her kindly, talk with her, gaze at the baby; but it was as always, and he neither felt of one flesh with her nor one spirit. She was a friend of his uncle York, he told himself; for that reason alone he could not trust her. They should never have married.

She knew his uncertainty well enough, lying back on her lace-edged pillows; the labour had been a hard one and had hurt her lame thigh. 'There is no matter more certain than that you will give me a child a year,' she taunted him. 'I mean nothing more to you than a brood-mare.'

He protested, and said with truth that he loved their children. But he could not offer Anna his love; in the same way that he tried never to break a promise, he could not now frame his lips in a lie. He might be sensual, braggart, thoughtless, profligate; but to love from the heart was to know many things he had

98

not known till now. He could not explain such matters to her; instead he mouthed some inanity about the baby, saying she was pretty, and must be called Anne.

CHAPTER TWELVE

'He raileth and is discontented.' That had been written about Harriet's father Thomas Wentworth, whom she dimly remembered; he had died when she was quite small. His portrait, of a slim young man with bright eyes, hanging nearby the mantel at Toddington, did not look discontented, but rather ready for anything; and many adventures had befallen Tom when he followed the King. Discontent was, however, rife after his death; when they were able to come back to England after the Restoration—the Commonwealth years had been spent in Middleburg, where Lady Philadelphia's sister Aletta had married a Dutch merchant—when they returned, it was to find the old manor ruinous and all the rents sequestered to pay off Grandfather Cleveland's debts. Cleveland himself had been an unrepentant Royalist who, they said, smoked a hundred pipes a day and at the height of Cromwell's power had threatened to 'thrash and cane' anyone who called him a Presbyterian. He had lived to welcome back

King Charles II with a following of a thousand gentlemen all clad in buff coats with silver lacing at the Earl's expense; then Cleveland was gathered to his fathers, leaving the bills. So Harriet, his grand-daughter, had spent a childhood of scant shifts and patched gowns, uneventful and poor except for the fabled visits to Saxham. Lord Crofts was a relative; the Lovelaces were relatives also, and there were other Wentworths living at Heaton Water, but they had fared well despite the wars. At home, there was Spanish as well as Dutch blood to reckon with; the one accounted for Lady Philadelphia's tempers and the other for her business head, and she set about recovering the estate at once.

Harriet herself had no business acumen; she was vague and careless with money. 'You are like your father,' Lady Philadelphia would rage, 'willing enough to be soft with the rents because a man's poor, or sick; but what about the landlord?' Yet the tenants loved Harriet as they would never love her mother; they knew the young Baroness would not be hard on them, would visit their cottages and come to their christenings. Philadelphia, despite her words, was devoted to her dreamy daughter; and Sir William Smyth, whom Harriet so disliked for his hard ways, was devoted to Philadelphia. The pair had their heads together often, though meantime Sir William had a wife elsewhere; but one could always make plans for the future. My lady, however, thought of little for long except Harriet's rich marriage, and when Duras and others offered for her was pleased, but the foolish girl would have none of them. No one could force Harriet; she had a quiet determination of her own, and after sighing and raging uselessly, Lady Philadelphia left the matter for the time; perhaps Harriet would meet some rich nobleman she fancied, and she was young yet.

If she had known, Harriet's heart had been given when she was younger still; to a tall beautiful grandly dressed boy dancing in Saxham Hall with his fellow-guests from Court. She had kept the glorious image in her mind for years; and when they met again he was not less glorious, with the laurels of victory on his handsome head, and no more thought of conquest, than he had been then. It was many weeks now since the masque at Court, and still she looked for him; and often met him.

That night after they had parted Harriet had gone to her mirror, fingering the zodiac sign which hung about her throat. She stared at herself; seeing the glory of the hair, a round young face, too round, she decided, like a baby's; a nose rather long than short; a sweet firm mouth, level brows, and her father's eyes, gentle, brilliant, and very blue. She decided there was nothing notable there; undoubtedly Monmouth would forget her after a few days, a few hours; yet their planets tallied. Now that she had been appointed lady-in-waiting to the young Duchess of York, newly risen from child-bed, undoubtedly she would see the King's son often, unless they sent him back to the wars. She prayed that that might not be; how would she live if Monmouth were killed or wounded? Till now, the stars had been with him ... but the war was changing sides; from being against the Dutch, England now was for them, by some process which did not survive the chatter in the maids' rooms. As for the vainglorious French, one fought against them now gladly. One man's glory against another's prudence; King Louis against the Stadtholder, William of Orange, who for so long had fought alone. William was by way of being a hero to some of the women; but Harriet saw only Monmouth's handsome face.

Meantime the Duchess of York was sad and Harriet comforted her; the baby, who had been born in January and christened Catherine Laura, died almost at once. The Duke also comforted his Duchess, but rather as a parent would console a child 'and that is not what she wants of him,' thought Harriet wisely. She felt full of wisdom by then.

*   *   *

The King sent for Monmouth, and uncertain what the summons might mean he obeyed it; it was some time since he had seen his father. Was this because his own life was so greatly taken up nowadays with honours, awards, portrait-sittings to Lely, sessions with Ashley who was now Earl of Shaftesbury? And thoughts of Harriet took up more of his time. Yet he would be glad to see the King.

Charles was alone; one of the spaniels had lately littered on the great bed, and the puppies' mewling punctuated their talk. Monmouth kissed the fine hand. The King seemed older, he thought; there were lines of debauchery on his face and his eyes were heavy. Nell, Portsmouth—Louise was a duchess now—and the rest were taking their toll.

'Why, Jemmy, I am glad to see you. It is long since we spoke together.' He looked at his son almost hungrily.

'I trust it is not because I have been idle, Sire.'

'No; I speak to a Chancellor and renowned soldier. I would have you now, if you agree, Lord General of the army here.'

'Sire!' It was beyond his wildest ambition. York cannot, he was thinking, have been consulted; joy rose in him, illumining his face. The King gazed at him fondly, aware of the inevitable tug at the heartstrings Lucy's son brought. It was a handsome devil he and the Welsh girl had aided into the world; and no idler, despite the rumours his brother would have him believe. 'You have used your sword to good effect among the French,' he said. 'The conditions of the new appointment may not please you if you have friends among them.'

'Tell me the conditions, that I may judge.' He felt no particular loyalty to Louis and his marshals. He had been, he supposed, a mercenary after a fashion. The King's gaze raised itself beneath the world-weary lids; he spoke earnestly, with none of his customary banter.

'Hitherto you have fought against the Dutch,' he said. 'Now you will fight with them and for them. The Stadtholder is the stronger since his alliance with Spain.'

'William of Orange? I, who have fought in Flanders, admire him as a brave leader even in defeat. His beliefs are mine also.'

'Do not bring religion into the question,' said the King drily. 'Your uncle hath wrought himself much harm thereby. Were I so honest a man as he, no doubt my head would have followed my father's by this, or else I'd tread the exile's path again; I cannot bear that thought. While I live there shall be ... compromise. I grant you one cannot outrage one's conscience over far. Were I free I'd bid each man do as he will, and think what he may. But a howling mob about Whitehall, led by your friend Shaftesbury, would be the result of that. So I suit my gait to their measure. At any event you will, if what you say is true, fight gladly on your own side.'

'I am proud to fight for the Stadtholder.'

'He is wily enough,' said the wiliest man in Europe. 'He hath got himself four allies, who together can subdue even Louis. I can no longer afford to honour my promise to His Most Christian Majesty, and he knows it. He was mistaken in attacking the Spanish Netherlands; he trod on a wasps' nest there.'

'He will be of a secret mind with yourself in the matter. You have known one another from youth.'

'Ay, when I was a beggar and he a damned supercilious young god. As for this William, he is my sister's son. Many times I have been moved to admire him, but not with liking. He is a prudent little fellow.' The jutting Stuart underlip grimaced comically. Monmouth smiled.

'He was not so prudent the night Buckingham made him drunk here.'

'Much is to be said for good wine,' the King admitted lazily. The newly whelped bitch jumped down off the bed and came to him, her great shining prominent eyes fixed on his face. The King caressed her. 'You had best not make William drunk when you meet again,' he said, smiling.

'Where are we to meet? And when?'

'You will make your way to Bruges as soon as you may. It is probable that he will need your help to besiege the town of Mons, but he himself will tell you of it.'

Monmouth had heard the French discussing Mons. He bowed. 'I will make all speed, and strive to be worthy of the honour you have placed in me.'

Charles gave a little shrug, and turned to talk of his grandchildren. That was a theme which would not be seized on to put before Shaftesbury. He frowned at his own suspicions, knowing whence they came, and talked amicably until Monmouth took his leave.

*　　*　　*

Shaftesbury himself was engaged in reducing a letter to ashes. It contained tidings which at the same time made him glad and justified his foresight. It amused him to be a secret pensioner of King Louis and to know that most men in high places, whichever side they were on, received a French pension to keep England divided. To place a figurehead before the mob, in place of the unpopular York, was Shaftesbury's task; and who better than Monmouth Jemmy? It was all the more so now that Monmouth went to fight a Protestant war; as an ally of the French he had seemed out of place. Meantime, the Catholics must suffer; soon, he himself must cry out for vengeance in a howl for blood, knowing that where he led men would follow. He had always been a notable leader, free and outspoken; the King called him Little Sincerity. He smiled at the thought, staring down at his ugly hands. The paper had burnt to grey ash and he dropped it, and ground the ash into the hearth.

CHAPTER THIRTEEN

The bright coats of the regiments Monmouth had brought—five hundred of Hobart's, four of the Duke of York's, a hundred of the Guards—deployed before Mons. Monmouth himself felt less strange than he had foreseen at attacking his old superior, Luxembourg, in the enemy lines. War, like chess, was played according to the rules. Yet he was cheered at meeting with the Prince of Orange. William had aged in course of the war; already he looked older than his twenty-three years; his mouth had hardened into an obstinate patient line, and the bridge of his nose had developed a hook. But he was the same courteous, if somewhat dour fellow; they sat together over the fortress map, tracing the plan of attack.

'You see,' said William suddenly, 'I must rely on you. You owe me, after all, six towns, and Maestricht.'

'Sir, the fortune of war—'

'I know it. Let us not think of what is past, but get on. You have brought artillery; use it *here* and *here*.' He gave his sharp directions as though no time was to be lost. The French had been different, heavily aware of etiquette, inclined to take offence, even in the midst of battle, if it were not observed punctiliously. But William of Orange, descendant of nobles and princes, sat now like any soldier, plainly attired in dark armour and a leather buff-coat, with his own hair cut shoulder-length for greater ease. He did not ask for liking or devotion, perhaps even gave the impression that such things were a waste of time; but Monmouth saw why his people worshipped him, despite the bitter orders he had had to give for opening the dykes and flooding the land.

Monmouth himself would fight gladly for William. Amid the smoke and crashing of cannon he rode forward with the best, using his sword and his wits; later it was said that without the English there would have been no victory that day. At the end William, grimed with powder but unhurt, came to Monmouth and offered his hand. 'Thank you,' he said simply.

*　　　*　　　*

Bells rang and bonfires blazed for Monmouth's return to England, but he came home to an empty house; Anna had sailed for Holland in company with the Duchess of York. The Duke had been obliged to leave the country; his unpopularity had been fomented by the Protestant party, or, as it began to call itself, the people's party. No one knew when York might return. Monmouth had his own wild welcome in the shouting streets, and they called to him, 'The Protestant Duke! Give us the Protestant Duke!'

He shrugged it off; it was true he was a Protestant, and was to be seen on Sundays at St Martin's-in-the-Fields when he was in town. But he would use the prevailing wind to seek renewed friendship with his father. Shaftesbury had told him the King feared York; he need not fear his son.

*   *   *

Soon after his return Monmouth found time to visit his sister Mary, whose husband was ill. They had seen little of one another since Lucy's day; Mary had been brought up in Lord Carlingford's house in London. She was a beautiful young woman, with heavy-lidded eyes, the Stuart lip, and a long neck. She lived quietly and did not come to Court.

'It is good of you to visit us; you are a famous commander now.' She had held him away from her on arrival, admiring his coat and sword with its wrought iron figures of the late King Charles I and Queen Henrietta embossing the hilt. They kissed, and he left her; they met seldom, he thought; how swiftly life went by! The memory of Mary's small pale face brought

109

him to thoughts of Harriet Wentworth; would she have forgotten him?

When he arrived at his house it was to be told that visitors had been waiting an hour, and he went in. Shaftesbury rose to his small height, and bowed; he was dressed, as always, in notable colours, having once even been criticised in Parliament for having no black except his hat. Now he wore the suit he had worn then; an ash-coloured coat, striped breeches laced with silver, and his great periwig. His eyes gleamed with triumph as he beheld the tall figure of the King's son; he had helped to send abroad the King's brother; now Monmouth should work for him to some purpose. The second man, the Scot Armstrong, had risen behind him; he had made the great leap to the demilune at Maestricht, but had neither much wit nor many things to say.

'We come to congratulate you,' said Little Sincerity, smiling; his smile had a disarming quality. Monmouth murmured his thanks and apologies; but he had not expected them today. He motioned the two men to be seated, and himself sat down. Shaftesbury fixed his gaze on a gilded console decorated with putti, probably Italian work, that he would have fancied for himself. He loved fine furniture, and all his houses were models of taste and elegance, his gardens formally planted with herbs, flowers and exotic shrubs.

'Sir,' he said, 'we are also come to warn you.' Armstrong nodded agreement. Monmouth, who had been about to summon the servant to pour wine, rose and did so himself. He raised his black brows in enquiry, setting flagons before the two men. Shaftesbury ran an appreciative finger round the silver rim; it had been polished carefully.

'The first part is that the King will send for you. You will have expected that, and perhaps also assumed the reason; that you are to be made Commander-in-Chief.' Monmouth lowered his lashes to hide his pleasure. It was an advance from Lord General, a permanency.

'As you will have foreseen also, the Duke of York used his utmost endeavour to prevent the appointment, but I think—' Shaftesbury shrugged—'that we have triumphed in that particular.'

'You are my good friend, as I know well.' What was the warning? He sipped his wine, reflecting that he never had any notion how Shaftesbury heard of things before they happened. Perhaps his astrologers told him. He sat back in his chair, idly staring down into his empty flagon. The wine had been good, but he had drunk enough.

'I am sufficiently your friend to warn Your Grace that the victory is not yet complete. The King, as I have said, fears his brother so greatly that he will not dare vouchsafe you any honours that would not be expected for, say, a royal bastard of France.'

Monmouth sprang up with an oath, and Shaftesbury soothed him with a gesture. 'Read for yourself,' he said. 'To compensate the Duke of York for his banishment and for what may seem an extravagant regard for yourself in this appointment, this paper hath been issued and is already signed. I pray you do not be angered with us; we did not advise it.'

Monmouth stretched out his hand for the paper. It was a copy, made by some clerk. His cheeks reddened in anger as he read. The King denied marrying or being contracted to Lucy Barlow as stated 'in a false and malicious report industriously spread abroad by those who are neither friends to me nor the Duke of Monmouth.' Charles denied ever having been married to anyone but the Queen.

I would sooner see him hanged at Tyburn than acknowledge him my heir.

There was silence in the room. 'What are we to do now?' Monmouth asked, trying not to let his voice tremble with indignation. To have gained glory abroad, to have the prospect of the army appointment, and now...

'It is not yet public property,' said Shaftesbury. 'It was drawn up to placate the Duke of York, who also insisted that the words "natural son" should be written above your name. I believe—'

Monmouth brought his hand down on the table; the flagons jumped. 'I will erase it,' he

112

said. 'And I will move matters so that the Papist Duke never sets foot on these shores again.'

'Have a care for your person. It is not a task for one man, however illustrious, but for many. And they can be found.' Shaftesbury extended a deprecating hand, hiding his pleasure that matters should have sped so exactly as he had predicted. The hothead would do his worst; but there were cooler heads behind him. It was possible to achieve much more now that York was sent abroad. Little Sincerity kept one piece of knowledge, no longer very important, to himself; James de la Cloche, the king's supposed elder son, was reported dead in Naples. As a Papist he might have been little use to them or none. One could always plead ignorance of the death.

*   *   *

Monmouth kept away from his father. Instead he went, with a servant, to the office of the Secretary of State, Sir Leoline Jenkins, and demanded the offending paper. While he watched frowning, they erased the word 'natural'. The Secretary obeyed in some fear; he had not previously seen the affable Duke of Monmouth enraged. It would preserve one's person the more securely to make it evident that one believed the orders to come from the King. Charles himself might be angry, but his rages were brief and hurt no man. Sir Leoline rolled away the altered scroll for signature.

The unexpected happened, however, when it was put before the King. Charles saw the erasure, cursed, and forthwith tore up the document. He missed his brother, and would not see his son. The matter of the army appointment remained in abeyance.

*   *   *

Monmouth made pretence to be merry at the royal wedding, for everyone concerned, including both bride and groom, was glum. It was proof of the young Stadtholder's victory over his powerful invaders that now, after the long war, he had been offered the hand of Princess Mary of York. Mary was fifteen; her father and stepmother had returned to England, and York was loath to give his consent. He influenced Mary against her bridegroom, and as she loathed the thought of leaving England it was only one step to loathing William also; he was a Calvinist, and little thought of at Whitehall, and made no attempt at pretty speeches. The wedding took place with a red-eyed bride and dour bridegroom, and when the couple were put to bed the King called, 'Now, nephew, to your work. Hey! St George for England!' and pulled the curtains on the lugubrious pair. A few days later the Prince and Princess of Orange, the latter with eyelids still swollen, sailed through a fearful storm to their country. At the time it did not seem to Monmouth that he would see his comrade in arms again, and he bade William a sincerely regretful farewell. Why were the popinjays of his father's Court so taken up with themselves that they did not know a good man when they saw one?

But he and William would meet again.

CHAPTER FOURTEEN

'The Yorks were well received in Brussels; it's a pleasant rich place. I confess I should have liked to stay longer, but I returned for the sake of Lady Fox, who cannot longer be expected to look after the children. As it is, I am grateful to her.'

Anna lay back against the cushions of their coach and adjusted the filmy veil she liked to wear about her head. She was dressed with care, for they had been to Somerset House to pay respects to the Queen. Monmouth stared idly out of the window; he was only just aware of his wife's presence, and the sight of her fair hair made him think of other such, guinea-gold. His exchanges with Harriet were increasingly loving; he had never felt so about any woman. The thought of her eased the raw anger from his mind, for the day after York again left London the paper regarding his own illegitimacy had been read before the Privy Council and was now public knowledge.

'I know well you will not heed me,' continued Anna, on her now familiar querulous note, 'but His Royal Highness would be a good friend to you if you would let him. As it is, he blames me for having given you ideas above your station with regard to the throne, and I—'

'My ideas, as you call them, are not your concern; pray cease to trouble yourself with them.'

'*Will* you take heed of me, Monmouth? By this determined flouting of the Duke of York you enrage the King himself. He and his brother are the only two left of their family; naturally they are close.'

'Shaftesbury says—'

'You will only listen to what Shaftesbury says; well, your clever Earl hath had to cool his heels in the Tower awhile. To concern oneself with stirring up the country is dangerous even for a man of his cunning; whereas you have no guile at all.' She moved restlessly. 'Content yourself with what you have—God knows it is enough—and make submission to the King.'

'How should I do that?' he asked absently. He had been watching the teeming street, and suddenly saw a little space where two men spoke together. They were Coleman, the Duchess of York's erstwhile secretary, a convert to Catholicism; and Sir Edmund Berry Godfrey, the magistrate, in his familiar gold hat-band and sober clothes, recently returned from abroad. Monmouth knew Sir Edmund well enough; he was a vestryman at St Martin's. He raised a hand in greeting, and the man's harassed eyes slewed round; he returned the salute courteously. What was Anna saying?

'. . . and you would do well to give her some little attention, and flatter her; then the King will not think of you merely as a leader of the Protestant party to his brother's despite.'

'Give attention to whom? I am sorry; I was watching the street.' He realised that he was often discourteous to Anna because she irritated him; he turned his head towards her, and smiled. It was not difficult, and he knew he had charm. She tightened her lips for a moment and then repeated what she had said in order that he might hear it. 'I said you had best pay court to the Duchess of Portsmouth, and win her to your side if you can; she hath greater influence with the King than anyone.'

'My father's French whore.' His lip curled, and she gave an impatient laugh.

'All men have a whore. Some have several.'

His face darkened. 'What the devil do you mean by that? Keep a still tongue in your head, if you can; it is over sharp, and you will cut yourself.'

'I might as well do so, for I have little gratitude for using it. Cannot you admit that at least I have made a friend of York for your sake?'

'He hath many whores, they say, all ugly.' But he knew well enough Anna was nobody's whore; she was too cold in her nature. It was in fact her tongue, which he had lately derided, that kept His Royal Highness amused. He reflected that she might have stayed in Brussels longer for all of him; and then repented of his treatment of her, was charming to her, and promised to dance that night with Louise Portsmouth or, as the King called her privately, Fubbs.

*   *   *

He and Louise danced; her exquisite figure was displayed to advantage in the rose-colour and forget-me-not blue she affected; a wisp of lace, starched and pinned, was fastened at the back of her head in the latest fashion. She was graceful, fragrant and beautiful; so much he knew. The King's passion for her was lasting; it was seven years now since the little Breton maid-in-waiting had come from King Louis. Charles himself stood nearby, watching; he did not dance these days. He was as ever, careless-seeming and affable, ostensibly talking with young Bruce and Lord Ossory, Ormonde's son; but Monmouth knew his own gesture had been noted. Yet Charles was not in a forgiving mood tonight; his mind was full of his brother

York, honest, tactless, loyal York, who was his own worst enemy and always would be. To have to send him again into exile had been hard. The King did not watch the graceful figure of his son in the dance. It was difficult not to let his love for Jemmy break all bounds, but he was still angry and distrustful. Shaftesbury might be under lock and key, but his poison was already in men's blood.

CHAPTER FIFTEEN

Monmouth had taken lodgings near Charing Cross, within sight of the royal mews; their half-ruined buildings reared against the night. There had been activity in the streets all day; with the coming of night a wind got up, sending the autumn leaves and rubbish scudding before it down the alleys. Monmouth called for his servant to throw more coals on the fire; it was cold.

Staring at the embers, the thought crossed his mind that the coal-merchant he patronised was Sir Edmund Berry Godfrey. It was not Monmouth's habit to remember or care where his household orders were made; that he did so now must be due to the impression the magistrate's strained face had made on him the other day in the street.

The man brought the coals and made up the

fire and withdrew, then came back again: there was a lady to see His Grace.

Monmouth frowned. It was unlike Eleanor to disturb him in his lodging; she waited obediently enough for his visits to Bloomsbury. His wife would not trouble to come. As for Harriet, his heartbeats quickened. Had she evaded her mother, and come here? They could seldom meet alone.

But the woman who was admitted was too small to be Harriet. She put back her hood and the firelight shone on her dark carefully dressed hair. It was Louise Portsmouth, dressed in sombre clothing to avoid recognition, though she wore no mask. She set her squirrel muff down and dismissed the servant she had brought in rapid French. Beneath the rouge her cheeks were pale. Monmouth had risen and bowed; she went to the fire and spread out her hands to the warmth, then spun about to face him.

'You have not heard,' she said. 'It is still known to only a few. Sir Edmund Berry Godfrey—' she used the name without familiarity, straining over the syllables—'hath been murdered; his body was found with two sword-thrusts through it, and a broken neck.'

He was appalled; the sight of the magistrate the other day had brought with it a feeling of doom. He remembered that he must show concern for Louise; he came to her and pressed her hands. They were still cold. He made as if to go to the sideboard and pour wine, but she shook her head.

'I cannot eat or drink, I am in such fear.'

He soothed her. 'There is none would harm you in such a way. It must have been some private enemy. He made many, poor man, in the law-sessions.' As he spoke, he knew he lied; there were many who would gladly get their hands about Portsmouth's throat. Had Godfrey foreseen his own fate that he had been in such unease?

Louise brushed his statement aside impatiently. 'It is not that,' she said. 'If it were so I would close myself within the Palace walls and not venture out without a guard. But I am a Catholic, M. le Duc, and it is for my fellows that I fear. This murder will be laid at their door.'

'The Papists? Why should they kill Sir Edmund? He was a fair judge, not biased. He was one of the few honest men on the Bench. He was truthful and honourable; I regret his death. But what you speak of is fantasy.'

She came to him and laid her small hands against his chest; her height only reached his shoulder. 'You do not understand,' she told him, and the blue, slightly squinting eyes looked up at his own. 'Three years ago there was a plot, so-called, by the Catholics, they said, against a man named Luzancy who had changed his faith. They were blamed for—how do you say it?—attempting to murder him.

Afterwards there were many cruel laws passed against those of my faith. This time it will be worse, a witch-hunt. I am afraid for us all. I have come to you to ask you, who lead them, to be my friend.' The hands stroked his coat; he had the feeling that she would have let him make love to her, but he did not have such ambition for his father's mistress. He took both her hands in his own, kissed them, and bade her be seated by the fire. 'The King loves you,' he said. 'No harm will come to you. For the rest, I cannot say. I have no such power as you would credit to me. The King will not do injustice of his own will.'

'He could not save his brother, who had to go into exile for no greater reason than his Catholic faith.'

'York was never popular with the people,' he said, then flushed at his own obtuseness: Louise herself was unpopular. Clever Nelly Gwyn had thrust her head out of her coach-window the other day to face a milling hostile mob. 'Be at peace, good people; this is the Protestant whore.' Nelly had great wit.

'How can you suppose I could help you?' he asked her. 'The King loves me less nowadays; I no longer have his ear.'

She shrugged lightly. 'He will forgive you times without number. He loves us both, and York also. All I ask is that, with Shaftesbury in the Tower—ah, how that man hates me!—you will use your influence. You have that, for the people's party speak of you as their leader.'

'They speak in whispers. There is no substance in it.'

'Much is done by whispering. How do you think I had Shaftesbury sent to the Tower?' She smiled for the first time, showing tiny teeth like a child's. Monmouth stared into the flames; little spurts of blue-green fire were coming from it; it must have come from near the sea. 'I will do what I may, as soon as I may do it,' he said. 'When that shall be I know no more than you.'

He sensed that he could accomplish little in such ways; he had not the subtlety of the plotter, the politician. But to comfort her he agreed to what she wanted, as his father would have done.

*   *   *

The King's mistress had been right. The dead body of the murdered magistrate was carried in state to be displayed in public in London, that all might see it with the neck awry. There was the strange circumstance that the dead man's shoes were clean, although he had been found in a ditch in the country. On his coat were the marks of candlewax. Altar-candles, the cry went up; the Papists had murdered him in Somerset House, where the Queen was, and had looked down on him by the light of candles from the altar in the chapel. Papists! They had a plot to overthrow the government, kill the King, kill the Duke of Monmouth, overrun the country with French soldiery, yoke England again to Rome. Much of this came from the mouth of a drawling long-chinned miscreant named Titus Oates, a creature of Shaftesbury. Nobody liked the man; he was physically revolting, but full of certainty and of his own importance. He had studied the Catholics for years; he had even insinuated himself into the Jesuit college at St Omer, after coming from Valladolid in Spain. He had asked to see the King, and this was granted; Charles caught him out in two proven falsehoods, and dismissed him, later growing angry when it was demanded that the Queen be put under restraint for intending to poison him. Poor forsaken Catherine, terrified and alone in Somerset House where they said the Godfrey murder had been committed, found some comfort at last; Charles ordered that she be brought back to him, to stay by his side at Whitehall. It had not occurred to him or anyone else how fond he was of the Queen.

But the hunt was up. The whole of London was hysterical with imagined danger; Shaftesbury's devout wife Margaret went about with a pistol hidden in her muff. Men were put to the torture who had been in the service of the Queen; under the rack, they screamed out false information, nonsense, anything which would cause the agony to cease. Men were hanged because of what they had said; as someone put it, if a Papist dog or cat had been seen abroad it would have been torn in pieces. A Catholic goldsmith named Staley was arrested on hearsay evidence for supposedly saying he would stab the King; his own evidence was not considered and he was executed within the week. In the city itself there were riots, and the Pope burned in effigy; the Protestant supporters wore green ribbons in their hats and shouted for Monmouth for heir. Monmouth himself kept away from the riots and burnings; he did not wish to displease the King, but his name was being used and he could not prevent it. He himself had gone, on hearing of Godfrey's murder, to the chapel at Somerset House, which was full of shadows and told him nothing of any death except God's. But there was murder in the streets and in men's hearts. Coleman, the Yorks' secretary, was done to death; his letters had been under scrutiny for two years. Three Jesuits, a layman, and a Benedictine were tried for treason, and imprisoned despite the Queen's pleading; one, Pickering, was hanged, drawn and quartered in early summer. In the provinces, eight priests were put to death. In London, Catherine's servants who had given evidence were executed; Pepys' own clerk at the Admiralty was taken, and they hoped to get his master; but the servant kept his head and was freed. Five Jesuits and a lawyer suffered, their

125

quartered disembowelled bodies exposed in the streets: one had been the English Provincial. The arrests went on, no credit being given for truth in anyone now that the perjurer Oates had had his way. 'I sign the warrants with tears in my eyes,' said the King. But he could not refuse to sign; they would have had his throne.

Later he convened a Parliament at Oxford, and the Exclusion Bill for the dismissal of York as heir went forward as long as it might; then the King, with his robes hastily pulled about him and a subsidy from Louis in his pocket, dissolved the Parliament. He would never recall it as long as he lived.

CHAPTER SIXTEEN

The King's continuing disfavour to his son was not unnoticed. Monmouth found that he was cold-shouldered by certain persons about Court, including the Sunderland faction who were for the Duke of York. There was also a rival cabal to Shaftesbury's, founded by Lord Halifax, who had written to the Prince of Orange as prospective heir to the throne. Monmouth naturally had no dealings with them, though he remained on civil terms with Halifax himself. He and William had fought a war together, and he would not be manipulated into a rival's place. For once he kept his own counsel, and his own company.

There was a ball at Court and he attended it. Anna was soon taken up with her own friends, and he found himself alone. He made his way to the privy garden, leaving the heated stench of the rooms. He sat there alone for some time, with the night breeze stirring in the trees King Charles had planted about Cromwell's wilderness. It occurred to him that seldom in his life had he been solitary. He waited idly, feeling neither sadness nor joy.

Then joy came. Harriet was beside him, having hastened in a rustle of scented silk; her very flesh breathed essences. She sat by him and twined her arms about him. He set his mouth against her hair.

'I saw you go,' she said against him. 'I had to come to you.'

'My dear. My own dear. It is not good for you to be here.' He thought of her suitors, of the marriage she ought to make. 'I am a marked man, out of favour,' he told her. 'Go back to your friends; your name is untouched. Keep it so; do not be seen with me.'

'What do I care for that? Did you not know I must give myself to you wholly, in total love? Do you think I am a creature who lives for the fame of the hour? I had thought you wiser concerning me.'

They kissed then. He was so conscious of the warmth of her smooth young lips that he could think no longer of the occasion or the time; only that they were here, here, together, alone against a traitorous world; that she and he loved one another as it had not happened since time began.

'Harriet.'

'My dear, my own dear.'

They made love there, in the quiet place among the trees. No one passed, but anyone coming would have been aware only of another amorous couple from the Court, a lady with her leman, a lord with his mistress. That which was done was done tenderly; he did not take her lightly, as he had done with his other women. By the end they were rapt in one another, the very stars forgotten.

'I love you.'

'And I love you. We will meet again when . . .'

'Do not speak of the future. The golden time is now. I love you, and am yours. This night hath brought me much gladness.'

'I also. I was never as glad in all of my life. You are mine, I yours, always.'

'Always.'

The moon set behind a cloud, and still they sat with their arms twined about one another, his body within hers. They had been made for this; each day they had separately known from the beginning had brought them to this consummation.

He said, still against her hair, 'You are my

wife before God.'

Afterwards, she went back to the Court and her mother, he to his wife.

*   *   *

Orders came for him to ride into Scotland, to quell the rebellious Covenanters, who had murdered an archbishop, taken the city of Glasgow, and killed thirty-six of the King's men at a place named Drumclog. Monmouth summoned his men and rode north, without enough money or supplies; these were grudged. It had been a chill leavetaking despite the summer weather. Once the King would have sent for him to wish him Godspeed, but now there was no friendly arm about his shoulders, no parting farewell; merely an order in course of duty. So be it; duty should be done.

He reached Edinburgh on the thirteenth of June, seeing for the first time the grey smoke-grimed buildings tumbling down from the Castle Hill. This ugly yet beautiful place was the capital of a country his father had loathed ever since his coronation as a lad in Scotland, where the Presbyterians had exposed him to many humiliations including the betrayal of his friend Montrose. A dour uncommunicative set of folk, no doubt; but with courage. He prepared to meet them, and in a day or two word came that they were to the westward, no doubt hoping to retire to their Galloway bogs if all else failed.

He rode swiftly, hearing the clatter of hooves and seeing the men's armour shine in the sunlight; scanning the beautiful, almost womanish face of Graham of Claverhouse, the captain of the Duke of York's Regiment of Horse Guards. Claverhouse was in truth no woman and was not inclined to mercy after his losses at Drumclog. But Monmouth himself suspected that a show of power was all that would be needed; he had learned enough in Edinburgh to know that here was no organised army, and that the Covenanters were divided by squabbles among themselves. There was a preacher named Welsh who headed the moderate party, and another named Cargill who thought God would send down thunderbolts in defence of His elect. It would remain to be seen who triumphed; but they would know by now, at least, that the King's force had marched.

Shortly two men were brought to him. They wore the plain hodden clothes and linen collars of the Nonconformists; their mouths were set stubbornly, but their eyes pleaded. They had brought a petition to have the whole matter settled by Parliament, or rather what they described as the General Assembly. Monmouth had heard of the latter through his father, who abhorred it. He stared at the men and they at him; they would carry back to their wives and children the legend of Monmouth

Jemmy, in his scarlet coat with his rich dark curls blowing in a northern wind, and eyes which regarded them kindly from under the King's black brows. Kindness was not what they had expected to find; even so, his reply daunted them.

They spoke out, for they were used to the sound of their own voices; His Grace was a merciful man, they had heard, averse to the shedding of blood. His Grace affirmed that he did not desire that it should be shed. 'I cannot enter into any arrangement, or grant terms, till you have laid down your arms,' he told them. They had handed him a paper full of wordy declaration; he took time to glance through it. 'I come as a soldier,' he said to them. He was sorry for them; they might be mown down like sheep, but they were not penitent. They had talked of a parley, first for a day, then for an hour; 'Sir, you have the ear of the King,' they said. Have I? he thought wryly; but told them that if, again, they would lay down their arms he would intercede with the King on their behalf. If the troubles in the north could be stopped, success was just possible in such ways; Charles was not a cruel man. A memory, here on the windswept plain, beset him of the King striding down to feed his waterfowl, the shorter-legged courtiers striving to keep up with him till they almost ran. It was hard to keep back tears; he dashed his sleeve across his eyes, pretending it was the wind.

He saw their averted gaze, and knew that what he had suggested was useless. These men would fight to the last for their beliefs; well, then, let them do so.

*　　　*　　　*

There was only one ford at Bothwell Bridge. He looked at it, and saw the five thousand of the enemy laid out to the south. His own ten thousand faced them across the water, from the less favourable side. He looked at the bridge itself; a little stone four-arched structure, with the gatekeeper's house at the further end. They had blocked it with stones and brushwood. He could see the Kippen and Galloway men, the latter with straps made of conger-eel leather, wade out and make as if to defend the stone buttresses in the river. More men piled on to the bridge, behind the gate which was already shut against him.

Graham of Claverhouse rode up, his curls blowing in the wind. 'I put it to Your Grace that we should outflank them.' But Monmouth gave the order to attack. For a long time—afterwards they said it had taken two hours—the small force held through the clash of steel, the smoke of firing, and the cries of men falling wounded in the water. The movement of troops from the other side began; they were horsed on little garrons, sure-footed in the uncertain boggy ground.

'They are running short of ammunition,' someone murmured; there had been no firing from the bridge for some time, only the clangour of steel meeting steel. A shout arose; the order had come to quit the bridge. The rebels withdrew sullenly, with many wounded. Monmouth gave the order to pass the bridge and draw up behind the cannon on the south side. It had been different fighting from the time in Flanders; the lie of the land was less flat. The stones were slippery with blood and he felt his horse stumble. They reached the further bank; beyond, past the outflung bulk of the Southern Uplands, Anna's inheritance lay.

The sun grilled down. He had no doubt now of victory; only the spirit of the makeshift army held fast. They believed so implicitly in their stern God that perhaps even yet He would help them.

It was nearly so. There had been no attack while they were crossing over; once on the bank, though, a detachment of the Galloway men wheeled about, and began to fight. This was evidently against orders; there were shouts to them to withdraw, and they did so at last, leaving a few dead. Monmouth gave the order to fire at the cavalry on the left wing. Confusion followed, with every man for himself. Through the smoke he saw men riding away in some numbers; perhaps they had meant to re-form, but the chance was not given them. The army panicked, and sixteen hundred men, led by their inept leader Hamilton, fled the field.

Monmouth advanced; men were standing ready to throw down their arms. He let it be known that there were to be no more killings, and that prisoners would be taken. The brave fellows had lacked a competent leader and he did not want to shed their blood. Among the hawthorns and gorse-thickets, horsemen still hid. He could not stop the men who remembered Drumclog from murdering them in cold blood. Otherwise he was merciful; when the prisoners were taken on the field, he sent his own surgeon to dress their wounds before they were taken to Edinburgh.

The capital, relieved, gave him a gold casket and the freedom of the city. The prisoners were penned meantime in Greyfriars churchyard. Monmouth saw to it that they had bread and ale daily; after he left, the ale was changed to water. Less kindly treatment still was waiting for them; but Graham of Claverhouse had ridden into the west to avenge Drumclog. He would not, like Monmouth, be accused of trying to gain favour by merciful measures. But Monmouth had returned to London, having feasted greatly on the way with the Earl of Selkirk at Kirkcudbright. He looked for a last time on the peaceful sea-loch and castle where so much had happened in ancient times; now it seemed calm and remote from strife.

*   *   *

He rode south, with such speed that when he reached Doncaster, where Sir John Reresby had made haste to greet him with a roasted buck and much wine, he found the host in bed, for it was past midnight. Monmouth fell on the fare, ate heartily, then would not let Sir John change the sheets on the bed, but got in with him; sleep came as soon as his weary head touched the pillow. It was better to tire himself out riding than to lie awake and think. He was uncertain what awaited him in London; the times were like a stewpot, changing while being stirred.

He need not have been troubled; as far as that went, the people of London did not change towards him. When his coach—he had borrowed it from Sir John, as horses were in short supply—came in sight they ran out in their hundreds, took hold of the bridles and conveyed the Protestant Duke into town, cheering all the way. Monmouth Jemmy had beaten the rebels in the north; that was all they knew, and with their acclaim the memory of the dour brave faces began to fade in his mind. He would never ride into Scotland again.

*   *   *

'Damn them, they say the Prince of Orange is to come over,' swore Shaftesbury, released from the Tower and striding with his short gait up and down the room. 'I declare I will have the heads of those who put it into the King's to dissolve Parliament. Certainly it had become an abode of tricksters, but where is not? And liberty must be preserved. The French whore hath betrayed us; she is on William's side for her own sake. Your Grace had best court Nell.'

Later Monmouth rode to Nell Gwyn's lodging, and prevailed upon her good-nature with ease. Her large eyes filled with tears at his tale, and she promised to speak to the King. 'I will tell him you are grown lean-visaged and wan, and 'tis true, for so you are indeed, Jemmy.' She sat on his knee and caressed and kissed him; Nell never withheld her warmth from any man. She was different, Cockney to the bone, more trustworthy because simpler than Louise; but even Nell could do nothing with His Majesty. Monmouth waited, and no word came from Whitehall except the news that the King had not been well. It was thought by some that he was dying, then he recovered; he had gone for a long walk after a game of tennis, and caught a chill which later turned to a fever.

Shaftesbury came to Monmouth again. 'They say York is to come back in secret from beyond seas. How will His Majesty greet his brother? Better, I'll warrant, than he hath greeted his son, and for less labour.'

'I know not,' Monmouth said. He no longer

pretended to have control of the events which were happening round him. Somewhere, there must be a place where he and Harriet could be private; he had seen her twice since his return, each time in fear of interruption by her mother. 'If once I were of age!' she had wept. 'They could do naught then, neither Sir William Smyth nor my mother; and how I should welcome you at Toddington!'

'That day will come, sweetheart.' He knew himself to be older than she was, but felt no wiser; it had been too much to expect that they would be left to their happiness; events had come on like a flood, to bear him away, and there were proposals of marriage for Harriet. In any event he had not the heart to unburden to her all that chafed him; the coldness of the King, the threat of York's return, the new cabal favouring William of Orange, the Duchess of Portsmouth's betrayal. Louise was piqued, no doubt, in that he had done less for her than she had hoped. Her favour now was for the other party, whether led by Halifax or Sunderland.

*   *   *

The King was recovering, half hearing the dying whispers about Whitehall; what if he had died? who would have been his heir?

A tall man in a black wig had taken passage in a French shallop and landed at Dover,

137

posting immediately for London. There he knocked at the door of Sir Allan Apsley, the King's falconer who lived in St James's Square; slept there the night, and was at Whitehall by dawn. A word here and there sufficed; he came upon the King being shaved. Charles turned a drawn face towards him; it broke into a smile. He could never withhold his affection for long, and this was his brother. York had done no harm except to himself.

The tall man knelt. 'I crave pardon for entering Your Majesty's realm without leave, but when I heard of your illness I could not tarry.'

His tears fell on the King's hand. Charles looked down on the disguised head; there was tenderness in his face. His speech burst out suddenly, as if formality could no longer be endured between them.

'By God, James, I am glad to see you!'

The Protestant party was forestalled.

*　　　*　　　*

Monmouth was his own enemy. In the midst of a crowd of cronies as he was, he met York coming from the King's apartments. He could not afterwards have said why, but at sight of the uncle who had so often shown his disapproval, even hatred, and whom he himself had thought safely across the Channel, he did a discourteous thing; he stared straight ahead of him, and made no bow. York flushed, and passed by. Monmouth laughed loudly, and turned to his nearest companion with some jest.

As might have been expected, in a few days there came a summons to attend the King at Windsor.

*   *   *

He rode through the Great Park, hearing the squelch of his horse's hooves on the wet turf. He tossed the bridle to a groom in the yard and strode upstairs to where his father waited. Suits of armour and weapons looked down from the walls and stairs: Prince Rupert, Captain and Governor of the Castle, had been at pains to array them carefully over the years of his residence. Two children ran in and out of the rooms; a stolid fair-haired boy and a girl some years younger, an exquisite little dark-haired creature. She was Prince Rupert's daughter by the actress Peg Hughes, while the boy, Dudley, was the son of his former mistress. Their shouts and laughter faded along the passages; the chill of the stone struck home.

Monmouth announced his presence and was admitted. The King was alone, gazing out at the trees beyond the window. Presently he turned his head; he did not smile.

'You will know why I have sent for you.'

Monmouth took refuge in insolence.

'Because I am your son and you my father; perhaps also because I fought for you in the North.'

Charles frowned. 'Your ambition exceeds all bounds. Let me say again what I have already said clearly; to my acknowledged heir you will show courtesy. This was ... not the case ... recently. Why, you fool, do you not know that every word and action is reported to me? You were damnably rude to your uncle and should make him an apology.'

'That I will never do. The Duke of York hath his friends, of which he does not choose that I am one; and his confessor.' The tone was contemptuous. 'Can any man blame me if I cleave to the Protestants? They have been loyal.'

'You choose your words narrowly. The Green Ribbon Club hath caused much unrest and much harm.'

Monmouth kept his eyes on the changed face. Since his illness Charles had shaven his upper lip clean; the bare face seemed older, dissipated and discoloured. Pity suddenly took Monmouth. 'Sire, there have been factions since time out of mind,' he said. 'Your Majesty is well loved.'

'You seek, I believe, the throne.'

'Sire! Your life—'

'Let me make this clear. Many have striven with me not to acknowledge you as my son; they even say you are Sydney's. I have not listened to them, and have made provision for you as I might. You will not deny that I have been generous.'

'To your own flesh and blood! How can you doubt that I am your son?' He was perplexed and angry; he knew the brothers Robert and Algernon Sydney well enough; they had known his mother since she was a child.

'Let that be; in any case my heir is my brother. The matter hath brought much grief to me through his cause and your own. His reception when he followed me recently into the City was so bad that I have sent him into Scotland, to do what he may there.'

'How will such a King sway a nation, Sire?' Monmouth's lips were trembling; he could scarcely form the words. York to Scotland! And those poor devils of Covenanters would be at his mercy, and that of Claverhouse.

'I must do what will please all parties. It was expedient to send my brother away; and there are not lacking those who say that as he hath gone, you must go also. Understand this.'

'But not to Scotland, sire, where they love me a little.'

'I have told you York is gone to Scotland,' replied the King coldly. Monmouth turned white about the mouth.

'Sire, he will be harsh and cruel with those poor devils! The greater part are ignorant of why they fight, for their ministers will tell them nothing except to rant. Most are innocent and

141

would show loyalty to Your Majesty if charity were shown them.'

'York may practise charity if he will,' said the King drily. He had begun to stroke his coat-braid with a finger; it was a sign that the talk neared its close. 'You yourself must make haste to Holland,' he said. 'I grieve to have to send you away, and to ask for—for your resignation as Lord General.'

'Have I ever disgraced you as a soldier?' Monmouth asked hotly. The other's eyes grew mild; almost, he smiled at his son.

'Far from it, Jemmy. I'm proud of you; you must know it. But for all our sakes I must send you away; York's friends demand it. They crowd about me since he was sent into exile, saying that as he is, so should you be. In justice, I cannot deny that.'

The long fingers strayed to the dark periwig; Charles began to pull at its curls, as if it were one of the dogs he loved; there were none about him here at Windsor. Monmouth stood pale as marble. To go abroad, and leave so much!

He began to babble at his father, throwing accusations both just and unjust at the changed face. Charles raised a hand presently. 'Have done,' he said; the eyes were hooded and cold.

'Then ... then ... am I never to see you more?' Rank, majesty, all the required titles forsook him; this was his father, and he must go away.

The King smiled. 'Come to me at St James's

before we part. Never think I do not love you, Jemmy! But the crown, that is another matter.'

*   *   *

They said farewell when the King was taking the air in Arlington Garden. There was a carpenter working nearby and Charles borrowed pen, paper and ink from him to write the Duke of Monmouth's order to pass out of England. Monmouth took the paper mutely; they looked one another in the eyes, and tears were not far from the older man's; but his son's were angry. So did they part. It was still September; the dulling leaves hung idly on the trees in the Park.

*   *   *

He left England by way of Whitehall Stairs. A crowd lined the bank to see him depart. His barge, with the Monmouth and Buccleuch arms blazoned, waited on the river. Monmouth made his way down the steps unhurriedly, his face sombre beneath the plumed hat. They would see that his wife was not with him; one of the boys was ill, and it was sufficient excuse not to have Anna's company.

The rowers started up, and along the way which had seen royal pageants without number his barge drifted, down the tide to Gravesend where his yacht waited. He went below at once;

143

he did not watch the flat coasts of England fade beyond the skyline. He was assailed by a savage longing for Harriet; she understood him as no one else could, not even his father.

*   *   *

'My father will do nothing for me: he favours the Pope.'

It was a braggart saying, and William of Orange took it as such, not replying in words, merely looking gravely with his dark eyes at his guest. He had welcomed Monmouth to The Hague, would take him hunting and make the time pass for him as well as he might, though he himself had scant leisure. Shortly, he knew, a house would be made ready for Monmouth in Utrecht; it was the property of Prince Rupert, who had offered it to the fugitive.

Once Monmouth had gone from The Hague York and his wife entered it, ready to return home. It had been discreetly given out by now that York would accept the post of King's Commissioner in Scotland. He and his Duchess would stay at Holyroodhouse, filled as it was with memories of the Stewart Kings. Mary Beatrice would become well liked among the Scots ladies, notable for her tea-drinkings; it was their first introduction to the beverage. But meantime she and York took pleasure in the company of William and his wife Mary, whom her stepmother called dearest Lemon.

Mary had changed from the thoughtless young princess of Whitehall; she dressed plainly and sought to please her husband, with whom she was now much in love.

*   *   *

Monmouth held court in Amsterdam amid suspicious Dutch and out-at-elbows English; lonely, bedevilled, and missing England, he did and said everything he should not. Word would go back across the water of the ill-advised remarks he was making about his father, having even chosen an enemy of the King's with whom to lodge on arrival. Few except Shaftesbury and Harriet seemed to miss him; the former continued with his rabble-raisings, wearing a green ribbon in his hat for Monmouth Jemmy. He wrote that the Popish whore, Louise, had been disappointed in the Prince of Orange and was not completely their enemy. Louis XIV, on the other hand, was friendly; in cipher, Shaftesbury made it clear that he would pay for their support. 'Otherwise all is lost, with the Princess Mary married in Holland and the King not yet daring to call himself Papist,' Monmouth announced unwisely. In fact that goose was cooked, for the French King's historiographer, Abbé Primi, had mistakenly published news of Minette's Treaty of Dover as far back as 1681. A bottle of wine, the second, the third; what did it matter how drunk he got? No one cared for him except Harriet, and she was far away; he thought of her constantly. He did not believe flesh and blood such as theirs would withstand long separation; soon, by whatever means, he must return to England.

CHAPTER SEVENTEEN

Harriet had received a letter at the town house in Portugal Row. For moments she stared at the seal, with its device of plumed feathers redeemed by a small stag's head; as near the Prince of Wales's escutcheon as Monmouth dared. She smiled tenderly, but at the same time felt anxiety for her lover; he was too rash, not thoughtful enough on his own account; harm must not come to him through her. She opened the letter, read it lovingly—his writing was careful, like a schoolboy's, his spelling atrocious—it was a love letter, saying only how greatly he missed her, how he longed once more to lie in her arms. Tears filled her eyes; with the King still disposed against him, how could he come home? And if she went to him her mother and Sir William would fetch her back again, for she was not yet of age.

She was still staring at the letter when Lady Philadelphia burst joyfully into the room. She wore a gown of black velvet, not new but amply trimmed with rich lace, which her sister in Holland sent her from time to time. Her swarthy face was rouged, to be in the fashion, but she kept her hair dressed plainly. 'Hear the news I have, and maybe you have heard it too,' she cried. 'The Duke and Duchess of York are to return to Court, and they request that you continue in your post of lady-in-waiting; it will do us much good. The Duke pays his household expenses promptly, not like some. A little money will help.'

She broke off, staring, for Harriet had not been in time to thrust the letter into her bodice unseen. 'What have you there?' Philadelphia demanded. She was not too perturbed; many suitors had asked for Harriet: Shrewsbury, Duras himself, perhaps Bruce, though the latter's father wanted him to marry money. Duras had the prospect of an earldom, though he was too old for Harriet. Countess of Shrewsbury ... One must remember that Harriet was dowerless, though she herself had done what she could regarding the Bedfordshire properties; they earned rent now. 'If I did not know you so particular in your choice I would swear 'twas a love letter,' she said teasingly. She was pleased with Harriet; the girl was beautiful, decorous, and gentle. She would make some nobleman a perfect wife. 'My dear, what are you at?'

Harriet had evaded her deftly, thrust the letter in the fire, and watched it burn. She knew what it had contained; the words were in her heart.

Lady Philadelphia stamped her foot; this was no dream, such as her daughter looked to be forever in; some man had written to her secretly. She peered at the seal, rapidly melting in the flames. 'You dare to thwart me, your mother! You have a lover that I do not know of? None of the offers need write so.' Her face had flushed with vexation beneath the rouge.

Harriet faced her. 'Forget the offers, mother; I will have none of them.'

'Then you have a lover. I should have known it, mim as you kept. After all I have done—'

'I have a lover indeed, who loves me as I love him. I would have made no secret had you asked me sooner; I am not ashamed.'

'Not ashamed? Then he hath made you his whore.' Her mother began to scold and wail, and Harriet went quickly to the door to ensure that none of the servants lurked outside. It was as well, she thought with humour, that they were not lodged at the Palace; Sarah Jennings' mother had once pursued her daughter down the warren of passages with a shovelful of flaming coals. But Sarah had made a satisfactory marriage to John Churchill only last year. I am in no such market, thought Harriet.

She turned back into the room. Her mother had fallen into one of the rages for which she was famous; Harriet half heard the hysterical

148

words and reproaches. She did not love her mother, though she was dutiful to her; since she could well remember, Monmouth had filled her heart and soul. Fears lest his name should somehow come to the angry woman's lips forced her to speak at last, when she might make herself heard.

'Mother, you will be listened to in the street; lower your voice, I beg you.' But this only served to heighten the storm. 'We will go to the country,' swore Lady Philadelphia, 'where I may have you under my eye. You'll not steal a march on me at Toddington as you have at Court. Lover, indeed! Slut that you are, a wanton, and my daughter! What your father—'

'Father would have approved it, I do believe.' Somehow her heart was singing. It would be a relief to be at Toddington again, among the trees and smooth water she loved. Reminder of her dead husband's gay charm made his widow angrier than ever.

'Tomorrow we go,' she said; her high colour had receded and her face was patched and ugly. 'As for the York appointment, what good is that? No man of repute will wed a whore. Is there question of marriage between you?' Her eyes were suddenly beady; Harriet smiled a little sadly.

'There will be no marriage,' she said. Her mother rounded on her. 'No marriage?' she shrieked. 'Is he a married man who hath your maidenhead? That I should live to hear it!'

'I love to be at Toddington,' said Harriet calmly. It would, she knew, be as empty there as at Court, lacking him. Perhaps when she was free of guardianship—it was not very long now—he would come to her, or she go to him. It did not matter in the whole world where they lived, so long as they were together.

*   *   *

The Wentworth coach, old and leaking at the leather roof-seams, set out for Bedfordshire amid a cloud of gossip. Lady Philadelphia was not prudent, and had loudly given out that she was taking her daughter away to make ready for marriage to the Earl of Shrewsbury. That personage had indeed proposed, but had not been accepted. Why had Lady Harriet gone away when there was the prospect of the York appointment? That might have brought her an even richer husband. Gossip spread, wildly because uninformed; then interest waned with the return of the Yorks to Court.

No one yet linked Monmouth's name with Harriet. He was not forgotten; everyone missed his beauty and grace, which had adorned Whitehall in the dances of an evening. One man kept in touch with him, however, and that was Shaftesbury. Soon, he was writing to Holland to advise a return to England; the uncle had been recalled from exile, why not the son? He would put it to the King; did so, and received a snub for his pains, such as Charles knew well enough how to administer.

But Monmouth set out secretly from Maeslandsluce, and was home before his uncle, who report said had indeed used the Covenanters with harshness in Scotland. The country rejoiced at Monmouth's return; bonfires blazed, bells chimed, and in the King's closet were sharp words, for the King had been disobeyed in that Monmouth came home without leave. The commons cared nothing, and exchanged the news by the light of beacons from church-towers, flaring against the night. They said the Protestant Duke had returned by the advice of the Prince of Orange, who was himself coming soon.

*   *   *

Monmouth Jemmy rode through the streets of London and his head was high. He heard the women sigh for him and the men approve him. He had been right to take Little Sincerity's advice and come home. Now he would go to Shaftesbury at his town house, sleep there, and proceed in the morning to his own house in the Cockpit. Tonight he could not face Anna. He wondered how the sick boy fared.

Shaftesbury's house had great flambeaux lit; he was bowed in, put by the fire, given wine, and presently the master of the house came, his diminutive figure decked out in satin and velvet with a rich cravat of lace. The firelight shone on his handsome face and shadowed the stunted body; he might have been a god. He came to Monmouth, bowed the knee and kissed his hand, as though the King sat there.

Subtly, smoothly, the comfort of Shaftesbury's house soothed Monmouth's hurt spirit; they talked over the wine, and he stared at the light wood surfaces rich with beeswax, the exquisite curtains and carpets. Shaftesbury had chosen them tastefully; that he himself should have been chosen by such a connoisseur flattered Monmouth. He asked what he should do, as the King was still angry.

'I had thought of going to the Cockpit tomorrow to see my children,' he said. 'My father cannot prevent that. Francis is sick, and hath ailed from his birth; there is a curse on me and mine.'

'Curses do not outlive their day. Your time will come.'

'To whom shall I go?' Monmouth trusted Shaftesbury; the little man had been working on his behalf all through the time of his exile, spending his own gold to whip up enthusiasm for the Protestant Duke with bonfires and bell-ringings, and the shouts of the Green Ribbon Club.

Shaftesbury regarded his fingers. 'First of all try the Protestant mistress,' he said.

'Nelly? I know and love her. But hath she the

ear of the King?'

'Try her again. If that fails, I say you should go to the country, as the politicians do. Stay out of London; take yourself on a progress through the loyal shires, in particular the south. Many people love you who have not yet seen you. Remedy that.' He smiled at the tall handsome figure. If he himself had had such height, such looks and charm, what might he not have achieved!

I will pass by Bedfordshire, Monmouth was thinking; his love had smuggled word to him that she was kept close at Toddington. In time he would force the lock of that cage, but meantime he must look to his cause.

Shaftesbury had not done speaking. 'It is you the people love, never the Prince of Orange. Also you have children, which he hath not. You and your heirs may fashion a Protestant dynasty for Britain, having the blood of the Stuarts running in your veins without their taint of Popery.' He moved slightly. 'They say,' he said slowly, 'that there is a document of your father's marriage to your mother, contained in a certain black box belonging to the Bishop of Durham lately dead.'

'Cosin? They say he married my father and my mother. I can remember my mother saying a paper was taken from her when she was lodged in the Tower with me and my sister, when we were young. Bradshaw kept it.'

'Well, Bradshaw swung alongside Cromwell on the gallows a year after they were dead; they stank together. You have friends, Your Grace; Russell, Essex, Halifax, Temple, Sunderland.'

'Sunderland is in the King's councils, and those of my uncle York.'

'Ay, but secretly concerns himself with you. It is of value to have a man who can guard his tongue.'

'And you, my friend? I know you have worked well for me.' His voice was warm. Shaftesbury laughed, showing his ruined teeth. 'Why, I will die of the gout ere you are crowned; an astrologer said so. Do you have mind of Dr Lilley? This past year, he died.'

They began to talk of other things.

*   *   *

In the morning Monmouth took horse and rode openly to his lodgings in the Cockpit at Whitehall. He was refreshed after his night's sleep and his talk with Shaftesbury. York might cozen the King against him, but he had his answer. The list of supporters Shaftesbury had given him lay in his pocket.

He made his way to the Cockpit, defiantly; these premises were part of Whitehall Palace. He ordered them to bring him something to eat; he was hungry, even after Shaftesbury's hospitality. They brought him meat, and he fell to on a mutton bone; halfway through the meal

154

he heard the rustle of silk at the door, and turned his head. A woman stood there. It was his wife. He gazed at her as though she were a stranger.

'Word hath come from the King,' she said. She advanced into the room with her limping step. 'He is very wroth that you have come home without his order.'

'I care not.'

'Perhaps you should care. All your appointments are stripped from you. He would not receive your letter which came. You are no longer in charge of the army; that you know. The Duke of Albemarle hath your Life Guards. Your governorship of Yorkshire is at an end; the Earl of Mulgrave hath it. Lord Chesterfield himself hath your wardenship of forests. You are nothing now, whereas you were once great.'

'And you are glad of it. You never loved me.'

'Nay, it is you who never loved me. I would have given you my love, but you scorned it always.' She stared at the tapestries which adorned the walls; he might not have been present. He looked at her, as if seeing her for the first time; she was a comely woman, fair and without defect except her lameness; why could he not have loved her? Yet the thought of Harriet was with him, like a warm beam of sunshine against cold stone.

'How is the boy?' he said.

'He is ailing, and hath been so since you left.

You may see him if you choose.' She spoke coldly; he had refused her offered reconciliation, and she had withdrawn into herself. She knew well enough that there was another woman.

'I will see him presently. Leave me now; I would put my affairs in order.'

She rose, and he heard the rustle of her skirts again as she withdrew towards the door. She must have stood there some time, looking back at him, for he did not hear it close at once. But he did not turn his head again and in the end she went; he heard the little click of the latch, and was thankful.

* * *

He betook himself to the mews, to think what he might do; first he would go to Moor Park, his place in Hertfordshire. Anna might join him if she chose. He looked forward to the sight of empty heaths and bushes of furze and gorse; in Holland there had hardly been any trees, and he missed the sight of them. While he pondered on it, a message was brought to him from the King. It contained a threat to clap him in the Tower if he did not return to Holland.

* * *

Sadly, the illness of the little boy Francis

softened the King, who said the child's father might stay by him a while. Monmouth returned to the Cockpit hastily; by the boy's bed was Anna, her eyes bright with tears. The child was breathing irregularly, his cheeks flushed with fever. Monmouth reflected that he had hardly seen this son, who was just over a year old, and who had been called after Anna's father.

Francis died as the others had, and would be buried beside them at Westminster. When his breathing had stopped Monmouth bent and kissed the plump cheek, still warm; then he laid his hand on his wife's shoulder. Her flesh felt like that of a stranger; it was incredible that he had ever been married to her.

'Perhaps some day you will find love, Anna,' he said; and went out.

*   *   *

He went to Nelly. Shaftesbury had been right in saying that she was on his side; she looked up tearfully through a tumble of auburn curls.

'It's of no use, love,' she said. 'I spoke to him, told him you were pale, like I said, and he bade me be quiet. When he says that it's useless to speak any more.' She gazed at him mournfully. 'I wish you were friends again,' she said. 'I'm certain he longs for you. You're his own flesh and blood, when all's said: the pity of it! He makes himself ill; he's not like he used to be.'

softened the King, who said the child's father might stay by him a while. Monmouth

         *   *   *

On the fourteenth of December Monmouth attended morning service at St Martin's. The congregation rose to its feet as one man on his entry, crying, 'God bless the Duke of Monmouth!' 'He took the sacrament then and there,' noted a recorder. There was no lack of love for the King's son. He stayed on after the service chatting with men and their wives, his hat in his hand. He had always known how to reach the common people.

         *   *   *

The King was still without a Parliament. Most of his advisers had left, and only Godolphin and Lawrence Hyde, uncle of dead Duchess Anne, remained. The King seemed heedless of the state of affairs. He liked better to hear Godolphin's tale of having found a neglected milk-horse in Paris, bought it, and brought it home to use as a teaser till the stallion should come; but instead one day it had run off with the chosen mare, they had mated in the woods and a beautiful little foal had afterwards been born, with Arab features. Godolphin said he would make it the foundation of his stud. Charles listened idly; half of his mind was filled with the need to see his brother again; he relied on York. He and his Duchess had returned quietly to London on the twenty-fourth of

158

February.

By April, Monmouth was turned away by the King's warden from woods where he wished to hunt.

*   *   *

'Your Grace, here is the man Robert Ferguson.'

A fantastic figure in dark clothes entered, clutching a bundle of pamphlets under his arm. He wore a fuzzed wig, had a great hook nose and shambled in his walk. Monmouth already knew something of him; he taught classics at a school in Islington, having been ejected from a Church living at Godmersham. He extended his hand smiling, and studying the man's queer face from under his hat's brim; had not the King himself shown that he might wear his hat in company? The plumed beaver shaded the handsome face, discontented with lack of news. The room was full of figures; he saw Shaftesbury's little shape among them.

'Sir, I have written and had printed at my expense this broadsheet which you see.' Thrust beneath his eyes he saw the title *An Appeal from the Country to the City*. 'It pictures the evils we may suffer under a Papist King,' said Ferguson hoarsely. Monmouth cast an idle eye over the paper; he had little time for printed matter. Ferguson waited for his comment, and when none came, thrust forward again, egregiously.

'Sir, if the cry could be "God and my People" instead of "God and my Right" there would be justice in't. There have been many publications of late.'

Monmouth lowered his lashes. One of the publications had been about the King's marriage to Lucy Barlow. His mother; how long ago she had died!

He returned his mind to the present, and tried to see the future. How would England indeed fare under a Papist King? And he himself, as Shaftesbury had said, was more greatly loved than the Prince of Orange; two of his sons yet lived, and two daughters. Why should he not enlist the services of such as Ferguson? A friend in adversity would be a friend in wealth.

His doings were remarked, with Shaftesbury's. By the spring a declaration appeared in the *Gazette* denying the tale of that early marriage; saying, again, that the King had never been married to any but his 'new wife' Queen Catherine.

* * *

Monmouth began to receive anonymous letters. *There are a sort of men who have made it their business of late to advance you higher than the wisdom of the King hath made you*, one ran. *We do say they are your enemies, and would seek after your Ruine.*

160

He paid no heed.

*   *   *

The Duchess of York received a petition; would she admit the Duchess of Monmouth?

Mary Beatrice inclined her dark head. Since being with him in Scotland she had grown to be on better terms with her husband, for there had been none of his other women by; he had been troubled by her riding accident there, when she had been dragged along the ground by her stirrup, and was miraculously little harmed; she had promised him never to ride again. Also, they had both shared grief at the death of their little daughter Isabella, whom they had not been permitted to take with them out of the country. A healthy son had also died, because York had visited his daughter Anne who had the smallpox; other children had hardly breathed. Mary Beatrice was sad, therefore; and disposed to listen to those in trouble.

Monmouth's wife came in and knelt before her. The Duchess of York extended a hand; the gathered linen fell back from her white forearm, showing the flesh. 'Do not kneel,' she said. 'I know you are lame.'

Anna was weeping. 'It is for my husband I come,' she said. 'He cannot find favour with the King, and hath made an enemy of the Duke by his rashness. I fear greatly for him. Madame, in the name of God will you do what

161

you may?'

I have little influence, thought Mary Beatrice sadly. At the same time she remembered hearing her husband complain that the King made no effort to reconcile him with Monmouth 'though it were but a little thing.' The two women, fair and dark, stared at one another; they had both had much to endure. York's wife smiled suddenly, the smile lighting up her sad eyes.

'I will pray that matters may go well for you,' she said. 'Only God and His Blessed Mother can help us when we are in such sore straits. Have faith, my dear. I am glad you came to me. I will do what I may, but it is little except for that.'

*　　　*　　　*

In May the King was ill again. Shaftesbury made ready for a rising in Monmouth's favour should Charles die. But he recovered, and was soon well enough to be seen out fishing at Windsor when, as they said, a dog would not have been abroad.

CHAPTER EIGHTEEN

Monmouth had no wish to remain in London awaiting the King's displeasure. He was troubled and annoyed, ready for anything as he had been at the time of the beadle's murder; he flirted outrageously with Ford Grey's wife. Grey packed her off to Wark in Northumberland, and there was no ill will to follow; the big loose-mouthed, red-cheeked fellow was conducting an affair of his own. A member of the Shaftesbury set, he had already attracted Monmouth by the devilry of his talk. But that was not enough; the empty places in Monmouth's heart and mind yearned for Harriet. She would send him letters secretly when she could, and he replied to them by way of her cousin John Lovelace, who could ride without suspicion to visit Toddington. 'By the spring she will be free, she says, and then she herself will welcome you to her house.'

But it was still only summer. He set forth at last, surveying the half-remembered country to the south of London. He could recall from his boyhood riding this way, bound for the Charlton Hunt; his mentor had been ... York. A pang took him, mourning those better times; he recalled the sport they had had together, the stirrup-cup and farewell the Bishop of Chichester had given them, for they had lodged in his palace; then the start, the headlong ride with hooves thundering; the streak of red in the distance with the hounds in full throat, then at last the kill; it had been a good day. York would not hunt with him now.

Other things had changed also. They did not

stay with the Bishop; that dignitary held aloof. But the common people turned out in their hundreds to see the King's son ride by, with his plumed hat set on his rich dark hair, and the Stuart features affable and gay. Soon the Mayor of Chichester thought it prudent to call, but said pompously that the Civil Wars had been started in just such a way, riding about the country. 'I hear they have petitioned the King for a Parliament,' he said. 'That is not a godly thing.' Parliament in his memory meant buff-coated soldiery, laying waste the land and folk's houses; even the church had not been safe.

In fact there was high feeling; a citizen of Taunton, named Heywood Dare, had collected signatures for the request, but all that happened was that he was bound over for three years' good behaviour and fined five hundred pounds. Monmouth heard of it, and spoke pleasantly to the dissenter; the man had honest eyes. 'Why, then, Dare, you have dared,' he said, and they laughed together. Some day, he promised, the man should follow his conscience.

The commons loved him; they made up the crowds that pressed about him. Most were weavers of wool cloth, who like the Scottish Covenanters must hold their religious conventicles in secret because of harsh laws, despite the toleration they had been promised. They had heard of Monmouth's mercy in

Scotland, and clamoured after him. Some of the squirearchy were for him also, notably outspoken old George Speke of White Lackington, in whose lodge Monmouth stayed awhile and ate refreshments under a great Spanish chestnut tree, while hundreds watched. At Hinton Park a strange thing happened. A young girl named Elizabeth Parcet, with her hands in gloves, fought her way to him through the crowd, peeled off her glove to show red diseased flesh, and touched his wrist; afterwards they told him she had been cured. Touching for the King's Evil belonged by right to the King alone. Some said it was all a plot of Shaftesbury.

At Ilchester Monmouth was met by two thousand horsemen, which company increased, they said, to twenty thousand; palings had to be pulled up to allow them to pass. He smelled the familiar acrid smell of horseflesh pressing close, and knew the joy of his own triumph; these people would not have turned out for York. He was heady with success and full of memories, remembering glorious Longleat where he had stayed with Tom Thynne, his friend; Sir John Sydenham had met him in Pound Lane, and made him drink strong cider of his own brewing before taking him on to a great feast at his pretty Elizabethan house. At Barrington Court near Ilminster he ate well again; new names, Chard and Ford Abbey, sounded in his ears, and their squires toasted him and made him welcome. There was Colyton, where he stayed at the great house; Otterton, where ducks quacked in a pond, and at last Exeter, where a thousand young men in white ran to meet him and shouted, 'God bless the Protestant Duke and the devil take the Pope!' There was no violence and none were even armed: there was only joy at the coming of Monmouth Jemmy. He would remember for the rest of his life the warmth of the welcome in this generous country. He stayed near Yeovil, then rode back to London; one could see the great bowl of smoke approach and still remember the clear West Country air, the great trees and loving company. 'God bless King Charles and the Protestant Duke!' they had shouted, and had strewn flowers in his way and decorated their houses and waved their banners. It was as if they wanted him for King when his father should die. He carried the knowledge back with him to town, holding his head as high as when he had left. They would never break his pride.

CHAPTER NINETEEN

Shaftesbury's men still clamoured and grumbled; as a result, Parliament was called against the King's wish for the twenty-first of

October. Monmouth knew that his father thought of the House only as a means of raising money; Shaftesbury held the views of Cromwell, that it represented the people. Monmouth himself cared neither one way or the other, and they did not argue the matter. He took ironic note of the burning light in the little statesman's eyes. Shaftesbury would never change the King.

This time there were scenes. York and Portsmouth, the Popish mistress, were attacked openly together as recusants. This made Louise perform one of her *volte-faces*, and again she promised to be Monmouth's friend. But he knew her well by now; he would sooner have honest Nelly, who knew when she could do no more. 'The French bitch will turn her tail again as it suits her,' Shaftesbury and the rest said among themselves, and looked on Louise's renewed offers with contempt. The King loved her as much as ever; but she was afraid of the mob.

As for the king's brother, there was no protection for him anywhere; nor would York change sides to procure his own safety. The King saw him at Whitehall and greeted him sadly.

'It is Scotland again for you, I fear. I cannot ensure your life if you remain.'

York bowed. The troubles of the last few years had scarcely changed him in appearance; his handsome, haughty face looked younger than the King's. York would not bend till he broke, and that would never be. Many had pled with him to resume the Protestant faith at least outwardly, for that would checkmate all his enemies; but he would not. He looked now at his brother, and the grey eyes registered a shadow of compassion.

'I can but obey Your Majesty.'

Charles began to talk, almost desperately; he could not tell when they might meet again. 'Is your wife well? I see but little of either of you; the Whig party makes trouble do I bat an eyelid. As for Monmouth, I will not see him; he shall never be put in your place, and that I swear.'

York kissed the King's hand, bowed himself out, and left again for Scotland.

*   *   *

Next day, Monmouth appeared in the Lords, with a procession of peers walking bareheaded before him. He was as nearly King then as at any time before or after. Everywhere there was cheering and adulation; on Sunday the congregation of St Martin's stood outside the great doors to see him emerge, and he stood talking among them for as long as half an hour, while his coach, with the arms painted on it, waited for him; they still bore no bar sinister.

Lord Mayor's Day came in November. Monmouth was present, with Grey and Tom

Thynne, Tom o' Ten Thousand, by him. His health was drunk in the absence of the King; Charles had sent a message to say that the Queen was ill. Since the Titus Oates plot he had been attentive to Catherine, and kept her by him, which gave her great pleasure.

*　　　*　　　*

The Exclusion Bill obtained its third reading in the Commons. Afterwards, Charles likened his son's speeches against York to the kiss of Judas. Monmouth stood to address a hushed company, sometimes not sure of what he was saying, at other times aware that he said what Shaftesbury told him. He made a resplendent figure in his ermine robes; those watching were reminded of the young Louis XIV. That deity meantime pursued his policy of greasing certain palms in England.

But the Green Ribbon Boys had reckoned without the King's friend, Halifax, called the Trimmer as a rule; the Lords rejected the Bill, and Shaftesbury grew livid and hysterical, crying out that the King must divorce his Papist wife. He cried other things, which summed up meant treason. Later the public hangman was ordered to burn the speech. Outside, armed bands roamed the streets; the country was unguarded, as it had been during the Civil Wars before Cromwell assumed power. War was again spoken of, but there was

169

no Cromwell now. The Whig opposition continued to meet; in one another's houses by candlelight; at race-meetings; anywhere they might be undisturbed and not spied on. No one knew which way the wind was blowing, and York was in the north.

Then the King moved. Without a flicker on his bland face, he dissolved Parliament. Louis XIV had sent him two million livres after much persuading. Parliament, he announced, would be recalled at Oxford, the old centre of loyalty to Charles I. The Protestant party made a great outcry. 'We are in the hands of the Papists there,' they shouted.

Carriages and horsemen stumbled towards Oxford; there, apart from the sessions, all was happy enough. Monmouth and his friends dined at Balliol, the King at Christ Church, the Queen at Merton. The rival mistresses, French and Cockney, were housed in the town, where much gaiety ruled. Meantime, a secret revolution was taking place in England, that stronghold of slow quiet stubborn thought. By the end, it would not be the King and York who were accused, but Monmouth and Shaftesbury.

The plot had failed. The people clung to the Establishment, the avowed succession, the true heredity. The alternative would have been war. The King relaxed, smiled again, and toyed with one or the other of his mistresses. He was said to be tiring of both of them and to have embarked on a new affair with one of the daughters of Lord Ranelagh.

*   *   *

But he had other things in mind. Hurriedly— not very decently, they said—His Majesty came to the House of Lords in a sedan chair, hurried on his robes, called the Commons, dissolved Parliament, disrobed again and headed for Windsor. His haste looked like fear, and impressed no one.

*   *   *

Monmouth had donned a plain cloak and hat and set out with only two servants, riding at speed by way of Aylesbury and Leighton Buzzard towards Toddington. The letters and loving messages he and Harriet had exchanged by way of Lovelace were not enough; their longing to see and touch one another was like a hunger, and today Lovelace had promised she would be free to ride a little way, and meet Monmouth in the rise of woods that surrounded the estate.

He was there at the hour, having clattered through the village with its market square and church and cottages, each one housing a tenant who loved Harriet, for she was kind and would come when they were sick. Her mother and Sir William Smyth were not liked, for during

171

Harriet's minority they had been harsh over the rents, being busied with managing the estate so that it was in a fair way to become rich again: the debts of the old Earl of Cleveland were paid at last.

The great garden was still wild with overgrown trees and hedges; Monmouth saw it as he rode past, and the places which had been avenues in Queen Bess's day when she stopped at Toddington. He could not see the maze Harriet had spoken of; he craned his neck from the saddle, and perceived the great house itself, half ruinous. It must have been beautiful in its day, with a turret in each corner. Perhaps that day would come again.

Harriet. It seemed half incredible that they should come to one another; it was long since he had seen her, the Parliamentary business and affairs, Shaftesbury, Grey, the rest, had come between.

But she was waiting. He saw her slender cloaked shape among the high trees, and slid from his horse and made his way to her swiftly on foot. They embraced, wordless. Presently she took her hands and placed them one either side of his face; the clear blue eyes looked into his own. What did she see? A popinjay, as his enemies would have him? A fool? He would not be her fool; if she desired it, he would be staid and wise, hardly with leisure for laughter among his sayings. Between kisses he murmured of it. 'I would not have you other than you are,' she said. 'Monmouth, it hath been long, so long.'

They lay on the grass and let their horses graze. He found pleasure even in looking at her; she had grown more beautiful than he remembered, no longer a child. He reproached himself now for the Grey affair; that had been to pass the time, and meant nothing. He would tell her of it if she asked, but she did not ask. For her part she could not stop touching him, his face, his sleeve, his cloak. He seized her hands and kissed them, turning them palm uppermost; he tried to read the lines in the flesh; her life must be long and happy. Presently they yielded to one another and made love, there on the grass; and having fulfilled themselves lay back again in each other's arms. The sky was pale blue overhead like a bird's egg; the late summer trees were in heavy leaf.

He heard her murmur against him. 'When will you come again?'

'When I may. The first instant I may. So many matters press; I care not for them, but those who busy themselves with them are my friends, and do it for my sake.'

'Your friends. You have many. I heard of your visit to the south parts, and how they loved you. Can anyone not love you?' She took a lock of his hair, pulled it between her finger and thumb, and let it go to watch the springing curl. She smiled; he was beautiful as a god, and he was her lover.

'Your cousin Lovelace is our friend,' he told her. 'But for him I'd not have known I might come today. Soon, I must ride into the north parts as I did to the south. Shaftesbury advises it.'

'Not all love Shaftesbury,' she said thoughtfully. She sat up and he joined her, while their hands kept hold. He laughed. 'No man is loved by all. He hath been a good friend to me.'

'But for his own gain. Lacking him, how would you fare?' She turned to him tenderly; she knew her Monmouth, guileless, trusting all men, even his enemies.

'My father loves me still,' he said, and fell silent.

She smoothed the hair back from his brow. 'Cannot you make friends again with your uncle?' she asked. 'Will not any speak for you to him now that he hath left the country? There is much enmity between you; it would be better sped.'

He frowned. 'You speak as my wife doth,' he told her. 'She spoke to the Duchess, and is a friend of the Duke. I cannot stomach my uncle. He is cruel, I think: a harsh judge. If he is to be made King I must die, or stay abroad.'

She shivered. 'Do not speak so; you have made a goose walk over my grave.' He turned to her anxiously; she had paled despite the sunshine and her eyes were closed. 'You are not well, Harry? Tell me what ails you; you must not be ill.'

She passed a hand in front of her eyes. 'I am not unwell,' she said. 'It is only a sensation which comes for no reason; a blurring of the eyes for a little while, some headache, then it goes again. I want to have clear eyes, to look upon you.' She smiled, and he thought he had never seen anything so lovely as her face; the golden hair was dishevelled with the light wind and their loving, and her hood had fallen back to display her white throat. A slender chain was about it, hanging down beneath her bodice; he knew it held her zodiac sign, the lion. She was like that golden beast, queenly and unafraid.

She was watching him, her eyes full of love. 'I would like to show you Toddington,' she said. 'Let us walk a little way, and there is a place where one may look down on the house. I want you to know it; soon you shall come there as of right.'

Afterwards he rode back leisurely, savouring his happiness. It was destroyed when he reached his lodging. Shaftesbury had been arrested that day at his house in Aldersgate Street, and now lay in the Tower.

*   *   *

To horse again, with Grey's tall slender figure by him, and others, all friends; by Tetsworth,

High Wycombe, Beaconsfield they rode, in the long summer light, saying little, urging the horses on. Monmouth had left his own mount at Oxford, for it was tired; himself not so, for anger revived him. They had chosen a time quietly to seize Shaftesbury while Parliament, in which Little Sincerity made such a stir, had been sitting elsewhere. There was nobody in the capital to cause a disturbance; the Green Ribbon boys were at ease, or in the west. 'There is no trust in the King,' his son thought. York's influence was still strong, whether he were in the north or here; nothing would break it but death. And what of himself? Lacking Shaftesbury, who would advise him fairly? Politics were dangerous and he did not understand their twistings and turnings, or their lies. Now there was only Ford Grey— hot-headed, slippery, good-natured, without morals; conducting, as his wife was in the north, an intrigue with his wife's sister Henrietta Berkeley, whom he had seduced— and Lord William Russell. Russell was an old friend, and close; the man was as sound as a bell, though he spoke little; and he would never betray anyone. Maybe with Russell at his side he was not entirely forsaken.

*　　　*　　　*

Shaftesbury was angry and ill. He had been taken from his house early that morning when no one was abroad, hustled by two men down to the water, and so to the Tower. Had they waited longer, there would have been six hundred brisk boys from Wapping to stay them, he assured himself; Wapping was his constituency and from the beginning he had greased palms there. Bribery, double dealing ... had he not acted so, he would not have survived a day.

He glanced down at his dwarf's body, aware of the stench that came from it. Of late he had had a cyst, which required to be kept open with a silver pipe. Tapsit, his enemies called him. Soon he would be dead. He would have liked once more to see and touch his beautiful horses at Wimborne St Giles in Dorset, where he had been born. Their physical beauty and strength had atoned for his own ugliness; he had taken pleasure in watching them, owning them, having others race them. If they kept him too long in here he had best sell the stud; without an owner's eye, the grooms would not take enough care. So many things must go; but in any event a man could not take them with him.

He thought of death, the unconquered enemy. It was unlikely, so well had he covered his tracks, that the King, on behalf of the Duke of York, would find enough evidence to sentence him. But they might keep him here for a year, perhaps two. He faced it; there were men he had himself had put away. The face of one was before his mind now; the murdered

Papist Archbishop of Armagh, Oliver Plunkett. Plunkett had been a handsome man, with long curling hair, a fine forehead, classic features and beautiful expressive eyes. At the end they had lopped his dripping head from the butchered body; he had died on a gallows with the fingers of his right hand poised in a blessing. Papists! They had a different view of death; for them it was not defeat but victory, and the means a glory in itself. The last stirrings of the plot that had begun with Godfrey's murder had, no doubt, made a new saint. Shaftesbury's mouth twisted bitterly as he thought of the way things had gone awry since it had become evident that the King would not jettison his Catholic wife. In due course, despite all he himself had done, York would ascend the throne. It would be as though the past were forgotten; the past of England, red with Protestant blood. Shaftesbury conveniently forgot the rest; he must be bolstered up in his own estimation, or his bigotry could not survive or with it, his manhood. He stiffened his thoughts again. It was better for the country to have the King's son, bastard or not, a Protestant, than the King's brother, a Papist without male issue. And Monmouth was loved. It was not necessary to pay the mob to run cheering after his coach; they ran of their own free will. The people would decide, in the end.

He turned his head; Buckingham had been

arrested also and that lightweight fellow might have asked to visit him. But there were several voices, growing louder as their owners approached. He should have seen them from the window; it was the same one Laud had stood at to give his blessing to Stratford on the way to execution. It sounded as if a concourse made haste to visit him now. So soon? The thin-lipped mouth curved in a smile. He was flattered that he had friends in adversity.

Monmouth himself burst into the room, not waiting for the Lieutenant's man to announce him; he embraced Shaftesbury, almost lifting the little man from the floor. Behind him was the tall lanky form of Grey, with Armstrong and others. Soon the room was full, the voices loud and unhindered. It was a disgrace that Shaftesbury should have been brought here so; what might they do to aid him? Was there aught of which he stood in need? Had his wife been here? There was wine; Monmouth raised a toast to the Earl's health and freedom. 'I will have the King take back the order,' he swore. Little Sincerity smiled inwardly; you cannot, he thought; the King hath ordered you to keep a respectful distance at Whitehall. But he smiled, and acknowledged the honour of His Grace's interest. He said little thereafter, merely repeating the tale of how they had come and taken him, the two men, at dawn of day.

'Knowing we were in Oxford.' Grey's voice was loud, his face redder than ever with riding and with wine. 'Had we been in town they'd not dared do it. They watch us as well; who is to say that we do not all end here?' He laughed, with a foolish echo. 'We may drink then to others' confusion, as we do now.' Grey would never count for much, except as a name.

Shaftesbury was watching the handsome head of Monmouth Jemmy as it towered above the crowd. What a King he would have made, with himself as first minister! Was it the chill of death which came upon him and blurred his sight?

'We will have you out of here within the month...'

It was silent when they had gone. Shaftesbury closed his eyes against the dark, against which he could still see Archbishop Plunkett's handsome face.

Next day they declared him a close prisoner, who was to receive no visits.

CHAPTER TWENTY

There was nothing else to be done, so the friends took a holiday. Tunbridge Wells was gay as always in summer, though neither the King and Queen nor Prince Rupert were there. There was dancing on the green by night, by day toyshops and haberdashers in the market; everyone diced for high stakes, and by day, especially mornings when goods were fresh, everyone went out to buy at the stalls. These were presided over by pretty girls in straw hats, selling vegetables, milk, fruit and cheeses. Armstrong and Grey flirted with the maids, chucking them under the chin and peeping at the clean shoes and hose beneath the neat gowns. But Monmouth kept quiet, and was notable for his sober gait: he even went to chapel, where the preacher ranted at him. In truth he was missing Harriet and regretting the ill favour in which, more than ever now, he stood with the King. It would have been pleasant had his father been here; they could have walked and diced together, or watched some great scandal unfold itself, as when years ago Prince Rupert had come down from his great height to court a play-actress. But there was no such diversion, and Monmouth began to regret coming. He would repair again to town as soon as might be; but he was tired, and Shaftesbury's arrest still preyed upon him. He felt at sea among the plotters without that shrewd mind to guide him; what was best to be done? He was not a politician at heart; how pleasant it would be to go to the King and say, 'Father, forgive me, for I have sinned,' and hear the deep voice say, 'Think no more on't; these things befall us, Jemmy; naught but death will part you and me.'

But it would not happen now. He was too deep in the game, and had no notion of how to

181

extricate himself. Wherever he went he was hailed as the Protestant hero; when he did leave, they gave a dinner for him at the Gun on Mile End Green, and crowded after his coach as it carried him back to town. He went to the Buckinghamshire horse-meeting, and was mobbed; those who were no longer in power since the King's dissolution of Parliament flocked to him.

One thing disturbed him more than all the rest; William of Orange was at Windsor. It might be that the late dissolution did not suit him; everyone said that he had an eye to the throne after the King's death by virtue of his wife, instead of the Papist his father-in-law. Where does that leave me? Monmouth thought, then regretted his own lack of trust; he and William had liked one another when they fought together against the French. Should it matter, therefore, that William might go to visit the King, whereas he could not?

Father, forgive me. He would go back to town.

*   *   *

He left on the twentieth of August, and a great course of people rode with him to Riverhead and drank his health there at the Bull and Bush. He had heard that Shaftesbury, chafing at his imprisonment, had asked the King to allow him to retire to his estates in Carolina.

But Charles would not set him free.

CHAPTER TWENTY-ONE

Shaftesbury's trial for high treason—one of his accomplices had been executed, and his secretary lay in the Gatehouse gaol—took place on the twenty-fourth of November, with the assembly coughing and spitting in the chilly fog that seeped through the courtroom's closed windows. The sheriffs had been hand-picked, the witnesses suborned, the jury kept in the dark as to evidence. The accused man sat shivering with cold in his box, his gaudy clothes not sufficing to hide the fact that he was an ill man. He was said to have had fits and attacks of ague in the Tower and had had to be moved, in the departed heat of summer, to cooler lodgings there. Now, the handsome head on the stunted body itself looked shrunken, as though its owner withered while he lived. Shaftesbury's eyes slid round the courtroom to where the brisk boys from Wapping sat packed together with lowering faces, and was comforted. If he were convicted there would be a riot at the least, and the King knew it. Charles had already tried to tamper with the evidence, as witness one Henry Wilkinson. Framing the bill of indictment would be difficult; in its way, it was amusing.

He looked for his high-priced friends, and found them; Monmouth's magnificent presence dominated the gallery. The man on trial gave a little smile. It did not matter what evidence, true or false, was brought forward: he would win the day.

He won it, after many confused renderings which were proved false with ease; sharp practice almost cut itself, and by the end 'the people fell a holloaing and shouting' making a noise in court for the next hour, and would not be suppressed. Outside, the bells began to ring, and when Shaftesbury came out into the yellow dusk it was to the light of bonfires. Moreover the King's son, tall, pale and nonchalant, standing head and shoulders above everyone else in the hall, had stood surety for his bail.

The King was much distressed. About then John Dryden, the Poet Laureate, seized a chance to libel Shaftesbury in verse; he himself had secretly turned Catholic. *For close designs and crooked counsels fit*, he wrote with vitriol about Achitophel; he was kinder to Absalom, for Absalom was the son of the King.

*   *   *

The matter of Absalom concerned Charles still, as David himself may have yearned in secret. How long was it since they had known one another's company in joy? His other sons, by Barbara and other women, did not move his

184

heart as Monmouth had; he was kind enough to them, but did not single them out. If York were with him, he could strengthen his resolve; Monmouth had put himself beyond the pale, and there could surely be no question of open reconciliation now.

*   *   *

Absalom made no show of greatly caring, but took himself off to visit Ford Grey in Sussex. In the damp, cheerless winter days they stayed by a good log fire exchanging stories, or hunted when they felt like it and the scent was good. Generally Grey talked of love; he was open about the fact that he loved his wife's sister. 'Marriages are made by man,' he said, downing his draught of wine to make his red cheeks still redder. 'Heard you the saying of Buckingham when they let him out of the Tower? Shaftesbury was at his window then, in the Lieutenant's lodging, and called, "Why, are you leaving us?" And Buckingham—you well know he is a devil—answered pat "Such giddy fellows as I am can never stay long in one place." He made his submission, I doubt not, as soon as they had turned the key.'

Monmouth smiled a little; he had heard the tale before. He stared into the flames, watching a log as it fell and flamed in the hearth. In a little less than three months from now, he would be able to go to Harriet and her guardians could no longer stop him. That would be a marriage in the eyes of God. His other had been made too young. He had no idea at present of Anna's whereabouts or intentions, except that she was in France.

He returned to the city at the end of the visit, and found his life without purpose now that Shaftesbury had been freed but was not well. He missed the little man's acid wit and company. The capital seemed quiet and he sought out such friends as had returned to town. One evening he was driving in his coach with Tom Thynne of Longleat. He was silent, not thinking of his present condition and unseeing of the flambeaux shining brightly on the dark trees in Hyde Park, but remembering the last Pope-burning he had witnessed, at Smithfield. They had straggled down from Holborn cheering in disorderly groups, and the crowd by the end had drunk his health and the King's as the flames mounted. It was not so great nor so pressing a crowd as last year. The people were settling back into complacency now Shaftesbury's trial was over, though they had given Monmouth two great dinners of late; they were ready enough to bow the knee to Old Rowley, as everyone called the King after his stallion. A pang of love shot through Monmouth. If only he and his father could meet again, forget the past, ignore the future!

He made to alight at Suffolk Street and the chill air struck his face. 'Farewell, Tom,' he said, and Thynne from the interior of the coach answered, 'Farewell.' Then shadows moved; three mounted men—he was certain it was three—rode up, and fired. Inside the coach Tom Thynne slumped forward. Monmouth drew his sword, and would have made after the men, but they had ridden off, and Tom needed a surgeon. He called the page, who had shrunk aside in fright. 'Go to Sir John Reresby's house, and fetch him,' he told the boy. Meantime he held the injured man in his arms, trying to staunch the blood. A small crowd had begun to gather; he hardly dared order the jolting coach to move to Tom's lodging. The blood was warm and sticky; it lay on his hands and soaked his clothes. The shots had been at close range. Tom's head had fallen forward and was jerking like a doll's. Why should they kill Tom? For he was certainly dead.

Sir John came, with his servants, as soon as might be; but they could do nothing for Tom o' Ten Thousand. Monmouth, Reresby, and a man named Mordaunt, who had been his guest, roamed the streets till the cold dawn came, searching vainly for the murderers. By that time, Monmouth was increasingly certain that the bullets had been intended for himself.

*　　　*　　　*

On the face of it, he was wrong. The murderers were found and apprehended, and the man who had paid them identified. He was a Swedish Count, Christopher von Königsmark, and was the lover of Thynne's young wife. Monmouth's own servant stopped the Count at Gravesend, about to take ship for Holland where his lady-love had fled. She was very rich, an heiress; Monmouth himself had helped to secure her for Tom Thynne.

The nine days' wonder subsided; Königsmark was brought to trial, but it was rigged. Perhaps the King's hand was in this, for the Count had useful connections, his sister, who was a beauty, being the powerful mistress of the Elector of Saxony. But the whisper was still abroad that the bullets had been intended for Monmouth. It was not long since they had heard of a poisoned letter being sent to him. The King would not have him a martyr, however, for that would suit York's plans ill.

*　　*　　*

The King still kept his distance, and took his wife to Newmarket. By now it was spring, and the gales had started; York, recalled to Court, set out from Leith in a stiff breeze, leaving his Duchess at her tea-cups in Holyrood. Monmouth heard that his uncle had been cheered on landing at Norwich; then that he had had fewer cheers, except from a paid few, as he rode in his coach from a public dinner in London. One side would light bonfires, the other put them out and light their own. As for Monmouth, he was angry because the King had forbidden him a dinner in his turn; 'there would a bin a worlde crieinge after his coach.' But even the King would not keep the people down. Shortly York set off for Scotland again, to fetch his wife south; news came that he was wrecked on the coast of Yorkshire, and hearts were high and the King troubled; but York won to land. At last he and Mary Beatrice rode through London without mishap; but Monmouth's anger flared again when the Duchess of York met Anna. The two ladies kissed, and seemed friendly, no doubt as fellow-conspirators. Anna should not be his peacemaker, Monmouth decided; he had had enough of her; he would go his own way and she hers. He had in fact sent a submission to the King and it had been rejected as not submissive enough; which galled him.

*   *   *

Worse was to come; Shaftesbury had warned him of it, and that Monmouth's friends were in disfavour. He did not begin to credit it until he heard the fate of his portrait as Chancellor of Cambridge. It had been taken down by officious hands and burned by the common hangman, the painted likeness curling and shrivelling in the flames while the surrounding guard, primed accordingly, drank together to

Monmouth's downfall. Who had given the order, ensured that the thing was done? Halifax, he heard, rightly or wrongly. He met that nobleman a little later coming out of St Martin's-in-the-Fields on a May morning after service. Monmouth approached him, hot resentful words tumbling from him. 'There is no need of a proclamation to prevent my keeping your company,' he finished sullenly. Halifax made a cool reply; at that moment the King's guard passed by, and unthinkingly Monmouth saluted them. Not a man answered. The insult was public and inescapable; he felt as if he were standing naked to the day.

The King's servants are forbidden to salute or have anything to do with you. How York had triumphed! Good God, if these were his own deserts what would befall his friends? They were surely in danger. He suddenly felt death in the air, coldness and implacable hate. He must warn Shaftesbury.

But Shaftesbury had been warned, and was no longer to be found at his house; Monmouth knew that soon he would hear from him. He still marvelled at York's malevolent influence over the King. Surely some stronger intelligence was at work? Whose could it be? Halifax was too great a trimmer to lean his weight firmly to one side or the other.

There might have been more to be told by a tall man with the face of a cautious cat, newly returned to Court from Spain, where he had been in the foreign service. He was already high in the councils of the Duke of York, and his advice was taken in most things. His name was Sunderland. Monmouth would hear of him again.

*   *   *

There was comfort to soothe his hurt pride and aching heart; he rode to Toddington openly that mid-April, for Harriet was of age. He did not ask whether or not she had reconciled her mother to their love; it did not matter; if Toddington would not house them then he would find some other place. But his troop of bright-clad horsemen rode up the long avenue, and it was already growing dark; light shone from the windows of the great square house with its towered corners. As they approached the great door was flung open, and Harriet stood alone in her hall, a carved fireplace behind her in which logs burned. Monmouth threw his reins to a groom and slid down from his horse, clumsy with haste. He went to her; she executed a deep curtsy, and her eyes were shining like stars.

'Welcome, Your Grace, to Toddington.'

He would have taken her in his arms there and then, but there were the others; the servants, his own and hers, and a subdued Lady Philadelphia with eyes downcast.

Laughter took him; Harriet had put the old lady in her place, and there was no sign of the egregious Sir William Smyth. He kept hold of Harriet's hand. She wore a gown of green brocade, rich and low-bosomed enough for Court wear, showing how matters at Toddington had improved under the stewardship of Lady Philadelphia and her swain. He could be grateful to them for that, at any rate: he remembered the little girl of the country-dancing, in her patched linen gown. Now, looking at Harriet, he thought she was the most beautiful woman he had ever seen. Her hair was combed high, in the new fashion from France; its deep rich gold glistered in the light from the fire, and her face owed nothing to paint; she was like an English rose, he thought; all of his love for England was in his love for her. And she? No matter how long it had been, how many offers she had had for her hand, she had refused them all; she was his, always.

After supper she led him upstairs. The stairs were winding and steep, and she took him by the hand. It was like a boy-and-girl game to hasten, almost run, up after her into the tower; at the end they came to a door, which Harriet flung open.

'There,' she said, 'this is your room, for as long as you care to stay; for whenever you care to come here. No one else shall use it.'

He stared, amazed and grateful; she had

192

spent both money and taste on the room. Wax candles were already lit in the sconces, and flickered with the draught of their coming, showing up the great bed, upholstered in green velvet, surmounted by a great bunch of plumes. He could be a prince in this room. He turned to her, caught her in his arms again and kissed her mouth.

'I will stay long, and come often; but am I to sleep alone?' His hands slid down to her shoulders, fondling them. He saw the lovely colour rising in her cheeks, still in a blush like the rose. A delicate perfume came from her.

'Not unless Your Grace should wish to; you are free.'

'I am not free, shall never be free of you; you have caught me in a golden chain. I do not strain against it, only ask for it to bind me closer. Come to me tonight. They will not prevent you?'

'They cannot prevent me now in anything I choose to do,' she said. 'I will come.'

By night she was with him, sliding into the great bed and leaving her nightgown on the floor in a heap of crumpled velvet. Their passion might have been that of wife and husband, considerate, loving. At the end he murmured that thought that had often come to him.

'You are my wife before God. There hath never been any other in my heart.'

It was true; Anna had been forced on him;

Eleanor had passed the nights when he should have been with Anna. Neither of them meant anything now except that he would continue to show them kindness. But kindness was not love.

When he awoke, in the grand plumed bed in the dawn, it was to find her gone. Later he rose and went to her when she was dressing. Her room was within easy reach, down the twisting stairs. A fire burned in the hearth and he sat before it, talking at easy intervals as though this were his home. So he would always think of Toddington. It chafed him to leave; it would have been paradise to stay here with no affairs to oversee, no insult to avenge, no sworn accomplices. But those waited, and he could not betray them by dalliance even in so sweet a place. On parting he seized Harriet's hands and covered them with kisses. 'I will return soon,' he whispered; there might have been no one in the world but the two of them. They were always to be like this, rapt in one another.

He rode off with his train behind him, turning at last at the stone-flanked gates. He would bear her image in his heart as he rode; and would return, as he had promised.

*   *   *

Later that same day he went to a wine-merchant's house in Abchurch Lane in the City. The address had been brought to him by a man of Shaftesbury's; he knew without being told that the Earl sensed which way the wind blew and had already got himself a hiding-place. Once there, he found the others; Grey, Lord William Russell, his big frame looking ill at ease in the dingy room; and Armstrong the Scot. Monmouth felt his injuries rankle anew; he thumped on the table till the single candle rattled in its holder.

'Am I to submit to this fiat of my father's that none may call me friend?'

Shaftesbury smiled smoothly. 'Never,' he said, 'nor must Your Grace be lost to the public view. The commons are fickle; out of sight, out of mind.'

'I'll be damned first.'

'I have a plan,' said the Earl. 'Will you hear it?' Russell leaned forward; he was not adept at concealing what lay in his mind, but he kept silent.

'Assuredly we will hear it,' said Monmouth, and sat back, smiling at the room. His displays of temper were rare and always brief, and he had had much to try him.

Shaftesbury began to speak, his mind filled with a bitter clarity. He knew, none better, that after the late French subsidy King Charles could afford to please himself and govern as he wished. Accordingly, in the naming of sheriffs at the summer elections, his own friends had been outvoted by trickery, by false returns of the ballot, by bribes; none of which methods

Shaftesbury hesitated to use for himself but which he greatly resented when they were applied against him. He had moreover been meeting secretly with York's most implacable enemy, the escaped Argyll. It was dangerous traffic; so dangerous that he must meet his supporters here, in one of his many hiding-places about the City. If all else failed he could go to earth in Wapping, his constituency, where none would find him. He looked at the men with him now; Monmouth he knew well enough, and had weighed him up long since; he had not the mind of a plotter and must be carried. Russell was in the same category, but could be employed to a certain extent; one always remembered that old, old scandal of his grandparents, the Earl and Countess of Somerset in King James's day. The man had been a King's catamite, his wife an adulteress, poisoner, murderess. After a notorious trial she had been committed with her husband to the Tower; a commoner would have been hanged. The disgrace had bred such echoes that later, when the Duke of Bedford's heir had fallen in love with the Lady Anne Carr, daughter of the union, his parents had long opposed the match by reason of the tainted blood that ran in the bride. Yet that marriage had been a happy one and Russell's mother was one of the sweetest of women. Had Russell himself inherited the taint? Was he unscrupulous, ambitious as his grandparents?

One had to consider such things, and tread carefully; outwardly, Russell seemed no more than an honest fellow.

'I have thought on this matter a long time,' Shaftesbury was saying. 'I must speak frankly, sirs, and trust you will forgive my blunt tongue in the name of friendship. While I was in the Tower, in danger of my life, I had leisure to reflect on what should be done if events should turn out as they have, and a Papist be returned, honoured, and promised the throne. Our plans must prevent that, even if we must rise against the King in his lifetime.'

The voice stopped. Monmouth had raised a hand and his hazel eyes looked into Shaftesbury's. 'I will not have my royal father's life endangered,' he said clearly. Little Sincerity raised a hand in protest.

'Did I speak of danger to His Majesty? God forbid; but we must make our stand before our enemies make an end of us. You have seen, Your Grace, how His Majesty suffers you to be treated since the return of the Duke of York. No man of any standing at Court may so much as salute you openly in the street without losing his place and preferment.'

'It is so indeed, but my sire was forced to it by others,' said Monmouth. He was toying with his fringed gloves; they bore his initials in gold thread, which caught and flashed in the light of the candle.

'He may be forced further,' said

Shaftesbury. 'It may be the Tower for Your Grace, as it was for myself; and but for fair trial, which was long denied me, I should lie there still.'

'What do you want us to do?' put in Lord William Russell. His was not a powerful intelligence and he was willing to be directed, at home by his wife, in affairs by Shaftesbury. His heavy face was expressionless, his hands idle. Monmouth smiled at him with affection; they were close friends.

Shaftesbury turned to him. 'I want you, Will, to join me in mastering the Tower and the City. I will answer for the latter.'

'And I?' said Monmouth. Shaftesbury turned again, the fair curls of his periwig gleaming softly in the candlelight.

'Your Grace hath a more arduous task; to betake yourself to the northern countries which have not yet seen you, and where there is much support. If the success of the progress equals that of your late southern visit, victory is assured.'

Monmouth was frowning. 'How am I to gather the Whig support?' he asked. 'Any rumour of arms will bring my uncle's guards northward at the gallop. He is beyond himself after the wholesale hangings in Scotland, which were only worthy of a butcher.'

Shaftesbury laid a hand on his sleeve. 'Sir, are there not horse-meetings? You are well known to frequent those, and you have won many a race on the King's own horses, and borne away the plate both here and in France. Why should it alarm any if your friends were seen to gather about you at a race?'

'Well spoken,' said Russell. Monmouth seized the hand that lay on his sleeve. 'To the north I will go,' he said joyfully. 'Who would have thought of it except yourself? You are not a man we can lose; stay with us.'

Shaftesbury bowed, inwardly amused. 'Yorkshire, Lancashire, Cheshire, the great towns, such as Liverpool; they will flock to join you there, for they are not pleased, as the nation is not, with the prospect of a Papist heir.'

*   *   *

To the north he rode, leaving the rest to brew up their plot as they might; names of half-remembered villages fled by. At Grantham, Daventry, Coventry, the crowds were thick to greet him; afterwards he heard that twenty men had been bound over to keep the peace, but there had been no damage. Lichfield was different. The King's men—Charles knew very well why his son had gone to the north—hired the room next door to him at the inn, and had trumpeters braying and fiddles squawking while they drank to the Tory party. Later, when Monmouth was to depart and leapt into the saddle in the inn-yard, the hostile crowd packed the galleries, with their hats on; not a hat was raised to him. It was a relief to proceed to his friend William Leveson-Gower at Stafford, and the people were friendly, going down on their knees as Monmouth and his men rode in.

He parted from his host and rode on to Chester, to the inn called The Plume of Feathers. The name reminded him of Harriet's bed; but there was scant leisure to think of her, for the city was a Whig stronghold and a thousand pounds was brought to him, which had been collected from the willing citizens. So willing were they that cries of, 'A Monmouth! A Monmouth!' sounded far into the night. The mayor bowed himself almost double, and begged His Grace to attend divine service with him next day, which was Sunday: would he also stand godfather to his baby daughter, who was to be christened? Monmouth agreed readily, and when the child came to be named called her Henrietta, after his love at Toddington. He would see his goddaughter again; next day was Wallasey races, and he set out early.

Here was a gathering; he rode in, surveyed the flat field where the horses were to be run, then looked with satisfaction at the friends assembled; Derby, Macclesfield, Delamere, all stalwarts, and Sir John Bullen, whom he did not know. They placed their bets heavily, and later met together at Bidston summer-house;

Monmouth spoke out then as to why he had come. 'May I count on your support, gentlemen?' 'Ay,' they roared, and the little summer-house could not hold their voices; the sound reached out to the surrounding fields and woods, where others might be listening.

That this was so he already knew. A report had been brought to him that a meeting of Tory gentlemen had already been held in Delamere Forest; they would have them to reckon with if there were trouble. But trouble meantime there was none; only promises.

*   *   *

He rode over the heather-covered scree to Liverpool, which, like London, was disfigured with smoke. On the way a child was brought to him with its skin covered with red peeling patches and sores; he touched it, as he had touched Elizabeth Parcet. What was this faculty that had been handed down from his ancestors? At least it disproved what York was saying to the King, that he, Monmouth, was no Stuart, only the son of Algernon Sydney. The blood in him rose hotly at the suggestion. He would win this fight as he had won the last race at Wallasey; the Plate was his, and he would give it to baby Henrietta; he returned to Chester and did so. Her tiny hands and vague blue eyes did not focus on him, she would remember nothing of her godfather, but the

Plate would long have an honoured place on the mantel.

He set Chester afire. There were bonfires, his insignia whenever there was feeling running high; but the Tories came out in strength and tried to put them out. Smoke mingled with shouting in the timbered streets; windows of the rival party were smashed, the fragments of glass strewing the cobbles and making them dangerous to ride; then the crowd burst into the Cathedral, with its memories of the martyr King. The stained glass windows themselves were smashed to fragments, the font and monuments pulled down to become so much rubble; the very vestments were torn to rags, and in the hallowed places healths were drunk, and damnation to the King and to the Duke of York. Monmouth rode away from it all with distaste; he had neither started it nor could he stop it. Once the mob were free they would do anything. What was it Shaftesbury had said of the mob? His six thousand brisk boys from Wapping had secured the verdict at his trial, and might yet do more for him. But such a wayward force might well be more dangerous than it was worth. Monmouth disliked seeing beauty destroyed as they had just destroyed Chester Cathedral, yet he could no more have stopped them than he could have egged them on.

He went on with relief to Rocksavage, with its warm brick and timber from the old Queen's time: then to Dunham Massey and to Gawsworth Hall. At each house the hosts were ready to welcome him, grudged him nothing in bite and sup, and regarded his coming as a good omen. They did not want the Papist heir; they would support him, Monmouth, if it ever came to blows.

Then there was Trentham, and afterwards Stafford; and at Stafford the blow fell. He was feasting unconcernedly with the mayor and dignitaries of the city, when the doors were kicked open amid the merriment; men in the King's livery stood there with swords drawn. Monmouth turned his head; he was slightly flown with wine. They were speaking; what were they saying? 'Speak up,' he said. The sergeant at arms repeated his instructions.

'I am to arrest you, sir, for going about the country in a riotous and unlawful manner, to the disturbance of the public peace and terror of His Majesty's subjects.'

So it had come. He went quietly with them; behind him, the hubbub of the banquet soon stilled.

*   *   *

They took him to Coleshill for the night, then back to Coventry; Coventry, where crowds had welcomed him on his journey north. He dined there, well enough. 'Where now?' he asked the guard; the men were friendly. After his reception everywhere, save at Lichfield which had been hostile, it seemed unreal that he should be a prisoner, under guard.

'To Towcester, sir,' said the men.

'Then I trust we may sleep there; I am weary.'

But at Towcester a drummer made his night hideous, sounding the point of war, taarp, tarrap-tap. In the end the sergeant himself went out to quiet him, and Monmouth slept in peace till dawn. They travelled on; at St Albans, Tom Armstrong of all people was brought to meet him. It was good to see a friend's face. They talked together in low voices; but Armstrong knew little of what had happened in London.

'Do you come to escort me to Tyburn?' He jested of it; but the notion that the plot had been sprung was unpleasant. Armstrong laughed vapidly. 'Never that, Your Grace,' he said. 'We ride to London, that is all I know.'

'Maybe I should never have left it. What will the end be?' But Armstrong did not know that either.

*   *   *

It was better than it might have been. He appeared before the Secretary of State, Sir Leoline Jenkins, and was told his case must be considered. After that he went to Moor Park, thankful that Anna was absent. He regained his spirits in the Hertfordshire countryside; John Lovelace, Harriet's cousin, rode over and they went to the races together, and once more Monmouth carried away the Plate. It was good to feel a horse between one's thighs, the wind in one's hair; to remember the times when he had had permission to race every horse in the King's stable, at Newmarket.

*   *   *

His friends stood surety for bail of £10,000, but Ford Grey was not there. Grey also had been arrested; for the abduction of his erring sister-in-law, Lady Henrietta Berkeley. Monmouth went to visit him in the King's Bench Prison and found him in good enough spirits. Lady Henrietta was safely hidden away, though her father had advertised for her in the *Gazette*, describing her notable bosom. Grey had been in one odd situation after another because of her; he had even been hidden in a cupboard in her room for two days, fed from time to time on sweetmeats by his mistress. Listening to his light recital of his adventures, Monmouth felt his own spirits rise; surely the King would not appear angry for ever?

*   *   *

But Shaftesbury was beaten, and knew it. There had been double spying; some among those he informed of the plot had engineered it to suit their paymasters and incriminate Monmouth's friends. A general rising, in which the King's person was to have been seized, was said to have been going to take place on 19th November; but Monmouth's arrest had come between. The affair of Grey's sister-in-law had happened at a convenient time to have him watched; in fact, not for the last time, he escaped trouble by making his guard drunk and himself escaping. King Charles, half angry and half amused, had the guard put in the Tower instead of Grey. But the plot itself was beyond stopping; by now it had spread like a web, to incriminate all who had had to do with the King's son. Afterwards no one was to know certainly who was innocent or guilty. The abortive meetings which had taken place in London at the Fortune, the Horse Shoe, the King's Head, the Young Devil, ceased.

A warrant was issued for Shaftesbury's person. Little Sincerity lost his wits: one witness said that, 'fear, anger and disappointment had wrought so much upon him that ... he was much broken in his thoughts, his notions were wild and impracticable.' This was not the cool intriguer who three years back had employed Titus Oates to hunt down Papists.

He escaped abroad, disguised as a Nonconformist minister, the sober clothes and white linen bands sitting curiously on his shrunken frame. He reached Harwich with a servant and waited there some days for a favourable wind. At last, on the twenty-eighth of November, the sick man set sail. Arrived in Holland, he asked to be admitted as a burgher of Amsterdam. *'Nondum est delenda Carthago,'* mocked one who met him.

He was staying in an English merchant's house and there he sickened. Years before, the astrologer had predicted gout as his end; as that disease will, it had flown to his stomach; the silver pipe was blocked and the evil matter could not discharge itself. He was in great pain for eight weeks, then died at midday on the last day of January, while a bitter wind swept through the alien, gabled streets.

They carried the body to England, whose servant he had tried to be: and buried his body at his home of Wimborne St Giles in Dorset, in presence of 'the assembled gentlemen of the county of all shades of opinion.' He had not been a good man, though he had been a faithful husband to three wives; perhaps politicians can never be otherwise.

All that was later.

*   *   *

Monmouth had called a meeting of leaders, confused at the news of Shaftesbury's defection. There would not be an occasion when they met together again; Russell and Hampden, Argyll with his proud crafty face, Sidney, Essex and Howard of Escrick, examining his nails below the table. Among them were certainly agents for the Crown. Midway between the two opposing loyalties, there was a scheme afoot which if it had been presented clearly to Monmouth, he would have rejected with horror. Seated at the table's head, uncertain how to proceed without Shaftesbury's nudging, he knew nothing of it; that Howard and certain confederates were said to have a plan of their own to seize King Charles and the Duke of York and shoot them at a place called the Rye House on the way back from Newmarket. A man named Rumbold, a maltster, owned the house; it fronted a narrow place where two coaches could not pass. But nothing of this was said openly.

Howard at least had the place pat in his mind; by a paling which enclosed a narrow space a cart was to be upturned, causing delay. The King always took the same road home from the races, avoiding Bishop's Stortford, going by Hoddesdon past Rye House with its stables and granaries. Nearby, spanned by its bridge, ran the Ware river. The thing could be easily enough done; Monmouth's name would be used as bait, but whether as victor or victim was hard to tell. The son still loved his father.

*   *   *

King Charles won the day in that affair, perhaps without intention. A fire broke out at Newmarket, and after seeing the terrified neighing horses safely bestowed he made his way back to town earlier than expected, York with him. As always, the King's coach drove at speed; it drove past Rye House out of danger. The bells of St Mary's rang out, and candles were lit in all the windows; the plotters, if such they were, retired discomfited, hearing later that the royal carriage was 'very slenderly guarded, only with five or six persons, and those tired and ill-appointed.'

If the opportunity had indeed been lost, there would never be another.

*   *   *

That was in March. It was not till June that the scattered suspects were arrested and placed in prison or the Tower. Sidney, Russell, Essex, Howard and a man named Wildman were taken; search was made for the concealed Argyll, whom York loathed.

Monmouth himself was not arrested. He sulked in his house, recalling the affront that had been put on him in February at Chichester. There was to have been a repetition of his welcome in the southern towns, with young men in white carrying willow wands and escorting his horse into town. But an order from the King had stopped it. His father was still having him watched; any hope even of a hunt with the Charlton was spoiled. They had cheered him nevertheless; but he remembered the impertinence of the preacher in church on Sunday, whose text had been *For rebellion is as the sin of witchcraft, and stubbornness is as iniquity and idolatry. Because thou hast rejected the word of the Lord, He hath also rejected thee from being King.* Monmouth had stalked out of the church, leaving his friends, Grey among them, swearing aloud.

There had been other things. A servant of his had gone into a hatter's shop wearing his livery, and had been insulted and shears taken to his face. Monmouth had written to the King concerning it; had he not still a right, as much as any, to write to the King?

Grey brought him some comfort. 'There was 'prentices put in the pillory for crying long life to Your Grace, but nothing was flung at 'em; they were given a pottle of wine instead to drink your health, which they did gladly.' But all of that would not console him for the loss of his father and the freedom of Whitehall, or the averted eyes of hitherto acquaintances whom he met by chance in the street.

*   *   *

They moved to apprehend him for high treason in the heat of summer. He had been warned, and took refuge in the last place anyone would have thought of looking for him; the doorkeeper's house by the Lords. He had gone to bed there when they came loudly knocking at the door. He seized his coat and breeches, struggled into them, and with his shoes in his hand climbed out barefoot through the window which gave on to the roof. As he closed it he heard them come; he ascended the slope, agile as a boy, and paused where the dark shadow of a chimney-stack obscured the starlight. Seated there, he gave way to hysterical laughter; he, the King's son, sitting barefoot on a roof where last year he had led them in procession! He would give them a little while, then go to Eleanor in Bloomsbury. He had not been there for months; all the better, and she would shelter him in the house he had taken for her. He sat hidden in the shadow, waiting. After Bloomsbury, Toddington and the plumed bed.

The sounds of search and pursuit faded presently; they had not looked for him on the roof, or perhaps had been secretly bidden not to do so. He stared at the glistering leads, the vista of lit London with the river winding on its course like a great snake, the wherries on its surface like dark flies. Presently he put on his shoes, and let himself down cautiously to the empty streets, making his way north.

*   *   *

'They do say His Majesty visited your wife, and told her her rooms would not be searched for you; but it was the first place they went.' Eleanor, long neglected and long suffering, searched her one-time lover's face anxiously. She would die for Monmouth, and he knew it; there was a change in him since she had seen him last, he was gentler, more considerate. Had he fallen in love? Eleanor felt her heart give a lurch, then chided herself for a fool; she had been lucky to have him for a little while, being of no great beauty nor wit. Now she would help him gladly. The house was exposed for letting; no one lived in it. 'I will give you a certain signal,' she said, and tapped it out. 'I will bring food and clothing, and bed-covers, and money if you should need it.'

'There is nothing I do not need; I escaped as you see me, in my shirt.' He took her face between finger and thumb and kissed it. He was grateful to her for many things. He enquired for the children, realising with a start of guilt how long it was since he had troubled to visit them. James would be growing into a fine lad, the rest following fast; love-children thrived. He spared a thought for the little graves at Westminster.

She smiled, though the smile trembled; and told him they were well, the boys brave, the girls pretty and obedient. 'They talk of you often,' she said shyly.

'And you had not forgot me, I'll wager.

Remember me in your prayers, Nell; I may need 'em.' He grimaced comically at the pun on her name.

'Where will you go?' She was no gossip, and did not ask idly; he knew it, and regarded her kindly.

'I know where I shall go, but it were best not to speak of it; then if any ask, you may say with truth that you do not know. I shall not forget your kindness.'

She brought him what he needed, making several trips to the house under cover of dark. Even so, someone remarked on her coming to the empty place where the windows were kept shut and 'there is a back dore.'

However, his whereabouts was never certain; someone wrote a letter to say he had hired a boat at the Savoy stairs and would go to Scotland. Others said he was in Portsmouth, and still others that he was with Lady Grey at Wark, consoling her for the loss of her husband. None of them were right. By that time, he was again with Harriet at Toddington, and the busy world seemed far away.

*   *   *

He could not remember a time in his life when he had been completely happy and contented. His childhood had been uncertain, bandied about between mother and father and commons and Queens and preceptors of rival faiths; his marriage had been a failure, his children were strangers to him; friends had proved false, and his uncle was his enemy. Yet now he could put it all behind him and live for the present, and when that was past remember it, as a kind of paradise.

They were together; no one disturbed the golden enchantment, neither Harriet's mother nor strangers; one of these came unexpectedly upon him seated by Harriet's fire as she dressed, and remembered him as a tall gentleman much at home. Harriet scolded her mother for it, then turned to him; always, at whatever hour of the day, there was the reality of their love for one another. They spent their days in an idyll; he loved the house, with its ruined grandeur and its galleries which drew forth echoes, and its wild garden. Once he and Harriet had walked a little way with her greyhound puppy Silk, and sat beneath an oak, and Monmouth took his sword and carved his initials and hers, entwined with a heart about them, as any country swain might do for his love. An oak lived for many hundred years; it would outlast them, and the letters be read by those who had not known them or their children. The puppy lay quietly in the shadow, his head against Harriet's gown.

CHAPTER TWENTY-TWO

King Charles was in the Privy Garden at Whitehall, setting his watch by the sundial. This was the hour when those anxious for a word in the royal ear would approach: the shadows lengthened into evening.

Young Tom Bruce, Harriet's good neighbour and old friend, who would have married her, was within reach, but did not force himself upon the King. A long finger beckoned, and Tom walked over and stood by the sundial, staring at the sharp shadow its gnomon cast on the face. 'Time waits for no man,' said Charles. Bruce found himself gazing into the wise half-melancholy, kindly eyes. The King evidently liked what he saw; a well set-up young sprig of ancient Scots blood. He smiled, and brought his charm to bear.

'You will have been at Toddington of late? They say there is a ... visitor.' The heavy lids clouded the eyes; the King's face became a mask. Bruce answered openly, 'Sir, I know not of it.'

'You know not? But you are a familiar of that company ... of that lady.'

Bruce flushed. 'Sir, I honour her; she would have made a perfect wife if...'

'If?' said the King. 'Methinks that word intrudes itself in affairs too often.'

Bruce spoke out. 'If her mother had had a care to her, sire, she would have made a perfect wife. That I will declare to my dying day.'

'Which we hope will be far off. Do you ride often to Toddington?'

'Sire, I have not been there of late.'

'Because the Lady Harriet hath other visitors?'

'I know nothing.' He let his candid eyes meet the King's. There was sympathy between them. 'If,' said Charles, 'you were to ride there on the morrow, you might surprise the visitor.' The lines of his face hardened; at such moments he looked what he was, a descendant of the fabled Medici, of Henri Quatre, implacable and devious.

Bruce answered quickly; he was well aware of the King's love for his son. 'Sire, it would not be possible to surprise anyone at Toddington. If a troop approached, word would be sent at once from the village; and the house itself is so beset with nooks, crannies and vaults that anyone might hunt for a week, and find nothing.'

Charles smiled slowly. 'I thank you, sir, for your most pertinent observations. I shall not forget them.'

He was pleased, as Bruce well knew, at the other's refusal to arrest his son. He still loved him.

* * *

Bruce himself was not to be permitted to forget Monmouth. Not long after, he and his father led out the hunt from Ampthill, not far from Toddington. The stag led them a long chase and finally swam the great fishponds on the estate, thrashing at the slimy water. Bruce had gone out of the way of the rest and as he was in pursuit, a tall man dressed in countryman's clothes went to open a gate for him. It was Monmouth, with his face undisguised. Bruce rode on, not turning his head; it was no affair of his, and he would not hurt Harriet. But later on, at the stag's death, the indiscreet countryman was standing among the crowd, watching idly. Bruce moved silently aside to where his father, the Earl of Aylesbury, Lord Lieutenant of the county, was; it would be his duty to arrest Monmouth if he saw him. Bruce began to talk to his father to distract his attention, thinking of every subject under the sun, keeping Aylesbury's eyes fixed on his own so that they might not stray to that tall vulnerable figure not far enough off. 'You have taken a drop too much wine this morning, Tom,' said the old man. But he missed seeing Monmouth.

Later they were invited to dinner. There was no sign of the hunted Duke, and Lady Harriet appeared to be in ordinary spirits. Aylesbury congratulated Lady Philadelphia on the improvements she had made in Toddington over the years. Yes, she declared, it was fit for princes now; and Bruce looked down and bit his lip. Otherwise all went well, and in due course they left. But the prattling lady lacked discretion with the other guests whom at another time she showed upstairs; they remembered what they saw and Harriet was angry.

Afterwards came Bruce's thanks from the King. 'I will not soon forget the tale of the hunt,' Charles said. 'I owe you a debt, Tom.' But Tom Bruce had done it for Harriet, much as he loved Monmouth. Her beauty moved him and always had; if only he might have had her to wife! She was too good to be any man's whore.

*   *   *

Monmouth might have escaped trial, but Lord William Russell did not. They impeached him for his part in the Rye House Conspiracy on the thirteenth of July, with his devoted wife Rachel seated below the defendant taking down evidence with a quill and paper. Monmouth had sent a secret message offering to give himself up if it would aid Russell; but Russell declined with courtesy.

They found him guilty, for the plot had been brewed to incriminate Monmouth's friends if he himself should evade them. They beheaded Russell not before his own house, as York had suggested, but in Lincoln's Inn Fields before a large crowd of watchers; he died bravely. His wife wore mourning for the rest of her days, and his mother did not survive him six weeks.

Sydney was kept waiting for his death, but Essex did not wait; he was found in the Tower with his throat cut, and witnesses said later that they had seen a blood-stained razor thrown from the window. It was given out that he had killed himself. Howard, who turned King's evidence to help destroy Russell, was taken in a hiding-place behind a chimney. Armstrong escaped, but fled abroad to Holland; Argyll was already there. Gradually the echoes of the affair died down, and Sunderland closed his file. The news made Monmouth chafe even at Toddington, and he swore he would take service abroad, and Harriet should come to him there.

*   *   *

It was late on an October night when they brought Halifax to him from the King. The man's bland face showed nothing. Why had he embroiled himself? Monmouth thought, remembering their brush outside St Martin's in the early summer. Could it be that others in council were gaining place, and Halifax wanted a card in his hand? One could not tell, and he did not greatly care for it. He rose, and trimmed the candles while Halifax talked.

'His Majesty will never believe that Your

Grace knew of a plot to kill him.'

'That is as well, for I did not know.' He snuffed a wick, and relit it. It was eleven at night, and the thought of diplomacy wearied him; he yawned a little. 'Why cannot the King know his friends from his enemies, and send the last to the devil?' he demanded. 'In Russell he lost a faithful servant.'

'The reason for this particular pretence is for your sake, and will advantage Your Grace by the end.'

'When is the end to be? I see none of it.'

'As soon as you will write to the King, and offer your submission.'

'I did so, and he scorned it.'

'Matters are different now. It is long since the King set eyes on Your Grace; it is in his heart to welcome you back to Court, but he must have evidence that you submit.'

Monmouth frowned. 'Letters can be used amiss. I had sooner face my father.'

'I can bring Your Grace a letter tomorrow ready written, and you shall read it before signing, and not sign at all if you would not.'

He shrugged. 'Bring it then, but not at so late an hour as this. I am for my bed.'

*   *   *

Halifax brought him the draft next day; he read its fawning phrases, and disliked them. He had done nothing, he persuaded himself, that

220

should demand so extreme a remedy. *And for the Duke, that he may have a more firm confidence of the service I intend to do him ...*

He would do the Duke no service at all. Why pretend otherwise? His uncle, he heard, had advised putting him for a few days in the Tower, as a show of strength. Perhaps he would have had him murdered like Essex.

But a kind letter came from the King, advising him to keep hidden meantime, 'till he had an opportunity to express his belief some other way.'

*   *   *

Charles at last made an appointment to see his son, who was there at the required hour; but the King did not come; there was an extraordinary meeting of Council. He bade Monmouth be there the following evening at the same time, and to say nothing of his own letter unless it was spoken of first.

Next day, Monmouth saw his father. The King looked older, and much worn. Forms of etiquette failed them both; they embraced, as they had been wont to do in the carefree days of Jemmy's boyhood. How could anyone believe that he had plotted to kill so kind a father? It would be a worse crime than that of Cain. It was not permitted that they meet often. The Duke of York was an open enemy, though the Queen was a friend. She had spoken in

Monmouth's favour to Mary Beatrice, which Charles heard of and was very grateful to his wife. There was fondness between them, though she had no beauty and had borne him no heir; he had supported her through the Popish Plot, and Catherine now did as much for him concerning Monmouth. All were agreed that something must be done to blind York in the matter; he saw too keenly, and took shadows for substance.

*　　　*　　　*

They brought Monmouth another letter, more subservient than the first, which was for York's eyes. It was to be presented by Anna herself with a letter of her own concerning him. He frowned at the thought of Anna's loyalty and continued efforts to have him reinstated at Court; it would have accorded better with his own dignity had she been his own enemy and York's. He turned to Harriet, and forgot his wife. Shortly an official reply came from Charles, its words harsher than at their meeting. *He must resolve to tell me all he knows, resigning himself entirely to my pleasure.*

It was evident that his uncle had been consulted in the matter.

*　　　*　　　*

He was made to appear at a semi-formal

meeting before Charles, and give certain depositions about the men who were dead. Afterwards he was to go before the Secretary and Council 'as though it were his first appearing.' From beginning to end the pretence wearied him; why could he not be reconciled to his father and have done with it? York's hand removed all joy. As it was, he himself was seen making away from the meeting-place 'wrapped in a cloak' and an informant eagerly hurried to the King. Charles told the man not to be a fool; the Duke of Monmouth was in Brussels.

But the official recognition came soon enough, and must be got over. Monmouth knelt before the King and the Duke of York, said what they bade him, and claimed with truth that he had known nothing of any intended murder. As for the rest, he gave some names recalled from the northern horse-meetings; the owners were too far away for it to trouble them. He was less aware of memory than of the presence of York, whom he would be expected to kiss.

It was done. At the end of their meeting he was given formal escort by a sergeant-at-arms to the Cockpit. He went straight to bed without seeing Anna.

*　　*　　*

The Court of St James's, ageing despite its

flamboyance, was cheered by the return of handsome Monmouth, also by the evident pleasure his company gave the King. It was whispered that His Majesty, after the submission, had sent his son a gift of £6000 and had prepared a pardon for him. Monmouth had gone to the first reception thereafter in a sedan-chair, for concealment, and Lord Halifax and the Whig party were gratified. Perhaps, it was whispered, there would be a falling-off now of the influence exerted lately by the Duke of York. What was the hold York had over the King that he could so bend him to his will? Suggestions were made and discarded; the true one, which concerned the payment of French subsidies and the long-ago promise to Louis to embrace the Catholic Faith, must have been known to some who read publications which came from abroad. But on the surface Charles was a happy pagan; few guessed at the deep hunger increasing with the years. York had had the courage to declare himself and to abide by his choice; but a similar declaration would cost Charles his throne. York knew this, and could accordingly let it be seen at times that he was master. The matter of Monmouth came to a head again only a short time after the young man's return to Court. No doubt the King's love for his son, the pleasure he took in his company, irritated York as it always had.

Whatever the reason, trouble brewed again,

224

and men came out of York's apartment with tears in their eyes. Matters were still in train for the execution of Sydney, the man York swore was Monmouth's father. The King tried to excuse himself to his son. 'I would not have beheaded Russell, but that my brother would have it so,' he told Monmouth. He had postponed Sydney's execution time and again, but dared not free him.

Monmouth looked at this beloved father, the deep lines graven on either side his nose grown flabby now; the eyes seemed almost sunk in pouched flesh. It was still a face that could charm; this man had made his way all his life by indecision, by putting off the fateful hour, waiting, pleasing. He did both still; he hated having to make an unpopular gesture both for his own sake and because it would hurt those he loved.

He had to do this with regard to Monmouth's submission. This would preferably have been kept private among those closely concerned, but York decreed that it must be published. A whisper had also started that Monmouth had betrayed his friends over the Rye House Plot. This agitated Trimmer Halifax, who had engineered Monmouth's return, and he ran about Court with his smug expression sadly altered. Monmouth confronted him angrily; was this all he got in return for having taken advice? 'Lie low, sir, lie low,' murmured the cautious statesman. 'It will pass in time.'

'I will not lie low; I have my honour like the next man. I will start a counter-rumour to your rumour, and this time it will be the truth, for I knew nothing of the murder plot, only the rising.'

Some stir was accordingly made in the coffee-houses, among the fumes of tobacco smoked there by regular customers who came to exchange news. A Protestant plot was murmured of. The King heard the rumours and was angry and, in fact, afraid. Was he never to have peace from factions? Could he trust nobody but his brother?

He made out a statement in his own writing, for Monmouth to sign. The young man looked at it; more denials, more protestations; he was weary of them. He signed with a flourish, to be left in peace; but when his friends heard they made an ado about that; the document, they insisted, must be withdrawn. Monmouth withdrew it, and this infuriated the King, who demanded its restoration in council and said, his face darkening, 'Tell the blockhead to go to hell.'

On 7th December Algernon Sydney was executed.

*　　　*　　　*

Monmouth was forbidden the Court. He had removed, taking Anna with him, to lodgings in

Holborn, and was spoken of as being about to retire to Moor Park. Nothing more was known about his plans and as he was no longer among them, the gossip-mongers fell silent. The King was still enraged and showed it; there was no doubt he regretted losing his son even though he thought Monmouth a fool to spurn the help he himself had tried to give.

CHAPTER TWENTY-THREE

A rider cantered along the mud-rimed Hertfordshire roads in the bitter December weather, his hat-brim sagging with rain, his cloak sodden; it was York. He could hear the sullen thudding of his men's mounts behind him, but spared little thought for their discomfort; he himself made no complaint; men were bred softly nowadays. He had grown used to cold, high seas, and hunger during his years of seamanship from a boy; they had hardened his body till, despite his excesses, it served him well even though he was by now over fifty.

He told himself that his reasons for coming here were sound. He did not desire to live at odds with anyone; he must come to terms with his nephew. It was true that for most of their lives they had been opposed, even enemies; that was unfortunate. Lately, moreover, he would have used harsher measures against the young man than his brother had seen fit to do. Allowance must be made for His Majesty's inordinate affections; his children, like his women, could cozen him almost as they chose. But in the long run—or perhaps, under God, not so long—he, York, and not Monmouth, would be King: and it suited him ill to think of disturbances like the late Rye House matter recurring. He knew, as well as his brother, the bitterness of exile; the so-called Popish Plot had left him little leisure to stay at home, and he and his wife had lost their only surviving child in absence. York's mouth set bitterly as he thought of the inability of either of his wives to bear him a living male heir. Perhaps the fault lay with himself. He could not rule it out. Yet two daughters lived; Mary, Orange's wife, childless also; and Anne, married lately to a pleasant dull Danish prince. The succession was not assured; within himself, he recognised the fact that his wife's health was at present so delicate that she might not live. If that came about, he would marry again, this time to a woman of his own choice who could bear children readily.

The gates of Moor Park, his nephew's residence, were closed; York waited while they were opened, then rode through. The rain still beat down. Seen through it, the front of Monmouth's house was welcoming and elegant. He liked to think of Duchess Anna, his good friend—how well she could divert his mind!—living amid such surroundings in preference to the cramped Cockpit. It was incredible that such a woman had never had her husband's love.

He gave the groom his reigns and dismounted, handing his sodden cloak and hat to a servant in the great hall. The interior of the house pleased him, like a cool shell; its tasteful panelling and light hangings bespoke Duchess Anna's taste. That, for instance, was a woman he would have liked to have to wife; fertile, and with a ready wit to challenge his empty mind. He had no easy fancies or humour, and admitted it. His Faith, which was like a rock to him, filled his thoughts constantly with its daily prayers and offices; he could not now understand how a Protestant could prosper in himself.

He was shown into the large light room which looked out over the garden and the moors. A spinet sat there, and he recollected that Duchess Anna played well. Perhaps her sole remaining little daughter—one had died in September—would be now of an age to learn, and show aptitude. York had a tenderness for little girls, having been a good father to his own. Surely, if he saw him now with his wife, he would be able to extend some such affection towards Monmouth, who was young, when all was said! Misunderstanding accounted for much; it was as well to have come. Perhaps, if he could have private speech with Duchess Anna, they could between them light on some way to strengthen her unstable husband. The Faith? But Monmouth was a long way from that; prayer might help him.

He heard light dragging footsteps, and realised that Monmouth's wife was alone. She entered, and curtseyed in a rustling of pale silk. As usual she was dressed with fastidious care, as if about to go to Court. Her eyes were red, as though she had been weeping; York felt compassion for her. Of Monmouth there was no sign.

He upheld her from her curtsey. 'Do not discompose yourself,' he said kindly. 'I have not come in the guise of a royal visitor, but privately. I had hoped that the three of us might talk together; there is small opportunity at Court.'

'The three of us?' She echoed his words almost witlessly. Once she put a hand to her forehead, as if she felt faint. York helped her gently to a chair, and waited for her invitation before seating himself. He was deliberately making for ease between them, but Anna did not respond as she was wont to do.

She spoke then. 'My husband hath gone,' she told him. 'He went in the night, I know not whither. The servants know nothing. I have done what I could. I fear I shall not see him again.'

He consoled her as best he might, but left

shortly; the ride had been useless, and he must return to town.

*   *   *

In the winter gales that beset the Channel, a party of three men in broad hats set out in half-darkness; they were Monmouth with his two servants, bound for Tervere in Holland from Greenwich. The wind battled against them and made the crossing long and hard; on land it pursued them, two days later, when they took horse for Brussels by way of Bergen-op-Zoom. As last it died, and Monmouth reined in his horse and looked at the city's thickening streets. Everything had begun for him here, in childhood long ago; perhaps the wheel had come full circle with his return. There were friends near; William of Orange at least would not betray him. The handsome face beneath the hat's brim lightened. He would find some haven here, somewhere he might be at peace; he had already sent word of his whereabouts to Harriet at Toddington. If she willed to come to him, good and well; he was hungry for her. He gathered the reins into his hand, and rode into the city.

CHAPTER TWENTY-FOUR

At the beginning all was rosy; the Governor, the Marquès de Graña, received him with that solemn magnificence only a Spaniard can, and hurried an annuity through from Spain. This was before the ill news came from England; Sir Robert Bulstrode, the Resident, whispered in his ear that Monmouth was disgraced at home and no military honours were to be allowed him. There was some awkwardness at a review, for the officers, again, failed to salute Monmouth. The colour rushed to his face and afterwards fled, leaving him white as paper.

'Even my father cannot say I have not served him well as a soldier,' he burst out. The Marquès murmured soothingly to the effect that it was not from the King of England enmity came, but from the Duke of York.

'My uncle. I owe him much hatred and despite.'

'It were wiser not to indulge it, sir.'

'I cannot spend all of my life being wise, and waiting, and licking their boots.' It was almost as though he spoke to himself; the black brows were drawn together, the full mouth had a petulant curve like a child's. 'See you, I have some little fame of my own I may turn to account. I could take service with the Emperor, perhaps, though it is a far journey.'

'The Emperor would be glad of your services. But wait only a little,' said the Spaniard, who had taken a fancy to the handsome creature before him; and he understood hurt pride. 'Better news may come.' He smiled winningly.

Some good news in fact came, in the form of Monmouth's horses from Newmarket, which he was glad to see; and his plate. Best of all, one spring day a coach drew up at his house and a hooded figure got out, followed by another with a greyhound on a lead. Within moments, Harriet was in his arms.

'My love, my love—I have longed for you, but dared not hope—you have left everything—'

'Did you think I would fail you, or could live long apart from you? I've brought mother; she would not be left behind, and I believe fancies a visit to her sister in Middelburg. She will not greatly trouble us.' Harriet put back her hood, so that the clear light from above the street fell on her golden hair. She had had a smooth crossing and bloomed like a rose. He could not keep his eyes or hands from her; they embraced, and made love before she could tell him more. He was touched as well as thankful that she had come to him. 'But, oh, my love, your fair name! They will tattle of us now, I fear.'

'Let them tattle. I do not care for their tongues nor for anything in the world except yourself. How could I stay on in England playing propriety, dining with neighbours ... my dear, my dear ...'

He stroked the beautiful hair, and kissed her numberless times. If any asked, he would say she was his wife. It was true in the eyes of God.

*   *   *

The Marquès de Graña did ask; in Spain such matters were understood. As the Duke of Monmouth had replied that the lady was indeed his wife, the Governor sent his daughter to pay a courtesy-call. Harriet was confronted by an innocent young lady in wide hoops, a feather in her hair, a fan in her hand and her duenna behind her. They talked of nothing in particular and the young lady departed saying she would come again. But this was never permitted, for the true identity of the golden-haired beauty under Monmouth's protection was soon known, and when he heard the Marquès was outraged. Such a happening was a stain on his family honour, a mockery. Monmouth was confronted by a stamping Spaniard with a suffused face. 'When I leave the service I will call you out, señor el Duque, and either you will cut my throat or I will cut yours.' He turned his back, and from that day was no friend. Monmouth cared little; he had plenty of money, for sums were sent from England, supposedly by supporters who resented his treatment, but in reality by the King. And he had Harriet. He set up house grandly with her in Brussels, entertained those with whom he could be on easy terms, and ignored the rest. However the treatment of Harry by officialdom made him angry, though she remained serene. 'I do not care for balls and receptions,' she said. 'I am happy with you.'

He frowned. 'I do not care to see you ignored. We will go to Holland.'

*   *   *

He had not gone there sooner because it was known for a nest of late intriguers, the riff-raff left from the Rye House Plot and other discontents. Moreover, a terrible fate had overtaken Armstrong the Scot at Leyden: his servant, an old man named Marshall, was now with Monmouth. Armstrong had been living in hiding in Berlin—another nest of spies—for some time with Ferguson and Grey and the latter's mistress, and was boarding a boat to rejoin them there when he was recognised and seized by an English spy. There was a fierce struggle; Armstrong tried to stab himself or throw himself overboard, but was put in chains and taken to Rotterdam, and thence to England. There, the angel-faced Jeffreys refused him trial as an outlaw. He was executed within the week, and his head stuck on Westminster Hall beside the rotting skull of the

Protector.

But lacking Armstrong, there were still the others; the net closed round Monmouth again. Ferguson held meetings in secret places, where in the smoky half-dark a tall magnificent figure in a cloak would come, listen briefly, then be gone with none knowing of it. They would say they had seen him, they thought; then again were unsure. Another proscribed figure, Argyll, came and went: would listen idly to loud coarse sayings from Sir William Waller, an outspoken old fellow whom many compared with Cromwell himself; he was the deadly enemy of the Duke of York and also of the Resident at The Hague, Sir Bevil Skelton, a distant relation of Harriet's. Present always, though never seen, was the Stadtholder. William had already made it clear that he would welcome Monmouth and Harriet to Holland.

Monmouth was anxious about Harriet. She had had a recurrence of blurred sight and headache, and complained of prickling in her hands and feet. He and her mother had had the physicians to her, but they could make nothing of the malady. She seemed better today; she was playing the spinet which was in the house. He went to the room from which the melody sounded; the spinet was placed near the window for light, and he could see her bare forearms and wrists, delicately poised to follow the music. He went to where her head was bent over the instrument, and kissed her neck. She stopped playing, and smiled up at him, the clear blue eyes full of love. 'Here am I practising my scales and old Dowland, like a child at school,' she said. Monmouth stared at the meaningless pages; he had never been taught to read music, though he had a natural love of it for dancing. There was a great deal he did not know; since being with Harriet he had resolved to remedy his ignorance, and read more than he had been used, without wearying of it. Indeed everything he did in her company was delightful; how empty his former life had been!

She rose from the spinet, and came and stood by him, her head leaning back on his shoulder. 'I am glad that you feel better,' he said.

'It is the company. And I am intemperate; remember my horoscope.' They had laughed together over that, and he had even teased her that her pricklings came of too much wine. 'Keep it always by you, as I do mine,' he said, and remembered poor Shaftesbury; that man had had good reason to abide by the stars.

'You are to avoid the Rhine; do not forget it, now that it is near.'

'Believe me, I keep away from it even in war. In William's realm it need not trouble us.' He had sat down by her, and began to play with her girdle. It was a pretty thing, with pearls and rubies set in threes, and she would wear it either about her waist or else with a mantle, to fasten it over her shoulders. He spoke of it.

'It is one mother liked to wear, although it is mine. She used to wear jewels.'

'To divert Sir William Smyth?' That personage could not have been pleased to see Harriet go, and Philadelphia with her.

'He thinks I am the Scarlet Woman, and hath denied all knowledge of me,' said Harriet. 'He tried to prevail on mother not to come with me abroad, and having failed rode off in a temper. He is an upright person, I daresay.' She raised a hand and smoothed a crease between Monmouth's brows. 'Do not let a line set there,' she told him. 'It troubles me when you frown; you were made for laughter.'

'I will never frown on you. Truth to tell it is age; I am growing thin on the top of my head, and have tried remedies, but to no purpose. I must take to a periwig, which I have always abhorred.'

She kissed the thin place. 'Will you be happy in Holland?' he asked her. 'My uncle York's wishes prospered too well in Brussels.'

'Your uncle York is the father-in-law of the Stadtholder.'

'Yet they are not of the same religion, and love not one another, I believe, though they stay civil. But if he will be kind to you, that is all I ask.'

'I can live without all other kindness than yours.'

238

He smiled. 'The sun rises for you in the sign Leo. Yet you are less bold than a lion in your manners; hesitant, when one knows you.'

'Am I so?' She blushed, and the glorious colour came up into her face and throat. Lordly and golden, his girl; but no one except himself knew her inmost heart and how little ambitious she was for her own concerns, unlike her mother. He endured Lady Philadelphia about them, but wished her gone; such was his love for Harriet that he would have liked to display her singly, like a rare jewel. In Holland she would be seen and admired; it should be her setting.

*   *   *

William of Orange had altered less since the last time they had met; he made a charming host. Monmouth was introduced to his Princess again at the theatre, where there were Italian singers, not yet known in England. The clear notes sounded in the still air as he kissed Mary's hand; she had grown stouter, a little, but was still beautiful. Later there was a great ball given at The Hague for him and Harriet; they danced amid great Chinese vases filled with flowers from the gardens and hothouses, and more flowers reflected themselves from the paintings on the walls; William and Mary both loved these. The fiddlers played tunes Monmouth knew; with Harriet and Mary he threaded his way through the figures of the country-dances at which he was adept, bearing a lady on each arm, hearing the swish of silks and lace in the warm air. The room was crowded with Dutch noblemen and their decorous wives, dressed in fashion less extreme than that of Brussels. Yet it was easy to slip away, when the music stopped, to the royal apartments, where they could be alone. 'My father hath not this boon in England,' he remarked, noting the doors and planned walls which shut all unwelcome comers out.

William smiled, the smile breaking up his haggard face. He suffered much from his asthma, and went now to one of the new sashed windows and opened it. Monmouth realised that the ballroom must have been torment to him, but he had stayed out of courtesy. He murmured of it to his cousin, William's wife. 'My husband goes where he chooses,' said Mary tranquilly. Her piled hair was fastened to a tall column of lace, and she wore long perfumed gloves which she peeled off to show arms which were plump and elegant. Her liquid brown eyes slid from her guests to her husband; she watched him always, with love and care. Her happiness was always tinged with a little melancholy; they still had no children. Monmouth turned from contemplating the bright contrast of the two women, dark and fair, for Harriet was ablaze with jewels and very glorious; and began to compliment his host on the alterations to the palace. 'Your people have many talents,' he said. William smiled, and replied, 'But all here is not the work of my countrymen; much of it comes from France. You seem amazed. A Huguenot, you see; his name is Daniel Marot. He painted my *grisaille* ceilings and hath made a little panel of flowers in my wife's room, and other places. Many come here from abroad now that there is peace.'

'It is kind in you to receive us also.'

'You are welcome,' said William quickly. 'Are you not a comrade in arms? And Mary is glad of English company.' He watched his wife with tenderness; she and Harriet were in close talk. If only life could be always as peaceful, graceful and dignified! He was happy in his English marriage, though it was barren.

*   *   *

The Prince continued Monmouth's affable host; took him hunting in the woods about Het Loo, showed him his paintings at Honselaarsdijk, his gardens everywhere; took him to the menagerie, in which there was a spotted cat and two fighting ostriches, some camels and a pair of chameleons. 'See, they change colour like statesmen,' remarked William, letting the creatures, which were tame, crawl up his broadcloth sleeve and linen cuff. He was dressed for leisure, and seemed oddly less fragile than when in a suit of armour, for his presence grew with the surroundings he had helped to create. Monmouth stared at the velvet grass, where tame waterfowl had followed them; at the pheasants strutting in their pens, the statues standing a little way off amid flowered parterres. It was astonishing to remember that not long since, half the land had been under water at this man's order, to keep back the French; nor William had reclaimed it, and more. Louis XIV might well reflect that he had underrated the Stadtholder.

Monmouth followed William's comment. 'Statesmen, Your Highness? They are more your game than mine; I'm a plain fellow, and say what I feel.'

The brilliant eyes regarded him. 'The times are too difficult to do that unless one is with known and trusted friends,' said William. 'I have some few and consider myself fortunate. I am also your friend, because we fought together; as such, I welcomed you to Holland, not only because you are a relation to my wife.'

'You have had those here too,' said Monmouth flippantly. York and his Duchess had spent some time in Holland, and Mary Beatrice had made much of her stepdaughter; less was said about William's relations with his father-in-law. The two pairs of eyes met.

'You know well,' said William quietly, 'that I dare not have England fall into the arms of France.' His face had grown grave; the chameleons scuttled back to their branch. 'How do you suppose your visit here affects the Duke of York?' he said. 'We may talk here; none will overhear.' He glanced at the placid garden, the waterfowl on the grass. Monmouth scowled. 'Nothing I do affects my uncle pleasantly,' he admitted. 'He may indeed complain of my reception here; it hath been generous.'

'I am glad that the suggestion comes from your lips and not mine.'

'Then he hath done so? By God, he will never leave me in peace. What harm do we here?'

'Do not exercise yourself over it,' said William in a low voice. 'I have let you know, as I need not have done, how matters stand. If there is need, I may have to act as your father did and appear harsh, even to the extent of openly asking you to leave my dominions. If that should chance, I know little of what proceeds in Amsterdam; the authorities there are my enemies. At the same time you know I am your friend, as much as your father.'

'My father sends me money secretly, and must say it is from supporters. Why should he submit to it?'

'He must do so, nevertheless,' said William. Beneath their hooded lids his eyes glowed as they surveyed Monmouth's face. So beautiful, and so ill-fated! 'You have many advantages,' he said uncertainly. He was not adept at expressing his feelings in words, and as a rule it was not safe.

'I like best to be out of doors, as we are here,' said Monmouth. 'Your gardens are pleasant.' He spared a thought for Moor Park, where he and Anna had begun to make a garden; perhaps by now she had leisure to sit in it. He seldom thought of her.

'I too,' said William. He took the other's arm and they walked slowly back across the smooth grass to the palace. Monmouth was turning over their talk in his mind; he knew that William befriended him. At the last moment William stopped and said, 'If you must go back to England, take advice from me; let it be as though you follow Milady Harriet home.'

Monmouth was amazed; how did the Stadtholder know that it had been in his mind to try to see his father secretly? He could send Harry and her mother to their Stepney house, to await him.

It was summer then. By October, Monmouth was requested by the authorities to leave Holland. But he remembered his talk with William, and did nothing. The days passed without his arrest.

*   *   *

Winter came, bringing snow. A message was sent from the palace to the Old Court, where Monmouth was staying; would he teach the Princess to skate on the ice of the canal? He went gladly; Mary came down with her cheeks bright, in a skirt pinned up short, and skates tied on by her Oriental page, whose face was pinched with the cold. They tried the ice together; neither was expert. Laughing, floundering, they took one another's weight; by the end progressing a little way. The burghers looked on with disapproval at the Stadtholder's wife fooling in public with her cousin; her skirt was too short; they would never allow their wives to behave so. And it was said that he danced often with her, and dined alone with her. That was so, but it was with William's approval.

CHAPTER TWENTY-FIVE

The house at Stepney was pale, set back by itself, and had upper and lower windows; in one of these a light shone, and then went out. A few moments later a man in a cloak came out, shut the door quietly, and strode off down the street. It was Monmouth, without servants; he could trust none on his present errand. He took a backward look at the house, where Harriet and her mother were; then made his way to the river, meeting no one in the chilly November street. The Thames lapped quietly. At the water-stairs he slipped the ferryman a coin to take him across. Afterwards the man was to note it; it bore a profile of the Stadtholder, with the great beaked nose thrusting below a circlet of laurel.

Monmouth disembarked at Whitehall, and was admitted to the narrow stairs leading to what they had used to call Chiffinch's spy-office. Chiffinch, groom of the backstairs, went ahead with a candle. The sight and smell of the place was familiar to Monmouth, waking a hundred memories. There could be few men in England who knew more secrets than old Master Chiffinch; he had brought Nelly here to his father often enough, and others; and now himself.

He knocked at the door, which opened; and saw Charles himself seated in a chair by the fire, warming his hands. His skin was leaden in the dull light. He did not rise at sight of his son, but turned his head towards him, smiling.

'Why, Jemmy,' he said quietly.

'Sire!'

The tall body flung itself at the King's feet; tears fell between Charles's fingers. The King looked quizzically down at his son's dark head; how often had he received Monmouth Jemmy in forgiveness, and how many times could it happen again? Not often, now.

'Jemmy. Jemmy, my dear boy. It was unsafe to come. There are spies everywhere, and even William of Orange is to be petitioned again to send you away. You know well enough where I stand in all this; I must make a harsh show against you, else we are all undone.'

'Because of the power of York?'

'Because of the power of France.' The King grimaced a little. 'All know it who wish to; but we must preserve appearances.'

'I must tell you of what I have found, why I had to come.' He began to mouth some fallacious nonsense learned in Holland, some discovery of a plot by the Jesuits to kill the King. Charles smiled sadly. News of the so-called plot, and of Monmouth's visit, had already been brought to him by Lord Allington, Governor of the Tower, himself a sick man.

'Jemmy, how could such word have reached you abroad before I was told of it at home? A Papist may not lift a finger or stir abroad. But it was kind in you to come. You have never lacked kindness.'

'Sire, all I ask is to remain your loyal servant.'

Charles murmured, and rose. 'Come to my cabinet; I have a gift for you, and then you must go. It may be that we will not meet again.'

'Sire!'

The King raised his hand compellingly. 'Hush; let it rest. May not a father give his son a gift? I have always known that you were my son. That is one thing they have not been able to take away from me.'

'They have tried all things.'

'And so, my son, have you. Never think I do

247

not know you, or am not proud of you as a soldier; never as a plotter, you have not the facility. Leave such work to dangerous men, and make your own way as best you can. This should help you.'

He had opened a drawer and had taken out a satinwood box; inside were jewels of great value. Charles fondled the gleaming stones and let them lie against his fingers; he might have been caressing a woman's flesh.

'These should have been given to your mother,' he said. 'Keep or sell them, as you will; there will be a time when I can no longer help you.' The deep voice saddened; the dark lids half covered the watchful eyes. The King's face was melancholy, and he spoke rapidly.

'Your uncle is to be made to go into Scotland on March the tenth, to hold a Parliament in Edinburgh. I will try to have you brought back to England then, on condition that you plot no more.' The eyes raised themselves and the King looked at his son. Monmouth nodded agreement. He was filled with joy at the prospect of coming home; now he would live in honour and peace. With York gone, even for a time, he could establish himself, win his father's trust again.

'Your wife,' said the King, 'your wife tried to present me with a petition for your return; she is loyal to you.' Monmouth frowned. 'You have not treated her well,' said his father. 'I told her that she could not see me, that she

248

must leave Court. That is the manner in which I must act meantime. Did any see you come tonight?'

'The boatman and old Chiffinch. None else that I know of, or who would know me.'

'How did you come?'

'By Arnhem, Nijmegen, Tiel, Utrecht; then on to Rotterdam and so by Delft to Tilbury, to shake off spies.'

'Cheerless places,' murmured the King. 'I pray God I may never look on them again. Your love is well?'

'Well, and with me. She and her mother are at Stepney. They are heart and soul for me, and I can trust them.'

'But you cannot trust yourself. Look on every man as enemy until he proves himself a friend; most never do. Remember it. Now go; you must not be found here, and I shall deny that I have seen you. Till the tenth of March.'

Monmouth knelt and kissed his father's hands. 'How good you have been to me,' he murmured. Charles smiled sadly. 'Say no more, but go. God go with you, Jemmy, blockhead. I often called you so, yet in truth it was a name spoken in love.'

*   *   *

Afterwards, with Harriet by, he opened the package containing the jewels; they spilled out in her lap. She drew a breath. 'They are worth much,' she said. She watched her lover's face anxiously; such a gift might have been a parting one from the King to his beloved son.

*　　*　　*

They returned to Holland together, after a brief sojourn in Brussels; but de Graña was still unfriendly. They travelled northwards, knowing that William would protect them; Monmouth exerted himself to please the Stadtholder, and was later mocked in a letter from the French envoy to his master, for picking up a walking-stick William had dropped in the street.

*　　*　　*

The rider clattered through the streets of The Hague, urging his horse against the wind; he reached the palace and dismounted, flinging his reins to a groom. He was admitted hastily, murmuring of tidings which would not wait; he must see the Prince at once; he came from England.

He was shown into a small room to which, in moments, the Stadtholder came; the messenger knelt and was bidden curtly to rise. 'What is your news?' asked William, and held out his hand; he had been with guests, whom he had had to leave abruptly.

'Your Highness, it is terrible news. The King

is dead.'

'My uncle?' William tore open the sealed letter, and swiftly read the lines. 'They say you are informed of how he died,' he said, looking up. 'Tell me of it.'

The man told him. King Charles had had a sore on his heel, and had been obliged to follow the hunt that day in a calèche, which irked him. However he had returned to a supper of goose eggs, and had gone afterwards to watch the card-play at the Duchess of Portsmouth's table. Later he had been lighted to his bedchamber by the Earl of Aylesbury, who held the candle high to show the stairs, which were narrow. The page of the backstairs came to take the candlestick from him, and as he did so the candle, for no reason, went out. They laughed at it, however, and Charles was undressed and put into his bedgown. He was in a good humour, joking with the page, Harry Killigrew, and talking of his new palace building at Winchester. 'I shall be most happy this week,' he said, 'for my building will be covered with lead.'

He did not sleep well that night, though the constantly chiming clocks he kept about him did not disturb him as a rule. Next morning when he rose he was pale as ashes. He went to his closet to take some restorative drops he kept there, and did not return. It was bitterly cold. Chiffinch, the old groom of the backstairs, who had served Charles many years, went to fetch his master back into the warmth. The King came, and sat down to be shaved when the barber arrived; presently he collapsed, with the towel about his neck; it was an apoplexy.

The Duke of York was sent for. Next day, and the next, the King seemed a little better; but on the third day there was a relapse, the doctors put hot irons on the King's shaved head, and York sent for Father Huddleston, who had been with Charles after Worcester. 'That now this good father should be the first to save my soul,' Charles murmured, 'surely, Lord, Thou hast created him for my good.' He made his confession, and secretly received the Blessed Sacrament.

He passed away, 'just at high water and full moon at noon.' James II was King.

*   *   *

William dismissed the messenger and sent for Monmouth and Mary. They came, not knowing why they were summoned; Mary's dark eyes were troubled. In the little room, with only the three of them present, William broke the news. Monmouth's face was ashen. 'My father,' he kept saying, 'my father.' Mary was trembling and tearful. She had loved her uncle, and knew that weighty affairs would result from his death; they would change her life and William's so that it could never again be as it had lately been, placid and happy among their friends and their garden-plots.

Monmouth was still quiet and pale. Only later, when he was alone, would he give way to his sorrow. Afterwards they said that the sounds of his grief could be heard in the street.

*　　*　　*

Nothing could be the same now; there would be no joyous meeting after the tenth of March. The difference the new reign would make to his own fortunes was not apparent for some days. Meantime, William tried to cheer his sorrow; perhaps tried also to honour a friend with whom he must soon part for ever. James II would never tolerate Monmouth's presence in ease at The Hague.

On the twentieth of February—the news of the death had come on the sixteenth—an invitation arrived from William to dine and sleep. Monmouth went gladly; even Harriet could not solace him, and he would drink deep and drown his sorrow in company. It was good; there was Odijk of Nassau, the Prince's kinsman, with his brilliant eccentric talk flowing from behind the bowl of his everlasting pipe; and William's close and loving friend La Lek, whom Monmouth knew already; Zuylestein, lazy and handsome, and Montpouillon the Gascon, full of wit. They exchanged tales and ate and drank and smoked and talked again; the table was littered with fruit-peelings and stones, the candles burned low in their sockets. It was the small hours when Monmouth reached his room and hoisted himself into the gilded bed beneath the painted ceiling.

He must have slept at once, for it was still dark when he felt someone shake his shoulder. It was William, pale-faced and stern, in his bedgown, bearing a branch of candles. 'Monmouth, wake up,' he said hoarsely. 'You must leave before daybreak. You must leave The Hague at once.'

'Eh?' He shook himself out of sleep, and sat up. 'Your Highness says ...' Suddenly he realised the full import of it; the candles shone on William's face as though it were that of a corpse, showing the half-open mouth and sad eyes. He bent over Monmouth again, drawing closer as if to let no other hear him.

'You must go,' he said again. 'None must even guess that I came to you here; I must be a friend to England. Word came tonight from my father-in-law. You are no longer to be harboured at Court, and in the morning I must give orders for your arrest and return to your uncle. Go now, while there is time to escape. Believe that I come as your friend.'

Monmouth left his bed and went to the window. None stirred abroad; outside, the February rain bore down. It would be very cold outside. Already the warm friendly evening was a thing of the past, to keep in the mind for savouring later; not now. He turned to William, who had risked so much for him even before tonight. He must not drive England into the arms of France for ally. Amazingly, to the Dutchman, Monmouth was smiling.

'Your Highness knows well that I have ridden through rain ere this. I am sorry that this time you will not ride beside me. Perhaps again, when . . .'

'Get you gone, for all our sakes,' said William, his eyes bright with tears; it was impossible not to love and pity Monmouth. 'Do not let me know where you are; it is better to be able to say with truth that I do not know.'

'You were always truthful, Your Highness; and honest.' Monmouth was dressing himself. 'I will begone now; I'll not abuse your kindness. God go with you and prosper you. My duty to your wife.'

Within minutes he was out in the cold driving rain, his cloak about him. Back in his own apartments, the Stadtholder heard a horse clatter away. He did not go to the window. He sat for some time in thought, staring at nothing; not seeing the elegant hangings woven with gold thread, the idle nymphs on the delicately painted ceiling.

There was a faint sound; it was his wife. She had flung a fur wrap over her bedgown against the cold; her chestnut hair hung in a long plait over one shoulder. Her eyes were heavy, like an awakened child's.

'Some matter troubles you,' she said. 'I had to come and see. Forgive me.' She sounded timid, as if he might scold her. William smiled, and stretched out a hand.

'I am glad you are here,' he told her. 'A despatch came earlier in the evening from your father, to say Monmouth must be expelled from Holland at once. When I could, I warned him privately. He is gone.'

So he had waited till the company were abed and asleep, she thought; he was patient, careful. She took the hand he held out and they sat talking, holding hands like children in the rich room. She could not take her eyes from him, her brave little husband whom long ago she had hated; she was glad, had been so for a long time now, that they had married her to him. Poor Monmouth, with his country-dances and his lessons in skating, and his infectious laughter and beguiling ways; the hour on the ice of the canal, their walks in the Mall, their dinners and dancing together, seemed in another life. What would become of him now her father was King of England? What would become of them all?

'I do not want to leave Holland now,' she said aloud, as if William had been able to follow her thoughts.

He asked no questions, but said, 'Neither do I.' His face was in shadow and she wondered at first if he talked of war; then he saw that she was cold, for the fire had long died in the room. He bade her come back to bed, settling the furs round her shoulders. The icy rain still beat down outside.

CHAPTER TWENTY-SIX

He thundered on the door of the Old Court, hastened inside, changed his soaked finery for a suit of drab; and scrawled a note to Harriet. He sanded and folded it and gave it to her Dutch maid, whom he had wakened. The woman was in her shift, with a shawl flung over; she made to curtsy, and he sensed her goggle-eyes following him as he gained the door at last, the tiled passages echoing from the clink of his spurs.

Now he was in the rain again, alone; no one was yet on the streets, even such prostitutes as dared show themselves in William's country having stayed indoors in their wretched dwellings as better than the wretched night. Monmouth mounted, spurred his horse and dug his heels down; he was for Rotterdam, where Washington of the Great Brewery would give him a bed; then for Brussels. The Marquès de Graña would surely receive him again, not being York's son-in-law and having no need of England as ally. He had left word to

Harriet to follow him and he would take a house for her, so confident was he.

Then it was the rain-swept roads, with the sea howling cold in the distance; he set his teeth and when the way slewed round braved the force of the gale, riding almost blindfold the way he knew well enough. His resentment against York—his pardon, the King—had lessened with the need to ride; there was victory in beating the gale, as he would surely beat his enemy in due course; it had been foolish, and inconvenient, to have to leave Holland. He should have foreseen it. 'What harm doth he suppose me to do?' he asked himself, and found no honest answer.

The others had been at him, of course; they seldom let him go. Lately they had murmured Argyll's name, for that proud nobleman had been for years in Holland, almost since the Test Act which crippled him as it had York. He was a Presbyterian, as had been the poor devils at Bothwell Brig; thus far Monmouth was on his side. But the man's Campbell pride sickened him. Better to live in peace abroad with Harriet than find oneself in a cockatrice's den. Even Grey's amusing tongue had palled; seen with his little pregnant bitch of a mistress, he was clearly to be recognised for nothing more than he was. Yet his presence meant laughter; one would forgive him much. But De Graña would provide worthier company, and meantime the night, ugh, was ending, and dawn showed over

258

the Ijsselmeer.

He clattered into the streets of Brussels two days later, having picked up his servants and baggage and been remarked upon at an inn. He went to demand an audience of the Marquès. It was too early, he was advised; return later; well, that was reasonable.

In fact, it was already too late.

*   *   *

He grew angry, and sulked; he was not used to having doors closed in his face. And there was no doubt of their closing, not only against himself but against Harry; the news from England had come swiftly. A few days after arrival in Brussels 'Madame de Winton' was requested to leave. The affront was borne mostly by Lady Philadelphia, who said she would go back to her sister in Middelburg; Harriet looked at her mother and, without disloyalty, wished she would do so. She herself wanted to be able to give her whole heart and mind to Monmouth now that the world had turned against him. 'It is cruel to use him so,' she raged, nails clenched against her soft palms. 'He hath no wish to harm any man, why cannot he be let live as he will? As long as King Charles was alive they loved and followed him.'

'That is exactly the difference, you fool,' replied Lady Philadelphia roundly. 'All knew the King doted on him still; you will know he had his baggage freighted, ready for recall when the Duke of York should go to Scotland, and his servants were ready to leave at an hour's notice. I hear as much as yourself; you do not listen to folk's tongues as you ought. All know now that Monmouth is out of fortune, and they dare not offend the King of England.'

'By rights, Monmouth should be King of England.'

'Do not talk foolishly; and yet ...' Philadelphia's beady eyes surveyed her daughter. Would not delightful Monmouth be more popular than a Papist King, childless at that? If she might hasten Harriet back to Court as Queen of England, it would be her greatest triumph. The foolish woman brooded on it; and spoke of it now and again, for she was not one to keep silence. She thought herself justified; they could not live in this hole-and-corner way, out of one waggon into another, and Harriet insulted by foreign residents as a whore.

'Mother, you should go to aunt Aletta Quirenson, till we know what is to be done,' said Harriet absently. Her mind was still on Monmouth; surely they might reside privately at Middelburg for a while, and offend no one? Surely if they were quiet, he and she could be allowed happiness together? There must be other places in the world besides Toddington; dear Toddington, that she might never see more!

Meantime Monmouth angrily galloped the wet roads back to Dordrecht, for there was no hope in Brussels.

*   *   *

A comic incident happened then, for Harriet had an admirer. His name was De Valera and he had spent many years in England; he remembered Harriet at Court at Whitehall, and was carried away by her golden beauty. He named himself as her champion; how dared society shun her? He would give a ball for her, he insisted; everyone, from the Governor down, should be made to acknowledge the English Baroness. Harriet half heard him and let him do as he would; on the night of the ball her maid dressed her in satin and diamonds, and she gave her hand to De Valera in the opening dance, then said she would return in moments; the maid had signalled from the door that there was a message, and Harriet hastened out of the room, leaving the sound of fiddles and flutes, the scent of flowers, the press of bodies. Was the word from Monmouth? It was; he was at Antwerp, and asked her to join him at once.

She sent for her cloak, and fled down the back stairs; what happened to the hapless Spaniard she never did enquire, and she took a coach and rode through the night to join her lover. Her fair name was mud now; it did not matter; she felt Monmouth's arms about her again, and was content.

*   *   *

They were together again. But for Harriet his life would have been intolerable, hunted as he was from pillar to post. But he found a little brick-built house in Gouda, and there they were at last able to live without comment for awhile, happy as any man and his wife; he even bought two orange trees in tubs to set outside the windows. But one day there came a fuzz-headed figure to the door; Ferguson had found them, and where he led others would follow. The plotter brought news of Argyll; the Campbell planned a Scottish rising. 'If I might sail with him!' Monmouth cried, and Harriet looked at him sadly.

Her mother spoke to her; she must not weigh down her lover with reproaches, but spur him on. Was he not the hope of the Protestants, and would not a rising in England serve the cause while Argyll rose in the north?

'Do not speak of it, mother; where is the money to come from?' Harriet felt at times as if her mother were her daughter; the older woman's black eyes were sparkling, and she set her hands on her hips.

'Would you grudge the Wentworth jewels in such a cause, to make you Queen?'

'I?' Harriet flushed; the notion had not occurred to her, and she could not see herself in such a guise. But if it would aid Monmouth, if it should be what he needed . . .

'I grudge him nothing,' she said. She turned away, and did not say more; but each day, with nagging and whispering, Lady Philadelphia worked on her, and on Monmouth also; and he had Grey and the rest pouring the same tale into his ears.

The time came when the Wentworth jewels were indeed turned to arms and ships.

CHAPTER TWENTY-SEVEN

He came into the little house, peeling off his wet cloak and hat and flinging them to the servant; he went straight to Harriet.

She looked at his set face. 'You have seen Argyll?'

'Ay, rot his pride. That is a man I cannot deal with. He will by no means hear of my going to the north with him, for he envies the men I might raise; all must be in his Campbell hands and head.'

She raised a hand to her heart. 'What would they have you do?'

'Make a landing in England.'

'Alone?'

'Grey and the rest will sail with me; and we

263

would hope for many to join us from Cheshire and those parts. Say naught of it—' he caught at her hands—'but it is thought that I will go first to the West Country. Thousands rose for me there when I made a progress in my father's day: they will rise again.' He seemed already cheered at the thought of them, and she did not dampen his mood. It was long since he had been carefree, and of late men rode in day and night to be closeted with him; she feared their discovery in Gouda, where the Prince feigned ignorance of them.

'We will march on London,' he told her. He was smiling, with a light in his eyes; he looked young again. 'We'll run the old Papist out of his lair, never fear! And then...'

He grasped her waist, and whirled her about in a dance-movement. 'A good fellow hath joined me today,' he said, when they regained breath. 'He is a Scot named Hume, whom I met in the Rye House days. He was wanted for that, and hid for long beneath his house, while his young daughter fed him with scraps she brought daily. In the end he won out and made his way here disguised as a surgeon. He is one of many who are glad to strike a blow.' His voice lightened as he tossed out now one name, now another; a good soldier, a proven friend, a nobleman, a swordsman. When he had decided to go on the separate English venture she never knew; it had come to him gradually following his dissatisfaction with Argyll, and now filled his head. Only the previous week he had been writing of making no more bustle in the world, because he was happy quietly with her; at another time he had said they would go to Sweden. She listened, and soothed him when it was needed; she would not hinder him in anything he might decide to do. If it was to be a fight to the death now between uncle and nephew, the cold man and the warm, she was almost glad of it; at least Monmouth would not be harried constantly, as he had been these past months. He was thirty-six; it was not so old; he should have years of useful life left to him. He had been a good soldier, she knew, and had won renown in war. Now he must fight again.

He looked at her, standing silently by him. 'The Prince of Orange is our friend in secret,' he said. 'He pretends neither to hear nor see, which aids me; and my uncle may not know all that is done in Holland, for in Amsterdam they defy the Stadtholder. What a coil! But by reason of it I doubt if my uncle will know when we set out.'

He slid his hands over her body, savouring the slender shape of it beneath the plain summer gown. The only ornament she wore was a blue girdle with a silver clasp; he took it off, and tied it about his neck.

'This will be my talisman,' he said.

'The stars must aid you, also.'

'Pray for that. I would run the hazard of being thought anything rather than a rash inconsiderate man.'

*   *   *

In London alehouses they plotted, and letters in cipher were sent back and forth; in Holland the women's jewels were sold, and fetched enough to hire a ship; there was a stir about finding enough arms in Amsterdam. Arms and ammunition were found, and suits of silk armour, and eighty-two men who would be officers; but only twelve had experience of war.

William of Orange continued to protest to his father-in-law that he knew nothing. Monmouth said farewell to him late at night, when they had an hour's long talk at The Hague. He remembered the thin bewigged shape standing against the light, his face hidden; in some manner, William might have become a stranger. Yet this was the same man with whom he himself had fought, dined, laughed; they had hunted and danced and known much pastime together. He must remember William thus, not as the cold head of a state whose first concern must be with expediency. He went out into the June night, heady with expectation, glad that at last the die was cast; now he must say farewell to Harriet.

As soon as he had gone, William sent for his right-hand man Bentinck, who had never been close to Monmouth. He was despatched with all speed to England to inform King James.

William might have turned a blind eye to the arming and plotting in his own country; he might even wish Monmouth God-speed, but he could not say so to the courts of Europe.

*　　*　　*

Monmouth and Harriet were in one another's arms, saying farewell; against the summer light could be seen the delicate tracery of the little orange-trees in their pots. Now that everything was in readiness they were silent one with the other; words were not needed. She passed her hands once more over the beautiful face, as if she were blind and must use her fingertips to stamp it on her memory; and, as if in blindness, her eyes were closed. When she opened them they were dry of tears.

'Harry ... I will write.'

She tried to smile. 'When you have leisure enough; may that not be soon. I have prayed that a thousand may join you in the first hour in England.'

He kissed her fingers. 'Soon you will be there with me. Do you remember the bad verse I wrote at Toddington? I was happy then. Not all men know such happiness.'

'I too have been happy—with you.' All of her life had been a prelude to that bliss; if she died tomorrow, she would still have known what many women never dreamed or imagined. She could not thank him in words,

267

nor he her. And so they parted, and he went to
his ship.

*   *   *

They saw England, rising out of the smooth
Channel after dawn; there was a light mist on
the water, pearly and wreathed. Ford Grey was
beside Monmouth, puffing at his clay pipe;
they might have been on a pleasure-jaunt
together.

Suddenly Monmouth said, 'When I am in
Whitehall, Sunderland hath promised me to be
my first minister.'

Grey turned his head, grinning with the pipe
between his lips. 'I doubt not many will follow
him; he knows when he's bested,' he said. 'You
saw the declaration?' Ferguson, the plotter,
had written out copies of a paper they would
proclaim at the market-crosses in towns when
they landed. It contained a statement among
others that the King had poisoned his brother,
to 'gratify his own boundless ambition after a
crown.'

Monmouth was watching the mist. 'I signed
it,' he said absently. He had not read it. He had
always put aside tasks which wearied him.

*   *   *

He had got into the small boat with a few men,
Grey always by him. He himself wore a violet
268

coat and the Garter, sparkling in the early sun, on the left breast. His beaver bore black plumes and his periwig was curled. The boat made smooth headway; on shore, several watched them. A lad from one of the groups waded out, and bent his knee for Monmouth to put his foot on it and land dry, not spoiling his silken hose. He laid a hand on the boy's shoulder.

'You will join me?' It was lightly said, an invitation to adventure. The lad, whose name was Bagster and who was a lieutenant in the navy, shook his head.

'No; I have sworn to be true to my King.'

The landing was made. When they were all out of the boat and on the beach Monmouth and his men knelt down to pray. Then he pulled his sword from the scabbard; he could feel the swish of the metal and see the good blade shine in the sun as it had done long ago at Maestricht. This was clean, open war, no longer furtiveness and pursuing shadows, accepting insult; now he would fight. He was not wearing the silk armour they had found him, made to turn bullets. He began to walk along a field path over a cliff into the town; the little semicircular pier where they had landed was abandoned, and settled back among its waves.

*   *   *

'Eighty horsemen, supposed armed, did passe

about one o'clock this morning a by way near this town.' So had the Mayor of Taunton written in harassment some days previously. No one knew exactly what was happening; a letter written in London had been taken at Ilminster; there was word of a great success in the north, and 'all true Protestants' were advised to stay close pending the arrival of 'a certain person' among them. The June roads shimmered in the heat; a man would be better off attending to his garden; someone said ships had been sighted, others not. Many remembered the duking days, when Monmouth had ridden down amongst them on progress; but that was in the dead King's time; matters were different now. Last of all, news came that a vessel carrying arms and ammunition was indeed captured at Plymouth.

It was the eleventh of June when fishermen at the little village of Chideock saw a ship's boat with ten men aboard, pulling in to shore. They had talk with some, while others went about their business; it was pleasant enough, for the visitors gave them neat's tongues to eat and canary to wash it down. If they sighted three ships away to the west, flying no flag and firing no salute, it was maybe best to say nothing. But later, when the city fathers had grown suspicious, seven boats of armed men put off and landed at the Cobb in Lyme.

* * *

270

They marched in files, and he at their head, his gallant figure outlining the banner of deep green and gold, with 'Fear nothing but God' worked in stitchery. Harry had paid for it. Crowds began to assemble as he made his way; drums beat, but the fort did not fire. (If they had known, the mayor of Lyme, frightened out of his wits, had already fled to Honiton to spread the word.) The crowd called and shouted; it was as good as a fair. 'A Monmouth! A Monmouth!' There could be no blame in shouting; everyone was at it; they couldn't imprison everyone. How handsome Jemmy was! How many years would it be, three, four, since he was down here? Duking days, they'd called them.

'A Monmouth! A Monmouth!' He was King of this people; they shoved one another aside to kiss his hands; he was not a stranger, like the Popish King; old folk remembered when his father had come among them as a lad, further west. Tall and dark, he'd been, like this one. There was no doubting Jemmy was the dead King's spit image, say what they would. He had the charm about him, a way of smiling, of holding out his hand; you could feel it.

'A Monmouth! A Monmouth!' Where would he go next? They said old Speke of White Lackington had thought he was too old, and had sent his son and some men and run off. As for the rest, they were maybe in prison, or cautious; a man must wait and see. Nobody had expected his coming, that was it; and yet surprise was what was needed, in a war. A war? Maybe it would never come to that; best wait and see.

* * *

By late afternoon he was on the Church Cliff, listing names. He stood where he could see the tower of the church, the sun setting in the sky in threads of gold; Grey's lean form, Ferguson's thick one, stood against the light, jotting down particulars of those who would join; their plain honest faces and thick-fingered hands waited, having no swords. Swords were few; later he would have a smith beat them out of old ploughshares and parts. 'Men are useless without arms,' he thought; a plague on that boat that had been taken in Plymouth!

How many men would there be? What could he do with such a number? How would they feed them, arm them, keep them? It should all have been thought of before, but nobody could foresee what would happen, how many would join ... the best plan of action was to wait, as Argyll had done in the north.

Argyll. He still thought it would have been best for them to make a joint invasion, but the proud foxy Campbell would have no one as leader but himself. News would take long to come down...

Guard the towns. Land the arms. Mount the

272

guns. There must be a place to store ammunition; did the town have a hall? That was fortunate ... Swords, muskets, pikes, stored and numbered; a blacksmith had broken the lock open; let the townsmen rally, and they should have guns. What? To arm thirty thousand, ay, and more...

*   *   *

The Mayor had reached Honiton. An express had been sent off to the King at Whitehall, while Mayor Alford hurried on to the Duke of Albemarle, who was at Exeter. Two others rode to London to be questioned by the King in council, remembering all their lives the cold stare of the King's eyes beneath the great light periwig. James had lately written to his son-in-law in Holland, saying that if Monmouth had indeed landed he would have expected to have been sent the news. Meantime, there was a Bill of Attainder; five thousand pounds for the capture of the Duke of Monmouth; forty thousand more to suppress any rebellion. There was perhaps little danger. Twenty pounds apiece to the men who rode in...

*   *   *

Albemarle was mustering the Devon and Cornwall Militia, his heavy face intent; he relished slaughter. The Secretary of State had informed him that the number of rebels was now less than had been supposed. However it was as well to make certain, and he despatched troops to Salisbury. Taunton had been controlled by the Somerset Militia before there was an attempt to rise. The town would regret its welcome to Monmouth.

*   *   *

Monmouth himself was staying at the George in Coombe Street, but could not pay the bill; they had to rob a customs-officer, for money was short. It was said folk were burying their valuables. But he had guests for supper; Fletcher of Saltoun, Grey himself, and Dare the paymaster, who should have brought in the Taunton men. He was dogged by ill-fortune; they drank deep, and afterwards there was a scuffle about a purloined horse. Fletcher drew out his gun and shot the paymaster dead; Monmouth was forced to bid him return to the ship. He cursed at the necessity, for now he had lost two good officers, and these, like the money and the guns, were in short supply. The good rough fellows who had come in knew nothing of the art of war: they must be given clear orders, but by whom?

It was seen that the Duke wore a dejected air from then on. Had he supposed that all the West would rise to his piping, as it had done in the duking days? Time had gone by since that progress; and already the Dorset militia were stopping men from joining him from Bridport. A troop of horse came in, however, from Lyme; they had killed a couple of the King's men on the road. With the approach of night came word that Albemarie was marching upon Lyme, and Monmouth ordered out his infantry and cavalry in ambush. The rest waited for news; idly, the first flush of enthusiasm already dead with the coming of night.

*   *   *

Grey swore to bring the Dorset Militia to a rendering, and set out towards Bridport. The first news that came in was from a rider, slumped and bleeding in the saddle. 'We would have won all had the cavalry held.' Why had not they? He ordered out his own force and rode to meet the men near Charmouth. Grey had been a fool; forty muskets had been lost, and muskets were more valuable than men. He had intended to march on London by way of Gloucester, to allow for the vital support which must come from the north. As there was news of an advance pincer movement of the Somerset Militia towards Lyme he went early in the morning of the fifteenth towards Axminster. Soon the twin files of the enemy could be seen corkscrewing down from a high point on the road; he sat horsed, the hat with its great black plume shading his face, and watched them.

He was not at the head of three thousand men. He gave orders to guard the town and the hedged roads which approached it. At Shute an encouraging thing happened; Wade's advance post fell back, terrified by the rumoured numbers. A little further on the Somersets, who were for him in secret, retreated in disorder about a quarter-mile from the town, to the distress of their colonel, Edward Phelips. 'They are drawn hither to have their throats cut,' that officer unhopefully stated, but it had not happened. His own men had lain out all night on the heath and were footsore. 'It is of no purpose to go on, for the two dukes shook hands last night,' they were saying. But Monmouth had not seen Albemarle. 'I am sensible I have lost honour never to be gained,' wrote the poor colonel.

*　　*　　*

There were more men from Axminster, and recruits from the Somersets. These at least were armed; but he was beginning to realise the problem of so many raw numbers. They would beat farm tools, scythes, to sharp edges, and mount them on poles; these were useful enough. The armed file were still in good heart; this was the country of the duking days, and the Somersets had abandoned their officers.

He had entered Taunton on the eighteenth of June; this was his kingdom. Cheering bands ran out of town to meet him; it was said the gaols were open, and the militia fled; they waved weapons from the store in the local church, broken into. The streets were flower-strewn, the houses with tapestries and carpets hung from their balconies as they would do for a king. Men wore green boughs in their hats, from the days of Shaftesbury the colour of Protestant freedom. Crowds flocked to join the Protestant Duke; he sat his horse and smiled upon them, King Monmouth, whom they loved; any other monarch seemed far away and no longer real; perhaps he never had been. The mob cheered, shouted, swayed, and the Market Cross reared in the distance, without its magistrates. These were fetched out at last, robed with the threat of a sword through their bellies, and came in affronted procession, Grey leading them with a grin on his face. The proclamation was read aloud and pinned up for all who could read; James, Duke of Monmouth, was King of England. He heard the words borne on the summer air, like wine.

*   *   *

Next day Miss Blake, the schoolmistress, in her Sunday best, led her young ladies out, their ages being between eight and ten; they had made banners for him, and he took each child

277

up in his arms and kissed her, the fresh country faces and little white caps and aprons pleasing him with their purity. Miss Blake, blushing, presented him with a Bible and a sword, and he duly thanked her and made a suitable speech, his hand on his heart. 'I come now into the field with a design to defend the truths contained in that book, and to seal it with my blood if there should be occasion.'

They were turning him into a Protestant hero: now that he thought of it, the identity pleased him. In the midst of rejoicings the news came that the royal forces were already at Wellington; he rode out shortly with Grey to see to the guarding of the roads and entrenchments. Mr Whitling, a Quaker of Ilchester, held up by the crowds, saw him and thought him thinner than in the duking days, more thoughtful, and downcast. Monmouth stopped among the Quakers and took off his hat, which pleased them as a 'sweet regard of princes.' The dark eyes surveyed them without seeing them; his thoughts were elsewhere, with the two great guns which had been lately sent to the town's end. There were not enough guns, nor flintlocks, nor weapons; and God knew how many mouths to feed. He had already given orders that there was to be no looting, but how long could he keep them from it unless they were filled?

But for now, all was gaiety and welcome; he himself, with Grey, had stayed overnight with a young gentleman on honeymoon, without marring that occasion. A surgeon, Pitman, had offered to stay with him and see to dressings; there was even a report of York's death. If only it might be true! True or false, many joined him when they heard it; rumour flew upon rumour through the town. 'The said high and mighty prince James Duke of Monmouth, son and heir apparent to the said King Charles the Second' had himself proclaimed again at the Cross, with a further appearance of the unwilling magistrates, who did not seem cheered at the prospect of delivering their country 'from tyranny, Popery and oppression.' The tall man with the thin face and dark wig sat mounted while the crowds called, 'God save the King!'

Already it sounded unreal; where would they all be tomorrow?

*   *   *

He made out a royal order to suffer the posts to pass without interruption; he cited a statute of Henry VII's time to make it easier for landed gentry to adhere to him without future blame; but the county would not come in. Weavers, brewers, carpenters, shoemakers, masons, bricklayers followed him, but not their landlords. Albemarle had already sent a sharp reply to his offer of mediation. 'He doubted not James Scott would be convinced he had better left the rebellion alone and not put the nation to so much trouble,' the old Cromwellian declared. The son of George Monk was under no illusions.

There was a skirmish between a party of men and some of Churchill's scouts at Ashill, but they came off safe. He and Churchill had scarcely met since Maestricht; it was strange to think of his friend as enemy. As it was so, he decided to move his men, now about seven thousand, to Bridgewater as the church bells pealed for Sunday. Meantime Churchill and Kirke of the Lambs, hearing that King Monmouth was evacuating Taunton, also hastened towards Bridgewater. Onwards also, by Maidenhead and Newbury, came Harriet's one-time suitor, the Earl of Feversham, with a hundred and fifty horse guards and sixty horse grenadiers, under the gaze of his sharp eyes beneath their peaked brows; and a further fifty by Andover and Warminster, for Oglethorpe to find out Monmouth's position. Already Albemarle himself was in Taunton, and the proclamations torn down from the Market Cross to send to Whitehall.

*   *   *

He had wanted to attack at once, but the rest would not agree. At Bridgewater, however, there was no need to coerce the magistrates; they came out of their own free will, including the Mayor. Again crowds joined him, but they were unarmed. Already some of those who had come out earlier, discouraged by the lack of weapons, were returning stealthily home.

The ruins of Bridgewater Castle jutted behind him as he struck camp. It had begun to rain; the fires were dowsed, and the men leaned on their scythe-poles and stared at the lifeless columns of smoke above the spitting wood. But at Shepton Mallet there was some comfort, and he had a bed to sleep in and a great balustrade of twisting oak on which to set his hand. It had been decided to try for Bristol, which some said should have been done earlier; news was brought that the bridge over the river was out of action, and he sent men to repair it. There was accordingly a brush with the Gloucester militia, who were dispersed. Later he crossed and re-crossed the bridge, to try to feint direction before the enemy watching at South Gate.

*   *   *

'Above 1000 horse and 8000 foot, eight field pieces with thirty ploughs whereof was four teemes of good horses and the rest oxen; his men some well armed, others indifferent, and some not at all, only having an old sword or a stick in their hand ... many muskets and other ammunition in their carriages' followed the tall mounted figure with the star on its breast; he was beginning to feel hungry and knew the men were, and regretted an offer, which had come too late, of a hundred cheeses back at Keynsham. In the high road packed with moving men, accidents took place; once the enemy galloped through a village and mistook the men for his own. Fourteen men were killed in the encounter by Oglethorp's troop, but prisoners were taken after he was beaten off; these were tied securely and put in the old Manor stable, formerly an abbey site; again, ruins stared at Monmouth as he made ready to lie down that night. But the pause was brief, for during the night the army moved cautiously, silently, along the south side of the Avon to Bath, and halted on the hillside above the town. It was too late now for Bristol, with Feversham and his fresh troops in the area; northwards to Cheshire or Shropshire was suggested, to join the loyal array when it could be found; but there had been no word, except for a promise of 500 horse; and Churchill was in the way.

They sent a herald to Bath, but he was shot at once; upon which an order was given to march south again towards Philips Norton. At the same time Feversham's gleaming columns returned along the north side of the Avon to Bath, joining Churchill and Monmouth's young half-brother the Duke of Grafton, Louise Portsmouth's son. It seemed a long time since a frightened woman in a dark hood had come to implore Monmouth's aid in London.

Now the enemy was in strength. The broad band of armed and mounted men moved out in one body to Philips Norton; battle would be joined soon. Battle? It was hopeless, and he was already persuaded; pitiful small numbers poured in, unarmed, uncertain of anything except that they would fight for him, but with what? And the promised horse from the north had not come in, and never would now. Worst of all, he himself had been shot at; the large reward offered by James for his arrest tempted some. He half regretted that the bullets had not found their mark: death would have been quick. He should not have come here. What was it Grey, or a kinsman of his, had once said? 'If Your Grace were to land anywhere in England with a switch in his hand, he might safely march to Whitehall.' That information had come from friends in London, among their plottings in the ale-houses and taverns near Temple Bar. But London was far away, and he would need more than a switch to make his way past Churchill's battalions. It still hurt his pride to think of John Churchill arrayed against him.

*   *   *

They had their triumphs. At Philips Norton a poor man held open a gate for them to pass,

283

and they killed him when he said he was for the King. For which King? Monmouth should have asked him, as he rode on past the prone body. He himself did not feel himself James the Second, King of England, riding against the usurper York; there was a ring about it that was not true.

He saw the horses disposed in the village and the men encamped in fields nearby, and himself went to the Old House, with its timbered beams jutting over a lower storey of brick. He slept little, and early next day there came word of an attack by Feversham's men, led by Monmouth's half-brother. The infantry fired a volley in flank as Grafton rode down a narrow hedged lane, but he broke through the guard crowding at the lane's end, and escaped as Monmouth's horse, refreshed after a quiet night, came to cut him off in the rear. Having forced his way through, Grafton took up cool position on a hill a quarter-mile distant. His artillery fired, and met a response, ragged enough, from Monmouth's four great pieces. They brought word that Churchill's men had lined another hedge, and shot was exchanged till darkness fell. At the end of the day, counting his dead, there were eighteen killed in Monmouth's army; but they said the enemy had lost eighty men. He would have come to close quarters then and fought the main body, although dark was falling; but the enemy had withdrawn to the north-east.

They came to him then, haggard and powder-stained. It would be wisest to move south again, to Frome. Always the lack of weapons nagged at him. There were the numbers to fight, if they were only armed. But he gave the order to retreat. It had begun to rain; despite the little triumph over Grafton's army the men were not in good heart. During the darkness groups of disheartened fellows staggered off through the mud, heading for home and King James's pardon. By the time heads were counted at Frome two thousand had gone. But they had thrown down their arms, and other hands were waiting to take these up; Taunton and Bridgewater would make up the strength.

The entry to Frome was pitiful, the men exhausted and knee-deep in mud. Some of his officers billeted themselves outside the town; he himself found lodging in it. Unable to sleep for weariness, he heard the men go ransacking through the streets; he was too weary to give further orders; let them take what they might.

He had almost slept when they brought him a messenger. There was news from Scotland. Argyll was defeated, with a price on his head. Later they heard that he was taken.

*   *   *

Light flared on the weary faces of the men in council; should they abandon the attempt, and themselves make for Holland? There was a silence while he considered it; Grey was hot for it; but Grey had no head for war. He himself shrank from leaving these poor devils to their fate. 'Take horse to Poole, seize a ship and make off,' said Grey again. He was like a greedy child, eager only for cake.

Three who had advised flight slunk away afterwards by themselves, taking money with them. They claimed afterwards that they had meant to buy arms in Amsterdam.

*   *   *

Feversham, as Duras now was, had refreshed himself and his men at Bradford and closed in a few miles east of Frome. It was supposed that the rebels would come to meet them. But Monmouth had heard of it by then, and turned instead towards Shepton Mallet. So Feversham entered Frome, and made ready to follow and attack when he might. He had once been a suitor of Harriet Wentworth, but with French practical common sense had forgotten it and only did his duty. 'What we every day practise among this poor people cannot be supported by any man of the least morality,' he wrote, knotting his heavy eyebrows over the page and remembering what his men had done in the town, seeing again the soiled places where horses had been stabled in family kitchens, hearing again the useless cries of the women, and the driving rain.

*　　　*　　　*

Monmouth's own men were still taking their share of plunder, for there was no money to pay them. Wells Cathedral had the lead torn off its roof for bullets, and horses stabled there; the silver vessels would have been lifted, but Grey made a saint's figure of himself before the altar with a drawn sword. He could not stop other events. The ten thousand Quakers who had been promised did not appear; they would in any case have been useless as fighting men.

There were more desertions. They bivouacked on Pedwell Plain, to the east of Sedgemoor. While they were there a deputation came from once triumphant Taunton. They brought him the mud-splashed riders, hats turning respectfully between their hands. Would His Grace please not return to Taunton? There had been trouble since he left, and the proclamations torn down.

He raised a weary face to them. 'It would have been better,' he said, 'if you had persuaded me not to go there while I was at Lyme.'

Another large body of men deserted after this; it was a sign of the times. Perhaps they would still not be too late for King James's pardon.

*　　　*　　　*

They continued next day towards Bridgewater, while at the same time sending warrants out to call for labour and materials for fortifying the town. But the carpenters with axes and hatchets, the hundred and ninety labourers 'sufficiently provided' with saws, spades, pickaxes and barrows, were never to be made use of if they came. As for bread and cheese, sheep, oxen and calves, there were none. Nor was there any hay.

'They have more a mind to gett horses and saddells than anny thing else, which looks as if he had a mind to break away with his Horse to some other place and leave his Foot entrenched at Bridgwater,' wrote Lord Churchill. In fact Monmouth now intended what he had advised from the beginning; to march by Gloucester towards Cheshire and then to London. If the message which had come in lately were true, there were three thousand reinforcements there; and they would not be without arms.

*   *   *

There was a place called Weston Zoyland near Bridgewater. Feversham moved and quartered his forces there; five hundred horse and five regiments of foot. There were five more regiments encamping on the village moor. The militia were stationed at Middlezoy and Ottery, a mile further south.

A man came breathlessly running in; his neighbour, Master Sparke, had watched the King's forces with his telescope from the tower of Chedzoy Church. 'They are moving, sir! They are moving!' And he gabbled out recorded details, accurately enough.

They would have to fight, and under great disadvantage. If only he could have got away with them to the north!

CHAPTER TWENTY-EIGHT

He had drawn up his cannon and ammunition to one end of the town, hoping till the last moment to make the escape north; if he had known, Feversham knew all of it. That man had sent Colonel Oglethorpe with the Life Guards detachment to keep watch over the Bristol and Keynsham roads, and had expected to go in pursuit next morning. But for now, when dark fell he retired to a house in the village they had taken for him, after a good supper; he was soon asleep.

Monmouth and Grey climbed the tower of St Mary's Church and looked out with a telescope from the parapet. To his sorrow Monmouth saw the faces of men he knew, drawn up in file against him; 'if only I had been their colonel still, there would be no doubt of victory,' he said aloud. It was long ago that he had had to part with the command, in another life; such matters seemed too far away to be as poignant. He knew the men would fight well, for he had trained them. There had been no time and no arms to train his present rabble, untrustworthy as they were, slipping one after the other into the dark. He had it in his mind now to attack by night, and hazard everything on a single throw; surprise was with them.

The man—his name was Godfrey—who had come with the earlier information returned, still breathless, from his indefatigable neighbour Mr Spark; Mr Spark said that the enemy had dug no trenches, set no sentries, and were mostly drunk. It seemed the right moment. The prospect of some action cheered him.

*　　　*　　　*

There were five regiments of under a thousand men each; the Red, the White, the Blue, Yellow and Green; and there was Grey's body of six hundred horse; the poor devils with scythes, and the four cannon. He regretted having sent eighty horsemen, under Captain Hewlett, off to the quay at Minehead to capture half a dozen guns there: he could have used the tried men in key positions now. He had information about the numbers of the enemy; fourteen troops of horse and dragoons, with thirty-four companies of foot, and sixteen field pieces against his four. They must do the best they could before the drunken men grew sober behind slow-matches. It was dark, without a moon; a thought of damp crept up from the evening ground after the rain. They must march six miles along narrow lanes before the attack on Feversham in his high-placed camp. Someone murmured a thing to Monmouth then.

'He hath the great rhine at his shoulder; mark it.'

Monmouth turned his head. 'What is that you say?' He saw their faces as a pale blur against the dark, their mouths agape. They repeated what they had said, not understanding why His Grace should care about it; it was the name used hereabouts for boggy draining-places, unseen in the scree of the moor. 'There are two before then, sir, the Black Ditch and the Langmore Rhine, as we call 'em here, sir.'

Beware the rhine. The words from long ago sounded in his head, but it did not matter, nor did he even recall his care when riding with William between Holland and Germany. What was to happen would happen. He believed it now.

He began to give orders, unaware of the change in his face; the men saw only that he was downcast. Grey's horse were to fire Weston village from the back, attacking the enemy in his right flank and rear, while

Monmouth himself was to advance with his infantry to the front line. He tried to laugh, saying, 'We shall have no more to do than lock up the stable doors and seize the troopers in their beds.' If they believed it, well and good. 'There must be silence; whoever makes a noise shall be knocked on the head by his neighbour,' he added. Later, Ferguson tried to lift the men's mood by preaching from a text of the Bible; his voice sounded thinly over the night air. Then Monmouth rode out, attended by his guard of horse. 'Though then but a boy, I saw an alteration in his look I did not like,' remembered a man named Oldmixon, long after.

Godfrey, who had not thought to mention the rhine earlier, was their guide; at least he was honest. The advance guard was followed by Grey's Troopers, as they called them; then the four guns and baggage wagons. They trailed silently along the narrow sticky lanes to a farm, where they left the wagons under light guard. At Langmore Rhine the guide missed the ford. They floundered, but extricated themselves.

Grey's horse now took the lead. They dismissed Godfrey at Langmore Stone, the Devil's Upping Stock. All about it the moorland looked level as far as they could see; a white mist had begun to rise, making visibility difficult.

A shot rang out. Nobody knew who had fired it; afterwards a man suspected was to be almost torn to pieces in prison by the rest. There was no more surprise; the enemy was alerted, and they had only crossed two rhines. There was a sound of a galloping horse's hoofs; someone was spreading the alarm. Monmouth had flung round to the man, Hucker, of Grey's.

'Treachery! If you fall not now, you shall fall later; mark him.'

Grey meantime was bewildered by the breadth of the rhine itself; he did not know which way to turn for a ford, and being no soldier took the right. 'The further he moved to the left the more he would have turned the enemy's flank,' said someone afterwards. There were Dunbarton's regiment and a battalion of foot guards, stationed on the right of the line; and at the place where Grey should have crossed, Compton's horse waited.

A challenge came, and there was a great shout in the mist. 'King Monmouth and God for us!'

Then the muskets blazed from across the wide boggy ditch. In the wraith-like whiteness they seemed like stinging gnats, with small spots of glow-worm flame. A man would be stung, then fall.

Grey's horse had meantime reared and fled back to the Upping Stock, disconcerting the advancing infantry, who took them for the enemy.

*   *   *

293

A certain Captain Jones, at the head of three hundred men, had tried to force the barred passage over the rhine; but the hooves foundered in the bog. They retreated, but in better order than the rest, to Sutton Mill, a mile north-east of Weston. In the village where he had been asleep in bed, Feversham had heard the trumpet call. He dressed unhurriedly, taking time to look in a small mirror before tying his stock. There would be enough leisure; he knew what he had to do. Monmouth had a pike in his hand. He was leading the infantry battalions forward at a swift pace, until they were brought up short by the rhine. 'Cross,' he said at first; then he countermanded it, directing the men not to fire until they were inside the enemy lines. He had forgotten the shortage of ammunition; the moving sensation of the rhine beneath his feet unmanned him. But the Yellow regiment disobeyed orders and began to fire; then the Red, then the Green. They might have been shooting rabbits in twos and threes. The aim was unsteady and too high, and did little harm. He heard them helplessly. In the near distance came the roar of his cannon. That, at short range, mowed down Dunbarton's company and the neighbouring foot. The firing continued for an hour, until the enemy brought their own cannon within range. Later he learned that these had been dragged through the mud by the battling Bishop of Winchester, no doubt inflamed with rage over the loss of lead and dignity at Wells. He was an old man used to war. He had fought in Holland.

Monmouth's men had gone on firing. They would continue until the ammunition was exhausted, and then they would turn and run.

The guns, and the Queen's and Queen Dowager's Regiments, did much havoc now; men were stumbling away, and the Household Cavalry and Dragoons poured over the ditch at the ford. Oglethorpe's troop, returned from Bridgewater, joined them. There was a little encouragement here; they had learned nothing, and the commander charged a battalion of Monmouth's foot and regretted it. He lost several men and his place in the line.

Churchill by now was attacking the guns. Already the infantry had swarmed over the ford and re-charged; but the bulk of the Monmouth foot was unprotected by flanking horse, and panicked. Fleeing, they were slaughtered almost to a man by the Scots under Lord Douglas. Monmouth had been in the thick of the fight, leading his men forward as long as they would follow. But the sight of the scythemen being cut to pieces in the ditches finished him; without more words he and Grey together took to abject, disgraceful flight. Monmouth had left his cloak and star on the field; a button had been torn off his coat. He looked down at the missing torn place in the cloth, and his mind was blank. A lost button should not matter.

CHAPTER TWENTY-NINE

'Our men are still killing them in ye corne and hedges and ditches whither they are crept.' They would bury in a common grave those who had died upon the moor; the rest were left for the countryfolk. Those still alive were kept for the gallows, whipping, branding and banishment to slavery. The King himself sent word that there was to be no leniency. Twelve hundred men had surrendered, five hundred of whom had been herded into Weston Zoyland church 'of which there was seventy-nine wounded, and five of them died of their wounds.' More wounded were taken by the cartload into Taunton, where hanged bodies were already swinging from the inn-sign. They and the deep-dug grave on the moor, the chimneypiece where the King's men had sharpened their swords, would go down into tradition; other small things were preserved, like the great lustre dish from which Feversham had eaten a junket before the battle; and Monmouth's sword, with the heads of Charles I and his wife on its hilt.

There were atrocities; a girl who had brought information was raped, and a poor man was put in a halter and made to run beside a fast horse. They did not set him free at the end; they hanged him with his friends from a tree by the Bussex rhine. Others were hanged from a hook, at the town's gate, and still more at Glastonbury.

As for Monmouth, Feversham had his coat and his papers, and the Garter; these would be given to the King. Later, the plumed hat was found; he had exchanged it for another to help his disguise. A small boy in Chedzoy brought in a blue girdle which he said the Duke had given him; it had a silver clasp. Monmouth's pistols were found, and remarked on because they were beautiful, with inlay and fine polishing.

But Monmouth himself was nowhere to be found, and they set bloodhounds on the trail. The King's men scoured the country, north and south, to no avail.

*   *   *

If they had known, he had scrambled up the slope towards Polden Hill, Grey urging him on; behind them, men were still fighting. 'There is no stopping those fellows,' said Monmouth. 'They will fight on, and then they will turn and run.' It had not been possible to make a retreat; but he would not have left them except for Grey.

They changed clothes at the Woodyates Inn; Monmouth had already exchanged hats with

Dr Oliver the physician. Now, he put on drab clothes such as shepherds or country hinds might have worn; and could not forbear smiling at Grey's long figure in such gear. Once he himself had been a courtly shepherd and had danced in a masque; this was different, and the masque was one of death. He wondered how Harriet fared. Already she would be troubled for him, having heard no news.

They turned their horses loose, having thrown the saddles in the undergrowth; the heavy padded leather fell with a dull sound, rolled away and was hidden. With a piercing effort of memory he recalled the scarlet saddle King Charles had given him, scarlet wrought with gold. There was no splendour now.

They plodded on, weary and dispirited; even Grey did not jest. Once they were not far from Shaftesbury's mansion of St Giles at Wimborne; the feathery trees of the estate blotted it from sight. Little Sincerity would not have let them get to this pass; nor would he have welcomed them now.

They took to the open country, for the roads were by this time alive with Royalist troopers eager for the reward of five thousand pounds that had been offered for him, dead or alive: it was necessary to proceed under cover of the dark. They hid in the desolate parts to the north of Wimborne; there was no food, and he did not recall when he had last eaten. They lay separately in the wild places, so that if one were

298

taken it need not mean the fate of all. After a time he heard scuffling and shouts, and knew Grey was captured; he accepted it dully. It no longer seemed possible that he himself would win free. Yet he went on, with the instinct that keeps man alive and not dead. Fields and woodlands began to come into view again; the summer dusk was short. Long ago he had commanded men and had fought a battle; it seemed to belong to some other man who was not himself, this hungry tired self that trudged on and hid among trees. He tried to pull a few unripe peas in a field; at such moments he would remember things from that other life, and he recalled that Prince Rupert had hidden in a field of beans after Naseby, or was it Marston Moor? Rupert was dead. So many of his friends were dead. He himself asked nothing more now than to live, however humbly. But this, this crawling on amidst sodden bracken and bramble which tore at his poor clothes, this was not living.

He was now between Fordingbridge and Ringwood fields. Grey's captors were still searching for him; where one had been, the other would be found near.

* * *

There was an old cottage-woman named Amy Farrant, who was very poor; she had heard about the ransom, but could not think of a sum so large as several thousand pounds; they might give her something, enough to live on; at present she was almost starving. She looked out of her cottage door to the faint light and saw two men climbing over a hedge; they should not be there. Amy pursed her lips and went to the soldiers with her tale. Afterwards she would be accursed and shunned by everyone; the very place she had lived would be blighted and they would not rebuild on the ruins. But she told her tale. The Island on Shags Heath had already been well searched, but had yielded nothing. But early next morning, while the dew was still cold on the ground, a servant was captured who confessed he had been with Monmouth three hours before. He had been promised pardon. They beat the places he spoke of, without result; but three hours later again one Parkin, a militiaman, looked towards a great ash tree whose boughs were rich with green keyed bunches thrusting over the field. Below was a morass of bramble and fern, but there was a piece of cloth among it.

They dragged him out, scratched, footsore, starving and exhausted; later they turned out the pockets of his coat and found the unripe peas. The man they stared at had a grey stubble on his chin, and was no longer young.

CHAPTER THIRTY

'If I had a good horse under me I could still have made off.' He stared at the grave bewigged figure before him, the magistrate at Holt House; with capture, now that the dreary chase was done and he had eaten and been shaved and put into fresh clothes, he felt his spirit renewed.

But the exhaustion was still there, in his mind. He took pen and paper and wrote to the King; an abject, whining letter, begging to see his uncle, begging to be allowed to live, saying he had that in his mind which His Majesty should know, and thinking of telling him Sunderland had promised to be first minister in his kingdom when it should come. King Monmouth. There must be no more of that in his thoughts, but if they would let him live, somewhere quietly with Harry, he'd not figure in the world's chatter again, he would let all men forget him. Surely the King would show mercy; if he could see him, he could persuade him. They said that if the King saw a man it meant the man was not to die.

They kept him at Ringwood two days, under restraint, but he learned some things of the men who had fought under him, other than the hangings. Ferguson the plotter had got himself away, no doubt to Holland; he would live to see another day. Grey was brought here, and had recovered his spirits; he also hoped to live, and told Monmouth a story from one of the towns; a man had hidden himself in his home, dressed as a woman, and had rocked a cradle with his foot as the soldiers passed by the open door.

At the end of two days, they came for him, and bound his hands behind his back. He took the insult calmly; and being led to his horse vaulted into the saddle without aid. Someone saw him then and described him as a 'black, tall, genteel man, with a dejected countenance.' It had already been noticed that he had grown thin on campaign.

The escort took him to London by way of places he knew: Romsey, Winchester where the walls of his father's palace were still rising, but it would never be finished. Guildford and Hampton passed by; the King had been written to to ask his pleasure as regarded travel by water from Isleworth, and replied with an order to stab his nephew if there should be a rescue attempt on the road.

But there would be none; from Ringwood to Vauxhall itself he was surrounded by guards. He saw them ride close, and looked for Churchill; would not John come to pass the time of day, remembering Maestricht? But Churchill did not come.

They took him by water to Westminster Stairs. Soldiers with pistols stood guard on either side of him even here; beyond were the Yeomen of the Guard at their posts, their bright coats shining in the sun. A man slipped behind a yeoman, hiding like a shadow; it was Aylesbury. 'I wished heartily and often since that I had not seen him, for I could never get him out of my mind for years, I so loved him personally,' he wrote.

They took him to the Bell Tower. Once alone, with the cool stone cell surrounding him, he wrote, and wrote again; abject letters, to the Queen, to Clarendon, to the King again; and once to Sunderland, by a secret hand. He did not expect a written reply, and none came. But next day a tall cloaked figure slipped into the cell; the catlike eyes regarded him.

'The King will see you.' It was said in a whisper, as though the knowledge itself were dangerous. 'I have done this for you,' said Sunderland. 'There is a condition, which may mean your life. Say no word to His Majesty of our matter; he knows of it, but would not have it seen that he knows. Remember it.'

'I will remember.' He was weary of yea-and-nay commitments; if his uncle knew already of the matter, he had as soon get on with the greater one. He saw Sunderland slip out of the cell and heard the salute of the guard outside, and footsteps dying away.

*   *   *

The King would see him. Chiffinch again, and

the spy-office; how greatly matters had changed since he had last seen it, and met with his father!

He waited; his hands had been bound and he was turned towards the view of the river. London was rebuilding after the Fire; the great skeleton of the new St Paul's reared in scaffolding on the east, and behind it was the smoke of the City.

Footsteps sounded, even, measured, unhurried. He turned to face the door. The King entered, alone. Monmouth flung himself on his knees, head bowed; but he had seen the cold grey eyes upon him, and in them was no forgiveness.

'Sire!' How often had he said that? There had been another King, dark and kindly; this was a stranger. His very voice was cold. 'How can you expect pardon, that have used me so?' He had turned away from the kneeling prisoner: the sight was distasteful. 'To make me a murderer and poisoner of my dear brother, besides all the other villainies you charge me with in your Declaration.'

'Ferguson drew it, and made me sign it before ever I read it.' And Ferguson was free. Monmouth felt the degradation of running moisture from his nose; he had a cold, and could not wipe it. 'Your uncle will find a cure,' Grey had said. Looking at the upright figure with its averted head, he could not believe in mercy. Yet he must cling to the shred of hope

304

Sunderland had given.

'You wrote that you had some matter to relate to me.'

'It is of no import. I only wished to show my loyalty to Your Majesty.'

'Your loyalty!' James turned towards the door. The footsteps sounded again and died away. Perhaps he should have said more. It was still not too late, if he could find a listener.

*   *   *

'As I hope for salvation, he promised to meet me.'

Ralph Sheldon heard the sobbed-out words about Sunderland; maybe there was matter here that should be taken to the King. He heard himself promise it. He went to Whitehall, but was unable to see James except with Sunderland by him. The cat's eyes watched him cautiously; James himself was morose and silent. Blundering, Sheldon repeated what Monmouth had told him; both men laughed. 'Why,' said Sunderland, 'if that be all he can discover to save his life, it will do him little good.'

'Poor Monmouth,' said the King. 'He was always easy to be imposed upon.'

*   *   *

They brought Anna to him with the two boys;

the little girl was ill. He stared at the fair-haired woman in her dark clothes and veil; she might have been a stranger. He could not think of any words to say to her, but when had they ever been close? He began to speak hoarsely; the silence was impossible. A man stood behind her; it was Clarendon, the Lord Privy Seal.

'I knew you did not love me,' he heard himself saying, 'when you went to the play after my father died.' What did that matter? Yet it had been all that came into his head. Her face had crumpled and he was sorry he had wounded her. She would do better without him, often as she had tried to plead his case with the King; his mind registered it, but he could not thank her because of the coldness between them. He turned to Clarendon, who stood with his head bowed.

'Can you not aid me?' It was like a child crying in the dark. The other raised his head.

'I have come only to attend the Duchess,' he said. The reproof was less in the tone than in the words. Someone was begging his forgiveness and clutching at his knees; it was Anna. He looked away from her contorted face and would have liked to withdraw from her touch; but he kept still, and presently they took her away.

This night would be the last of his life; he had heard the hammers erecting the scaffold. He slept, and rose early, to see the sunrise fling a peach-coloured light along the river; small wherries surfaced it like black flies. He realised that never before had he looked on London with love; he had taken it for granted; this would be almost his last sight of it.

A scraping of keys came at the door; the warder was bringing in his breakfast. To go to the scaffold hungry would be foolish, and might make him tremble; yet he did not feel afraid. Why should he; he was a soldier, accustomed to wounds and death. In fact fear had left him now; he had not felt it go, but was glad of his present calm. He began to pray silently, as he had done at many times in his life; not kneeling, only talking to God.

The man took away his breakfast things; presently Anna came in again, leading the children. He stared at them and tried to think of words to say to the elder boy that he would remember. It did not greatly matter; they were their mother's children, he himself a stranger. There was a rustling sound shortly; Anna had fainted. He watched them carry her away.

The bishops came to him then; stout Tenison, whom he had often heard preach at St Martin's, and the slight dark figure of the Bishop of Ely. It had been kind in them to send Tenison. It was the fifteenth today; if he could have lived past the unlucky date, there might have been hope. Of what was he afraid, after all? Other men had died; his own grandfather most bravely on a scaffold at Whitehall. Did he fear pain, or being cut off from God? God was surely merciful. In his own eyes he had not sinned. He had never loved Anna, and a man should not be forced to try and love where he could not.

He would die today. 'Truly, sir, this is very short,' he had written to the King; and had sent a sop to James by betraying the men of Cheshire. To go out of the world as a Christian ought; they were talking at him now. He had tried to persuade them to give him time to change to the Popish religion; he would have done even that could he but live. He remembered the dark robes of Father Petre, the King's confessor. 'You are trying to save your body, sir, not your soul.'

His body. By tonight it would be hacked and bloody carrion. He himself would be ... where? What happened when one left the body? He had never truly asked himself. Harriet had loved his body, and his soul, and he her mind and flesh. He had not taken time of late to think about Harriet. On the very scaffold he would proclaim his love for her. That would bring comfort, and justify him. He must hope for no more than that, and to die bravely.

CHAPTER THIRTY-ONE

The time had come. The churchmen had come in at ten o'clock; they made him sign a paper of illegitimacy, and he did so for the sake of his children. Later Tenison, whose parishioner he had been, took him aside and endeavoured to persuade him to repent; he had been living as a sinner, and the late insurrection against the King was a crime, which he must disavow if God were to receive him. He and Ely asked foolish questions, pompous and unreasoning; by the end their lack of wit roused a devil in him. 'I am come this day to die,' he said repeatedly, but they would not stop their urgings. They talked of his wife, and of Harry; sudden anger rose in him that she should be discussed between them. 'Scripture says that a man may have one wife in the eye of the law, and another before God,' he told them. Within him his heart cried, you are my wife, Harry, Harry; my only wife in the sight of God and heaven: when we are dead our two ghosts will be without rest till we find one another again.

Tenison cleared his throat and did the best he could to turn the mind of his recalcitrant listener to better things. The Duke did not seem to be aware of the shortness of time left to him. Within himself the clergyman thought, it is only a week since his capture: the King is punctual. But Monmouth would not hearken. He 'had rather a cast of enthusiasm on him,' they said afterwards. It was regrettable.

His mind had left them; it sped already with the old servant Marshall, to whom he had given certain things, trifles to be given afterwards to Harry. There was his watch, a toothpick-case, a ring with a charm to ward off danger. She had hung charms about him when he left for England; they had been found on him and taken away.

It was time. He turned and made ready to take his place in the procession that had formed; the Lieutenant of the Tower, the churchmen in their lawn sleeves, the guards who would ensure that he would not be rescued. It was rumoured that there was much sympathy for him among the waiting crowd.

They entered a coach. Monmouth heard the trundling of its wheels over the ground; his mind flew back to the last time he had driven away from the Tower, with his mother. Out of the window he could see the clear summer's day, and England again; England that he had loved, over whose lands he had hunted and coursed and fought and made love and made war. He remembered the oak tree at Toddington with his initials and Harriet's carved forever in the bark. Nothing could destroy their love; it would last till the end of the world that he was leaving. He felt the coach stop and saw the massed guards and sheriffs waiting to receive him; three men with loaded pistols stepped to his side as he came out. King James had ordered that they stab him if any rescue were attempted after his capture in the West Country; he heard a scuffle and some shouting now, and then it died. A man had thrust his way through the crowd, but was overpowered. There were no shots. It was ill fortune to try to save him. The time had come to die.

The waiting crowd was large, and made a great groan at sight of him; women were weeping openly. Memory stirred in him and he heard his mother's voice, telling him how nobly Charles I had demeaned himself on the scaffold. She would not be ashamed, now, of her son. He saw the gaunt place waiting, and felt no fear. It was draped in black, a courtesy of the King.

He saluted the mounted guard and foot about the scaffold; the old smile flashed out briefly, with all its charm. He heard the sheriffs fuss behind and about him; would he speak on the scaffold, had he a speech prepared? 'I never was good at speeches,' he told them. 'In any case they would not hear me. It does not signify.' But they were persistent that he speak, that he show some sorrow, some repentance. He felt impatience rise; why could they not let him die in peace? Finally he said, 'I am sorry it ever happened.' He took thought for the rough good fellows who had flocked to him in the West; the carpenters, tallow-chandlers, ropemakers. There would be more suffering for them. His own time was now.

He could not rid his mind of Harry, waiting in Holland for news. They wanted him to address the crowd, did they? Well, he would speak. He spoke with a clear voice into the silence and the upturned faces.

'I have had a scandal raised upon me about a woman,' he said, 'a lady of virtue and honour. I will name her, the Lady Henrietta Wentworth. I declare that she is a very virtuous and godly woman. I have committed no sin with her; that which passed between us was very honest and innocent in the sight of God.'

The shocked bishops moved impatiently; moments to live, and he could speak only of his whore! Here perhaps was a true son of King Charles. Ely intoned prayers, and the rest joined him. The figure of the doomed man stood apart, as if he had separate hope of his own salvation; they would not give him the sacrament because of Harry and his lack of repentance. The churchmen prayed, looking at the dark unmoving head. Monmouth, they thought, was like a man who has drunk wine, too full of cheer to be dying. Whence could his trust come, unrepentant as he was? Surely from the devil. They had wrestled with it, but to no purpose. I cannot understand it, thought Tenison; His Grace was a regular worshipper.

The executioner, Jack Ketch, was waiting with the axe. Monmouth tried the edge with his thumb. 'It is not sharp enough,' he said.

'Ay, it is sharp enough, and heavy enough.'

He took his purse and counted out six guineas and gave them to the man, who seemed afraid. 'There will be six more for you from my servant if you do your task well. But if I am served like Lord Russell I make no promise to lie still.' He remembered the butchery of Russell; it had taken more than two strokes. None would mourn him now beyond the crowd here, and Harry: King Charles would have pardoned him, King James wished to be rid of him. He should have succumbed the sooner.

Now he would die. He took off his coat, showing the fine shirt he wore with its collar of heavy lace; and his peruke, leaving his shaven head clear to the view. There was a light wind. They tried to bind his hands again, to cover his face with a piece of linen; but he would have none of it. He asked for time to pray; his own prayers, not those of the pompous clergy. He had always felt that God listened, and He listened now. Monmouth prayed for himself, that he might make a good end; and again for Harriet, that she might not die under the affliction of his death. She was young and the news would be bitter.

Still with her in the forefront of his mind, he strode forward and fitted his neck to the block. He hoped the poor wretch who would wield the axe would shed his fear, 'for it is I who ought to be afraid.' But the new lightness, almost gladness, remained with him. It would be strange to have died.

It was not easy. A knight named Verney, writing of the scene afterwards, said of him,

'The Executioner had five blowes at him; after the first he looked up and after the third he put his legs a cross and the Hangman flung away his axe, but being chidden took it again and gave him other two strokes, and severed not his head from his body till he cut it off with his knife.'

They rushed forward, the crowd, after he was dead. He had touched for the King's Evil and had cured it; they dipped their linen and kerchiefs in his blood. As for the executioner, it was said they would have lynched him, 'for he deserves to be Hanged, or beheaded with an oyster knife.' Later they put the body on a black velvet-covered hearse with six horses, and returned it to the Tower for burial.

*   *   *

'King Monmouth will come.' They had begun to say it already in the West Country, for the grievous season of hangings, the Bloody Assize, was about to begin, with angel-faced Jeffreys dispensing small justice with ropes and scourges and harsh sentence. Through the news of blood and torture, the mockery of all pity, the men's lives twisted or made strange, they remembered him who had come to lead them; and as in the west they still talk of Drake when war threatens, so they talk of Monmouth in time of peace. For he will come again, they say, and there shall be justice and peace in the land. They remembered him as beautiful and strange, King's flesh, riding on a white horse down among them to their welcome. They remembered him in the time of Revolution, when men ousted King James at last and the Prince of Orange came to take the throne as King, his wife Queen; but Mary died young, and never forgot the handsome cousin with whom she had danced and skated and laughed and dined in Holland. He was dead, but he would come again; he would not be forgotten, and every house which had sheltered him would be marked with a blessing, and the house which had betrayed him would be shunned forever. For he meant love to them, and beauty; such things do not die. Whether in war, famine, pestilence or peace, he would come; King Monmouth would come again.

CHAPTER THIRTY-TWO

Harriet was walking in the Middelburg garden with the dog Silk. It was the dusty time of summer; in that almost treeless country the plants had lost their flowers and the prim bulbs William had made fashionable were over. Further off among the dug beds, her mother and her aunt Aletta Quirensen were doing embroidery; their curled heads bent together, gossiping.

Harriet walked out of restlessness; it was a fortnight now and she had had no news, except a hasty note Monmouth had scribbled to her on landing. Moreover she had been ill again; the prickling of her limbs had turned to a kind of paralysis, but it had worn off for the time. She walked slowly in the calm, heavy air, the greyhound sidling at her skirts. The sky was grey-blue, the sunshine muted, as if it dared not shine too brightly in this place of half-tones. The heat was heavy, making Harriet's gown drag and her hair hang out of curl. She felt foreboding come, a result of her own heaviness. It was not well with her or with him; she knew it.

She turned between the patterned brick paths, and across the borders of lavender saw the messenger come. It was the man Marshall. She felt her slippered feet strike softly, swiftly on the ground, to reach him while they were alone. Later her mother could ask concerning it. She put a hand to her throat as she came near; the man's eyes were bleared with weeping.

'My lady. These are from him.' He held out a package to her and she felt doom rise; why did not the man say more? 'Tell me,' she said; it was as though he had waited for her permission to speak.

He told her. He would have omitted the merciless details of the defeat, the escape and capture, the King's coming at last and the

316

bungling with the axe. But she questioned him closely, strangely calm. At the end she said, with the little package in her hand, 'Where did they bury him?'

'In the chapel of St Peter in Chains, to the east of the altar.' They had sewn on the head; he did not tell her of that. She said strangely, 'So he died in England. He would have wanted that, at the least.' Then she looked at the man, who was no longer young, and said gently, 'Get them to give you refreshment. You have travelled far.' She bowed her head and hurried into the house.

*　　*　　*

When she was alone she opened the package. It contained the little toothpick case he had used, his watch, his ring. She pressed the latter to her cheek. Marshall had told her that the last words on the scaffold had been about herself. She thought, 'Good God! Had that poor man nothing to think of except me?'

She could hear the hubbub as her mother and aunt entered the house; Lady Philadelphia was sobbing. Harriet herself had no tears. There would be time to shed them.

*　　*　　*

Later a coach came. She had been sitting dully by the window, remembering the little orange trees he had brought to Gouda; such small things henceforth must make her world. She saw a tall thin woman get out of the coach, her maid with her, and enter the house. She did not want to see visitors; when the servant came she would say she was not at home.

But the woman said, 'My lady, it is from the Court,' and Harriet rose. The woman who entered had red hair, with a plumed hat elegantly set on it; her figure was boyish, and she had a cast in one grey eye. Harriet knew her slightly; it was Elizabeth Villiers, one of the Princess of Orange's maids of honour at The Hague. She curtseyed, feeling her limbs stiff. Why had the woman come? She would sooner have been left alone.

'Lady Harriet,' said Elizabeth; her voice was low and pleasant, and Harriet recalled that there had been gossip about her and the Prince. She was an intelligent woman; no doubt her brain meant more than her body to him. She was talking now; what was she saying? The Princess, she said, had sent her.

'Her Highness cannot travel here herself, but she would wish to send her sympathy.'

'Her Highness is gracious.'

Elizabeth put out a gloved hand, and her face showed compassion. 'You know well that she would have said more could she see you,' she told the other. 'She had a great love for her cousin, and wept when she heard of it. The Prince too was grieved.'

'But may not say so. I understand all of it. Pray thank Her Highness for her consideration.'

'What will you do?' asked Elizabeth suddenly; she had shed the cool courtier's pose, and revealed herself as a curious woman, not uncaring. Harriet stroked the dog's head: he had stayed by her and knew that she was in grief. Later, it would be worse, she thought; but now she was numb.

'It does not matter what I do. I shall die ere long.' She spoke in a matter-of-fact tone and Elizabeth looked at her curiously. 'You are young,' she said suddenly. 'You may find happiness; do not despair now.' She saw Harriet's blue eyes regarding her and said of a sudden, 'Poor boy, poor boy. He seemed no more, although he was a man grown. Wherever he was there was grace and laughter. The Court is sad.'

'Now that he is dead, the Prince of Orange will be King of England.'

'My lady!' Elizabeth's face grew narrow and blank, as though something had been said which should not. 'My lady, even in Court circles that is not spoken or thought of, yet.'

'Not yet. But the time will come. A time comes for all things.' Harriet turned to the window, and went on speaking with the light falling on her face and shoulder. She has beauty, Elizabeth Villiers thought, and I have none; but I would not be in her shoes for anything in all the world, she is so broken in her grief.

'The Prince could not aid him,' said Harriet, 'for such aid would have turned against himself. As it was he had to dismiss certain ones from his army who were in sympathy with Monmouth. It does not matter; but soon, in England, they will call for another King; they will not long tolerate the present one they have. I may speak, you see. His Highness was friendly to my love, as two men together; but he dared do no more, maybe did not wish to. To send enough ships, arms, money, would have committed him against his father-in-law. Whichever way fortune had gone, William would win in the end.'

The other was silent and she turned back to her. 'My love told me all his heart,' she said. 'To be royal is to be different from other folk. I can understand it, though now it does not matter.'

Elizabeth's fine mind was spinning about the thing, which was not news; she kept her own counsel, but it was in the air that one day, if the King of England had no son, the Princess would succeed. When that time came, she, Elizabeth Villiers, would have her own place. 'Her Highness—' she began. One must be careful not to say too much.

The steady eyes regarded her. 'I wish the King joy of his kingdom,' Harriet said. 'We have known much kindness here, even in the days when we were exiles and suffered to remain in hiding in Holland. Do not think us ungrateful; half a loaf was better than no bread.'

She speaks in the name of the dead man as though he were alive, thought Elizabeth. Smoothly, she drew on her gloves and took her leave. The coach trundled away. When she returned to The Hague, it was to hear criticism of the Duke and his 'dancings', by those who could not dance. The Prince himself chided them.

*   *   *

Harriet died in England. There was not any reason for her longer to live, and she did not. She died at Toddington, where she and Monmouth had known happy love together. Spring had come by then, and the oak where Monmouth had carved their names was sprouting small copper-red leaves. The bed where he had slept was deserted, silent; the servants continued to dust the room.

One day a visitor had come, while Harriet still lived: the Bishop of Ely. He had been on the scaffold with Monmouth, and had received a further package from him which he was unwilling to deliver. He had asked the King. 'Let her have it,' James had said. It proved to be another talisman of Monmouth's, one of those which he had worn about his body when

321

he was taken at Woodlands. It had no significance as it lay in her hand. All those things were dead with him; the stars were blind.

She died soon. On the day before the funeral Sir William Smyth, her mother's officious admirer who had been Harriet's guardian till she came of age, went to the little church and cut the bell-ropes. The villagers would not be able to toll a passing-bell for Harriet; she had been a sinful woman, and they must bury her in silence. The villagers were angry and would have had his blood; they had loved their young baroness. Smyth did not dare come again often to Toddington, and Lady Philadelphia took no more to do with him. By then, matters in England had reached a head; Mary Beatrice of Modena bore James II a son, and revolution followed. William of Orange landed, and took his father-in-law's crown; one of the first officers to desert to him was Churchill. William and Mary became King and Queen of England; after Mary's death William reigned alone.

By then a monument had been erected over Harriet's grave at Toddington, bearing a likeness of her in marble. It lasted longer than the great house, which fell into decay after Lady Philadelphia died. The Duke of Monmouth's room survived longer than many, its plumes grey with dust, its cover black with damp; the roof was open to the wind and rain. The initials on the oak tree remained longer, for almost two hundred and fifty years; then vandals pulled off the bark. The oak died, the house was gone; only love remained.

Many years afterwards, the fifth Duke of Buccleuch was looking through papers in the muniment room at Dalkeith Palace; some of them remained from old Duchess Anna's day; she had died at a great age after two further marriages. The paper was dry and crumbling; he opened it carefully. There in brown ink was the marriage certificate of Charles II and Lucy Barlow. After considering the matter for some time he decided, as it might create trouble, to destroy it 'and thereon threw it into the fire and it was burned.'

We hope you have enjoyed this Large Print book. Other Chivers Press or G.K. Hall & Co. Large Print books are available at your library or directly from the publishers.

For more information about current and forthcoming titles, please call or write, without obligation, to:

Chivers Press Limited
Windsor Bridge Road
Bath BA2 3AX
England
Tel. (01225) 335336

OR

G.K. Hall & Co.
P.O. Box 159
Thorndike, Maine 04986
USA
Tel. (800) 223–2336

All our Large Print titles are designed for easy reading, and all our books are made to last.